One woman missing. One suspect dead. One killer still out there.

SERENITY'S SEARCH

A Novel

LINDSEY CACY

ISBN: 978-1-7368969-9-0

www.lindseycacy.com

For my brother, Joshua. Thank you for being not only my sibling, but my friend and my biggest inspiration. I love you, in this life and in all the lives to come.

PROLOGUE

"...an obsession is a way for damaged people to damage themselves more."
—Mark Barrowcliffe

The first thing that bothered me was the light.

Every lamp in Samaya's house was on. Not a soft glow, not a forgotten lamp in the living room, but every single bulb burning at full brightness like the house was trying to hold the dark back. She *never* did that. She hated wasting electricity. She hated feeling exposed. Tonight she had chosen both.

I stepped out of my car, and the air felt heavy in that strange way that warns you long before your thoughts can. My pulse picked up without my permission. Something was *wrong*. I could feel it in the quiet.

The front door was cracked open. A thin line of light spilled into the night. My mouth went dry.

I pushed it open with one finger.

Inside was silence. Stillness. A kind of quiet that feels staged. I set my keys on the kitchen counter, the sound far too loud in the empty room, and that was when I heard it.

A voice upstairs. A man. Low and angry.

Then Sam's voice. Thin. Trying to stay calm.

Another crash. Something breaking. A sharp scream that sliced through the house.

I froze at the bottom of the stairs. I could feel my heartbeat in my throat, in my fingertips, in the soles of my shaking feet. I knew I should call someone. But first I need a weapon

I opened drawers until my hands closed around a kitchen knife. It felt small. Insufficient. But it was all I had.

I climbed the stairs. The air grew tighter, heavier. The voices sharpened. Then stopped.

Silence.

I reached her bedroom door and pressed my ear against it. Nothing but my own breathing, rough and uneven.

Then my phone rang.

The sound blasted through the hallway like a flare giving away my position. I fumbled to silence it, but the damage was done.

The door flew open.

He filled the doorway. Broad. Sweating. Eyes wide and dark like something had snapped inside him. He looked at me, then at the knife in my hand, and smiled.

For a second, the world felt held in place, suspended between before and after.

I knew two things at once.

One: I had stepped into something I was never supposed to see.

Two: whatever this moment was, whatever I had just walked into, my life would not come out the same.

He took one step toward me.

And in that tiny, breathless pause before everything broke open, I understood the truth with a clarity that chilled me to the bone:

The danger was never the dark outside.

It was already waiting inside the house.

CHAPTER ONE

As I gaze out at the ocean, I can't help but wonder how I got so lucky. I get to live ten minutes away from this gorgeous scene.

I glance down at my watch and realize it's way past the time that I was supposed to leave for work.

"Shit," I mumble as I grab for my phone and toss it in my bag. I walk to my car, throw the large black purse into the passenger seat, and climb in. I consider stopping by Starbucks to grab an iced mocha. I mean, I'm already going to be late, so why not? It isn't like I enjoy going to this job anyway.

The thought of work makes me immediately feel less lucky. I sigh and begin pulling out of the beach parking lot, stopping abruptly to allow the tired-looking mom and her two very slow toddlers to pass in front of me.

I drive along the long stretch of large homes surrounding the beach and spot my sister Samaya's house. The gray paint and white trim look perfect against the dark gray sky and rolling clouds. I notice her car is in the driveway and check the clock in my car. It's only 10:26 a.m. She never misses work. I decide to call her.

"Hey, Sam," I say when she answers, "I just drove by on my way back from the beach and saw your car. What are you doing at home?"

She sighs heavily. "Just not feeling well today, so I took the day off to catch up on some rest."

"Really?" I frown. "What's wrong?"

"Tummy troubles," she says quickly.

Too quickly. Something is definitely off.

"Ok," I say. "Well, I'll check on you after work."

I pull up to my favorite Starbucks and see the drive-through line is wrapped around the building.

"Ugh," I groan as I continue to get onto the road that will lead me to Mario's.

Mario's is the high-end Italian restaurant I've been working at since I moved here a few months ago. The food is excellent, the drinks are even better, but the company, eh, not so much. I mean, unless you like uptight, rich people who start speaking incredibly broken Spanish to you because they have never seen a biracial woman before up close.

I get mistaken for Hispanic or Puerto Rican most often here, and I guess who can blame them, especially when I have my hair straight. Here, in Suffolk County, it's a land of pale faces and few races. There's not a lot of variety, at least not as far as I can tell. But it has only been since August.

In California, where Mexican people were almost the majority, I was rarely confused for Latina. People knew what light-skinned girls looked like, so most people knew I was Black and "something else." Although I don't miss the drama I left behind, I do miss the autonomy I had there. No one cared what you were, nor did they feel the need to ask, all too loudly and comfortably, if they could touch my hair.

I sigh again as I make the sharp left turn into the shopping center where Mario's is and park, scanning to see if Johnny's car is in yet.

Nope. *Thank God.* Johnny is the owner's son. I am used to getting hit on as an attractive woman, but he is relentless.

The man is handsome, but his cockiness makes him unattractive to me. The other reason I don't like him is that he's a tattletale. Anytime someone comes in, even just two minutes late, they will get side-eye from Johnny. He'll pull out his phone and start texting Mario, the restaurant owner, no doubt snitching in real time on the minor sins of the already overworked, underpaid staff member. Apparently, Johnny has never heard the phrase "snitches get stitches." But because he's obsessed with the idea of me someday being his girlfriend, luckily, he keeps my name out of his mouth.

I grab my stuff and exit the car, shooting one last glance over my shoulder, ensuring that I don't see Johnny, and rush inside. Looking at the clock on my phone, I'm only four minutes late. Not bad.

"Serenity! Don't you look stunning today!" a voice calls from my right.

"Hi, Stella," I say with feigned enthusiasm. Stella is nice enough, she just likes to talk. Like a lot. But because she is Mario's wife and Mario is the owner of this restaurant and, more importantly, my boss, I always feel obligated to engage longer than I usually would with anyone else.

"How's your day going?"

"Oh, you know," she says, "just the usual Wednesday preparations."

Ah, yes, I think. It's Whine Wednesday.

Whine Wednesday is the weekly, mid-week shit show where a bunch of rich, privileged (usually white men) come in and complain about their lives and their wives, all while guzzling bottles of $80–$100 wines. I think I'd like it better if there were maybe some guys under 55, but the tips get better as the evening goes on, so it's not so bad, I guess.

I walk through the kitchen to get to the break area and can already smell the spaghetti Bolognese being cooked. My stomach growls. I probably should have grabbed something to eat on the way to work, but I could always snag a slice of the freshly baked sourdough when it comes out of the oven. I wave at Roberto and the two other guys sweating over huge pots of bubbling goodness. This smell could never get old, and the smell of good things cooking almost makes the uptight customers bearable.

When I got hired in August, I knew this was just a temporary gig. Having just arrived in a new place, I really just needed something that didn't require a degree and would be easy money. They were high-end and had a bar, so I knew that I would finagle some good tips. Plus, it's near my apartment, and I absolutely love Italian food, so it works.

Since I'd left California so abruptly, I didn't have time to preplan a job, so I've pretty much had to wing it since arriving on Samaya's doorstep, tearstained and heartbroken, back in July. It's not like I had some epic career or even a life back in

San Francisco. I was fired from my part-time office gig, cheated on, and basically homeless before I arrived here.

There's something about walking in on your boyfriend with his face between the legs of a girl he claimed was "just his friend from work" that makes you want to move out — and far away. Since it was technically his aunt's house anyway, it's not like I had any legal right to stay there. The energy was completely tainted anyway. How could I stay there after what I'd witnessed?

Fuck that.

I couldn't even be that mad. I'd sensed that Dre was a bona fide fuck-boy, but damn, the sex was good, and he'd been so attentive in the beginning. It's interesting how we can hang on to something just because it's familiar, even when we know it's not good for us. His cheating had brought me closer to my sister, though, and while I am still not sure if I like Long Island all that much, being near her again after so many years of our long-distance sister-ship felt really good.

I hear a long, low whistle from behind me as I tie on my apron. I smile even before I turn around because I know exactly who it is.

"Hi, Jason," I say, my back still turned.

This is our usual routine: he whistles or makes some borderline inappropriate but allowed comments, and I laugh him off because I know he's harmless.

"Sis, if I didn't like dick so much, I'd be asking you to dinner."

"What a shame," I say, turning around, my face a picture of disappointment, "because I'm totally free tonight."

He rolls his eyes. "Girl, you free *every night.*"

He's right.

I fold my arms over my chest. "Jason, it's not my fault there are like no cute guys here."

He mocks surprise and hurt while clutching what I assume are the imaginary pearls at his throat. "No attractive guys?"

"Well, attractive straight guys. You know what I mean," I say, slapping his arm. He fakes hurt, as if I've socked him in the arm at full strength. I roll my eyes. "Such a baby."

We laugh and walk out of the break room and back through the kitchen. It's nearly 11:30 a.m. now, so we'll be opening and receiving our first lunch rush in a few moments. I run to the bathroom since I have a little time. As I fumble with the zipper on my fitted black jeans, my mind wanders back to Samaya's strange response on the phone earlier. I'll need some answers on that after work.

Heading to the sinks, I wash my hands and catch a glance at my reflection in the mirror. My brown curls are fairly tame today, but I put my hands in them to fuss with them, mostly out of habit. As I gaze at my reflection, I realize Jason was right: I look pretty damn good today. Immediately after this thought, I have a flashback of Dre eating his coworker's vagina like a Thanksgiving feast and instantly question my appearance.

This seems to be the chain of events mentally since the incident. Something about knowing Dre chose—no, preferred—her over me made me feel, well, less attractive. Why else would he go through such lengths to hide it and lie? That was his first choice, and I was just the dumb girlfriend he hung on to until I had enough sense to catch on.

He had told me it was my anxiety getting the best of me, so all those months when I felt something was off, he'd almost convinced me I was the crazy one.

Almost.

The day I caught him, I came home early on purpose. Call it a gut instinct, but something told me to stop home for lunch—which I never did. And sure enough, there they were.

Forcing myself to put these thoughts aside, I head back into the restaurant to start my shift. Work and Jason's wisecracks will distract me for at least the next few hours.

By the time 4 o'clock rolls around, I barely notice that I've been at work for four hours. Jason pushes past me, practically running toward the break area, also almost running over Stella as she walks through the kitchen with two fresh plates.

"Jason!" she exclaims. "You almost knocked me down!"

"Sorry!" he calls over his shoulder, slowing down to a half-power walk, half-gallop. I smile and shake my head. This is classic Jason, always needing to get the hell out of the restaurant the moment his shift ends. Unlike me, he has a social life.

I help myself to a to-go container and shovel some of the night's pesto fettuccine into it. One of the other perks of working at Mario's is the delicious food we get for free. I wipe the excess off the side of the container, lick my finger, and walk to grab my stuff from the break area. To my surprise, Jason is still there.

"Hey, Speed Racer, got a hot date tonight?" I tease. "What's his name?"

"Wouldn't you like to know?" he says, smiling devilishly with that all-too-familiar glint in his dark brown eyes.

"I'm just glad one of us is getting laid."

"Girl, you need to snap out of your little pity-party funk you got going on. There are plenty of guys who would snatch your ass up in a heartbeat—you just gotta put yourself out there."

I shove my apron into my bag, ignoring his comments. He is always trying to get me to "put myself out there," and I always politely decline.

"I just don't have time, J."

"I'm calling bullshit," he says, giving me an unusually stern look, his hands on his impossibly narrow hips. "I think you do have the time. You just don't want to go out for some other reason, I'm still trying to figure out why."

Like most people in my already small social group, Jason doesn't know the details of my last relationship and how abruptly it ended. Hell, I'm not sure I've even fully processed it for myself. Even though it's been several months, the idea of even attempting a conversation with a guy just feels… scary.

"I gotta go, boo-boo," he says, interrupting my thoughts. "Some of us want to get lucky tonight."

I grab my box of food and purse so we can walk out together. We say our goodbyes, and I watch Jason get into his car and peel off. I smile and turn my attention upward toward the sky. One thing I do love about this place is the sky; I've always been a sucker for an incredible sunrise or sunset, but even without the ascending or descending of the sun, these skies take the cake. The clouds look like giant pastel cotton balls against an almost purply gray sky. It's beautiful.

Lowering my gaze, I walk over to my car and get in. I decide to head home before checking on Samaya. I need to shower anyway since I smell like garlic and marinara sauce.

Driving to the sounds of Solange's "Weary," I make my way toward the apartment I share with my friend and roommate, Alyse.

Alyse is, well, different. She was born and raised in Brooklyn, and it shows. She's the kind of girl who won't talk about you behind your back, but she will most definitely say it to your face. And with her whole chest too. I love that about her.

When we first met, I was attending my first East Coast yoga class with Samaya, and Alyse walked right to us and started asking us about what kind of products we used on our curls. Me being the hair product junkie that I am, I knew right then she was cool as fuck. Since that day, we became sort of inseparable: she would show me the best hair stores in Long Island, and I would show her how to make authentic Mexican food — a rare delicacy on this side of the country. When Alyse told me her roommate had just moved out a few weeks later, I quickly asked her if she would consider me for the new housemate. She said yes, and here we are. She doesn't complain about my messiness, and I don't complain about her bringing random dudes home after nights out, so win-win.

As I pull onto the highway, it begins to rain. I turn on my headlights as I slow down enough to allow the large semi-truck to go ahead of me since he's barreling down the highway at an unsafe speed anyway. I accelerate again, turning the windshield wipers up to match the growing fury of the rain.

Suddenly, out of the corner of my eye, I see a black object coming at my windshield, and there's a loud *CRACK!*

I scream, "What the fuck was that?" Then I see the blood— and the crack in my windshield just under my passenger-side sun visor. I pull off to the side of the highway and jump out to check the damage.

"Goddammit," I mumble as I see the U-shaped crack that has a few droplets of now watery blood dripping from it. I just hit a fucking bird! Well, for the record, that bird hit me. I gape at the windshield dumbly, as if my eyes can somehow seal the damage done by the giant bird.

Shaking my head in disbelief and frustration, I get back in my car and scan the highway, looking for an opening to continue my wet journey home. What the hell is going on, like who gets hit by a crow in the middle of this highway?

And aren't blackbirds some kind of omen? Like a sign of death or something? I think I saw this in a movie.

I groan inwardly because not only have I hit some damn ominous bird, but it's now a dead, ominous bird, and I'm pretty sure a dead blackbird is somehow a worst-case scenario in the bad luck department.

Great.

CHAPTER TWO

"**W**ait," Alyse says, her dark eyes wide with disbelief, "you hit a fucking *bird?!*"

"Yes. Well, technically, the bird hit me."

Her eyes narrow. "What do you mean the bird hit you? You were the one driving the giant car, and that bird was just going about his business until BOOM"—she claps her hands together for a more dramatic effect—"here you come to kill it!"

I have to stifle a giggle. Another thing about Alyse is she can be a bit, let's just say, extra. She sees my poorly hidden giggle and puts her hands on her curvy hips.

"This is second-degree murder, Serenity," she somehow says with a straight face. I start full-on laughing at this point because she reminds me of my Auntie Bonnie with her stern Black mama spiel. I see the corner of her mouth rise and know she can't hold out much longer. Sure enough, she starts giggling too, covering her mouth with a perfectly manicured hand.

"I gotta see this shit, bitch," she manages between giggles, shaking her head and grabbing her jacket off the back of our shabby brown couch.

We walk over to the carport and look at the sad face-shaped crack in the windshield of my Camry. Somehow, under the harsh fluorescent lights of my carport, it seems worse.

"Do you think I'll need a whole new windshield?" I ask, not able to take my eyes off the crack.

"I don't know, girl," she replies. "But that's a pretty big crack."

With finances already stretched thin due to the brakes I had to get replaced last month, I'm not sure how I'm going to afford another unexpected car expense. The rain picks up even more, so we hurry back inside the apartment.

Once we get inside, I go grab my towel out of my room to shower. After turning the water on, I turn and face the mirror and stare into my own eyes.

You really fucked up, I think. *Now you have shitty bird luck, and you might need a new windshield.*

I stand there like this, staring at my reflection, hand gripping the small white sink. This couldn't be happening at a worse time.

The longer I stare, the image of my face and bathroom behind me becomes distorted, and my vision swims. I realize these are tears and snap out of my brief trance, wiping my eyes with the back of my hand to clear the tears from my eyes.

I am not going to cry over this. Yes, this is terrible timing, but I still have a windshield, so I can still get to work, and that's what matters most right now. I can figure out how to get the thing fixed in the morning, and it doesn't do any good to spend the rest of the night fretting over dead birds and bills. I get undressed and step into the hot water, hoping the steaming water will wash away not only the smell of Italian cuisine, but the recent events and thoughts of financial ruin as well.

As I get dressed, my phone pings with an alert. It's a text from Samaya:

Hey boo, call me after work.

I smile. Samaya is always right on time. It's almost like she can sense when I need comfort. I throw on a green tank and slip into some gray yoga pants that I've had since 2008. For me, comfort is key. I pick up my phone and text her back:

Girl... I hit a fucking bird!!!

I immediately see the three tiny gray bubbles come up as she responds. I put on my favorite fuzzy slippers, needing all the comfort I can get. Her response is in all caps:

WTF?????!! HOW THE HELL?

I was driving. Bird hit and broke my windshield, I text back.

I see the gray bubbles appearing and then stop. My phone rings.

"What did you hit, Big Bird?? How did your windshield shatter?" my sister asks, clearly mystified.

"Well, hello to you too," I say. "My windshield isn't shattered, it's just cracked, but it looks pretty bad."

"Can you still drive it?"

"Yes, but I'm worried I'm gonna have to replace the whole windshield. I do not have the money for that right now, I just got my brakes done."

"I know, babe," she says quietly. "Come over. I can even come pick you up if you don't wanna drive it."

I part the sheer white curtains that cover my window and see that it's still pouring outside. "If you don't mind? I mean,

I could drive, but I'm a little freaked out that I might hit another bird."

Stifling a giggle, she says, "I think you've reached your bird-killing quota for the day. I'll leave here right now."

After we hang up, I collapse onto my bed, wrapping the furry white blanket around me. Sam's house is on the other side of the town, so it'll take her at least fifteen minutes to get here. I text Alyse, too lazy and cozy to unfurl myself from the fuzzy goodness of my bed.

I'm going to Samaya's. Wanna come?

I hear her phone chirp with my incoming message and smile. We are constantly texting each other even though the only thing separating us is this flimsy apartment wall. I hear her desk chair squeak and her footsteps padding down the short hallway. My door swings open, and her short but voluptuous form fills my doorway.

"Aww, girl…" she says, coming over to my bed and sitting next to me, "you look like shit. Please tell me you're not going to drive over there."

"Fuck no. Sam's picking me up."

"Ok, good. We don't need you killing any other wildlife. But I can't come. I'm working on this graphic design project for the BFC."

BFC, or Black Female Collective, is a group of Black female entrepreneurs, artists, and business owners that came together each month, and they would be coming to Long Island for September. They'd reached out to Alyse to create the promo images since she's a local Black female artist.

"Ahhhhhh!!!" I squeal, sitting up, "I forgot! Are you excited?"

"I am, but I just want it to be perfect, you know?"

"You're going to kill it, girl," I say with total confidence.

Alyse is like me because she struggles with anxiety and almost crippling self-doubt. I think that's why we became such fast friends, almost like sisters. We understand each other.

"Oh!!!!" she exclaims. "Are you working Friday night? The girls from BFC are having a meet and greet here with a few of the Long Island members and their families and friends, wanna come?"

I grimace. "But I'm not an entrepreneur or an artist or anything…" I trail off.

"Not yet," she says smugly. "Also, you're a woman, and you're Black, so… you should come! Bring Samaya!!" She is practically clapping her hands and jumping up and down now.

"Fine, I'll see if Samaya wants to come. I know we both need to get out more," I reply dryly.

She actually claps her hands now and hugs me before skipping out the door. I check the time on my phone and see it's been ten minutes. As I finish getting ready to head out, I remember again the abrupt interaction I had with Samaya this morning and make a mental note to grill her about it when I see her. Then I remember my windshield and sigh.

What a fucking day.

CHAPTER THREE

As soon as we sit down in Samaya's pristine, all-white kitchen, she pulls two wine glasses from her cabinet and grabs a bottle of champagne out of her stainless-steel refrigerator. When she notices me watching her, she shoots me a sheepish look.

"What's the occasion?" I ask, a little puzzled.

"It's all I have, and I need a drink," she says.

"Ah, got it. Rough day?" I ask, then remember this morning. "Wait, I thought you were sick?"

"Girl, I'm so stressed. David is back on his toxic bullshit, and I am just so exhausted. We aren't even together anymore, and yet somehow, this dude is still way too close for comfort and trying to ruin my life."

David.

I sigh loudly.

David is Samaya's soon-to-be ex-husband, and he is a real piece of work—and that's being incredibly generous. Although their marriage didn't last very long, only about three years, it was volatile and tragic.

She'd moved to New York City to attend college to become a therapist, and they fell in love hard and fast. Within three months, Samaya was pregnant, and because David's family is super Italian and super Catholic, he pleaded with her to marry him. Because she was so in love and expecting the love of her life's baby, she said yes.

Probably one of the biggest mistakes of her life.

They'd had a small ceremony at their local courthouse and moved into Samaya's two-bedroom apartment. For the first month, things were good. Typical. When Samaya began finding empty liquor bottles in random places around their home, she felt that gut fear because she knew what she was dealing with. Our mother is an addict who still struggles with it to this day, so she recognized the signs. Samaya approached him about it, and that was the first day he got belligerent with her.

She'd known he drank, but thought it was an average amount until she discovered all the discarded and hidden bottles. I remember the first day she mentioned it to me. She was about twenty weeks pregnant at this point. I told her to come to California for a while to stay with my then-boyfriend and me.

She didn't come.

The next time she called, four weeks later, he had "gotten rough" with her after an argument (about his drinking, of course), but she said she "was fine."

"What the *fuck*, Samaya? This is not ok. You are pregnant. What if he goes too far and hurts you or the baby??" I had asked, fuming. How was she downplaying this, this was abuse!

"*Shh, shh,* I'm fine, girl. He just grabbed me on my arm," she said quickly. "I just needed to vent."

Then, I got the call that I will never forget.

It was 11:30 p.m. in California, so it was 2:30 a.m. in New York. I answered groggily. "Hello?"

"Serenity?"

It was Samaya. I immediately sat straight up in bed; her voice sounded strained, and I could tell she was crying.

"What's wrong? Are you ok? Is it the baby?" Then I realized it was way too soon for the baby to be coming. My stomach clenched and locked up. "Samaya, what is going on?!"

"I-I'm at the hospital. I'm ok, but I… I fell."

"You fell? At two o'clock in the morning? How?!"

"David—"

I cut her off. "What the fuck did he do to you?" I growled.

"We got into another fight after he got home from Charlie's. I am fine, Serenity," she said as her voice cracked. She had begun to cry now openly.

"He pushed you?" I asked in disbelief. "Please tell me you called the police?"

"No, he-he didn't push me, I just kind of… fell. And we were right in front of the stairs—you know the few stairs by the kitchen entryway? I just tumbled down and fell."

My jaw had dropped, and I just stared blankly into the darkness in front of my face as I sat in bed. Now Sam was covering for David? I hadn't known who to be madder at, him or her. Luckily, the baby had been fine, but I knew then that if she stayed with this man, he would hurt her or the baby, or worse, kill her accidentally in a drunken rage one night after she dared to confront him about how out of control his drinking had gotten.

My sweet niece, Samantha, was born eight weeks later, and things were good for a while. He'd seemed to slow down on his drinking, or maybe Sam had just stopped telling me about how bad it was. I'd flown in to meet her when she was six months old and fell in love immediately with her curly black hair and chubby cheeks. She'd somehow wound up with these beautiful hazel eyes that shone with so much life. Sam teased me because of how much her daughter loved me.

"She doesn't act like this even for me!" she'd said. "Are you sure this isn't your baby?"

I had no idea then that that would be the last time I ever saw my only niece.

A few months later, Samaya was in Baltimore for a weekend seminar where she was providing a training to other mental health professionals about effective practices working with at-risk teens dealing with addiction. David had Samantha for the weekend. I remember Sam telling me she was a little nervous since this would be the longest time she'd been away from baby Samantha.

According to Sam, the police told her that the car accident occurred around 10 p.m. that Saturday night. Only twenty-four hours after she'd left for the event. David's car was found upside down in a ditch near the highway in Nassau County.

David and Samantha were airlifted to Mount Sinai Hospital. David received surgery that saved his life. Samantha was pronounced dead three hours after arriving at the hospital.

She was only eleven months old.

"Did you hear me?" Samaya asks, pulling me out of my thoughts.

"I'm so sorry. What were you saying?"

She rolls her eyes, clearly annoyed. "David called this morning. He sounded furious and possibly already drunk. He said I ruined his life because I left him and that he's going to come after me for money since he lost his job."

"Wait, didn't he lose his job because of his drinking?" I ask.

"Yes, but according to him, he lost his job because I left him and kicked him out of the apartment. Oh, and also, it's my fault he got arrested and that that led to his current unemployment," Sam says incredulously.

I can't believe this. After everything that man has put my sister through in the last few years, the last thing he could do is blame someone else for his actions.

"Fuck him," I say. "He's all talk anyway."

"I don't know, Serenity. He said I have it coming. Like what the fuck does that even mean?" she says, and although she keeps her voice even, I can tell she's nervous.

After everything she's been through with this man, I don't blame her. But I don't think he's stupid enough to do much more than talk all big and bad since he's got domestic violence on his record.

"Try not to stress about it too much. I know you're nervous about it, and I totally get why—I just don't think he's crazy enough to take it to a place where he's going to end up back in jail," I say gently. *At least I hope not*, I think to myself.

Samaya takes a long gulp from her glass, draining the remainder of the contents. "You're probably right. I just get on edge even hearing his voice."

"Understandable—he's a fucking looney toon." Then I remember Alyse's offer earlier. "Hey! You should come with me to this event at the Bayport Inn on Friday evening, I guess there's a whole little event space and bar there. Alyse roped me in, and I told her I'd come if you came." I smile sweetly at her, fully aware and unashamed of the full-on guilt trip that I just placed on her.

She reaches for the bottle of champagne and takes a swig directly from the bottle. I raise my eyebrows. "When is the last time you've done anything social?" I ask.

"You know I don't go out like that," she says.

"Then come with me! It's all women, and it'll be nice to be around some color."

"I don't know these women, girl."

"Neither do I," I say, exasperated.

Samaya takes another gulp of the bubbly liquid. She's quiet for a while, gazing out the back window of her stark-white kitchen into her green yard. With the skylight above, it looks almost ethereal on a bright day.

"So…?" I say, picking up my own, almost untouched champagne.

"Fine," she says. "I'll go. But I'm not buying anything."

I roll my eyes. "It's just drinks and some food—they aren't there to sell. They just want to meet up with the people who are helping with the event, you know, so everyone can meet each other and connect before the day of."

She sighs. "I guess it would be good for me to get out of this house for a few hours."

"Exactly! You can do something besides go to work and Stop and Shop." I playfully push her shoulder. She pushes me back, but I can tell she's on board. I feel myself begin to smile too.

"Who knows," she says thoughtfully, swirling the bottle of champagne in her hand, "maybe we'll even have some fun."

CHAPTER FOUR

My alarm goes off with its usual shrieking intensity, and I groan, pulling the blankets up over my head. Yesterday, I had to cover my shift and Jason's shift because he decided to call out sick. I knew he was either hungover or laid up, exhausted with his latest beau after a night of drunken sex.

At least it's Friday, and I don't have to go back to work until Sunday evening.

Thank God.

I roll onto my back, put my hands behind my head, and look up at my ceiling, already thinking. I hope this event tonight is low-key and that the ladies are welcoming. I'm usually pretty quiet around new people due to my anxiety, but the fact that this event is for women only made me a little more comfortable going. The last thing I need is a bunch of drunk guys asking me what my sign is and if they can buy me a drink.

I peel myself from my bed and slip my feet into my baby blue bunny slippers and make my way to the window. Still raining. Luckily, I love rainy days. I make my way out of my room and into the hall, mindful of tiptoeing past Alyse's door since she's such a light sleeper. The last thing I want to do is wake her up early. I love her to death, but she can be cranky as hell in the morning.

Once I safely make it back to my room, sans-grumpy roommate, I throw on my CAL hoodie and my Uggs so that I can make my typical day-off journey to Starbucks.

As soon as I approach my car, I wince. I'm still not used to the massive crack in the windshield. I'd spoken with a guy at Safelite yesterday morning, and he confirmed that I would indeed need to replace the entire windshield. This clocks in at $589, and I will have to wait until I can get some overtime under my belt at work.

I slow for the yellowing light above, and then I flick my eyes downward to scroll through the playlist. I select Bryson Tiller's *"Don't."* The light changes to green, and I can't help but sing along with this song I've listened to an infinite number of times.

The line is, of course, wrapped around the building, but I don't mind. It's my day off, and just reminding myself of this glorious fact makes me sing a little louder.

"Welcome to Starbucks. What can I get started for you?" asks the tinny, mechanical voice from its speaker heaven. I order my usual white chocolate mocha with coconut milk and whipped cream. Then, I pull up the millimeter the red Kia in front of me allows me to.

My phone chirps. It's a text from Alyse:

Can you get me a chai latte?

I already ordered, I text back.

The gray bubbles appear, preparing her response. *Ok, grab me a coffee?*

You spoiled, you know that, right?

She responds with three kissy-face emojis.

When I get to the window and ask the acne-covered, college-age redhead if I can "please also get a grande coffee," he sighs loudly, as if I'd asked him for money. I get it. As someone who also works in the service industry, I know these kinds of last-minute requests can be incredibly annoying, especially in the drive-through.

"Sorry," I say with an apologetic shrug. "Last-minute roomie request."

His face screams, *I couldn't care less,* but he smiles a forced smile and says nothing.

Pulling out of the drive-through finally, I call Alyse.

"Girl!" I say when she answers. "You just got me the worst death-stare at Starbucks with your last-minute shit."

She yawns and says lazily, "My bad. But I have a big day, and all they gotta do is fill the cup with coffee."

"Well, tell me how you really feel," I say, laughing. Alyse laughs too.

"I'm sorry, girl, I just need to get ready for tonight."

Oh shit, tonight's the women's thing. I'd already forgotten.

"What's the dress code for this?" I ask, mentally raiding my closet, realizing that I will need to go shopping since, besides work clothes, all I have is workout clothes.

"I'm wearing a short black dress and my pick heels. Nothin' major."

I know exactly what pick heels she is talking about; they're the ones that if my feet were three sizes smaller, I probably would've stolen because I adore them so much.

"Well, I am definitely going to need to go shopping."

Alyse squeals, "Just tell me where to meet you!!" Alyse is a self-proclaimed shopaholic. Of course she wants to come, even though she has her outfit already picked out.

"You're addicted to clothes," I laugh. "Meet me at the Smithaven mall in twenty minutes."

The whistle I receive from Samaya when I walk out my front door lets me know that I picked the right outfit.

I chose a nude-colored dress from Forever 21 that left little to the imagination. I figured I should go out with a bang if I'm going out. Also, I knew this was the kind of dress that my ex-boyfriend, Cheating Dre, would be very wary about me wearing out for a night on the town with the girls.

This makes me smile. I paired this award-winning dress with my brown and black snakeskin pumps and a black, ankle-length wool coat that looks straight out of a 1950's fashion magazine. Last winter, I got it for $12 at Goodwill, and I am so glad it gets cold enough in New York to actually wear it.

"Girl, *ok!*" Samaya praises me with an actual round of applause after closing the passenger door.

"I figured I couldn't go wrong with a tight dress," I say, flashing her a big smile. "I'm actually kind of excited!"

She looks less enthusiastic. "Do I look ok? I feel like I haven't gone out in ages."

I turn my head so I can see her entire outfit. Cheetah print blouse with just enough cleavage to be sexy, but still be classy, black pants and, from what I could see of her feet, some black heels?

"You look great," I confirm. "And I am so glad you are coming—we both need to socialize more."

We get on the highway, Samaya telling me about the day's events in her office with one of her regular patients.

Samaya is a counselor, a Marriage and Family Therapist. She is telling me about one of her regulars, a fifteen-year-old she works with weekly, who recently got in trouble at school for fighting again.

"I don't know what is going on at home exactly, but something seems off with the mom," she continues. "I legally can't give you the details, but there's something neither of them are telling me. I just don't have enough info to contact CPS."

"You think he's being abused?" I ask, realizing she means Child Protective Services.

"I don't know. But I do know the signs of an abused child, and he *is* showing a lot of them."

I shake my head and turn to look out the window. We both dealt with abuse growing up due to our mother's drug addiction. Sometimes it was her hitting us and telling us we were worthless, usually when she was out of money and drugs and men to buy it for her. Other times it was one of the many boyfriends who came around. As kids, we never knew what to expect when coming home from school. Would mom be drunk or awake or even home? Would there be dinner tonight, or would Samaya have to play mom again and "figure something out"? Although Samaya is older by a handful of years, we were just kids. No wonder we both have such intense anxiety—we spent our entire childhood just trying to survive.

"What about the other guy you mentioned a few months ago? The guy who was pissed when you had to refer him to a different therapist?" I ask as I apply yet another coat of lip gloss to my already glossy lips.

"Oh my God, girl, yes, Spencer. I actually saw him. Twice." She shoots me a sidelong glance. "The last time I saw him, he approached me at the coffee shop I go to near my office. It was a few weeks ago."

"What did he say?"

"He just kept asking how I was doing and saying how much he missed me. He even brought up Samantha, which was super uncomfortable. That was kind of why I let him go originally—he was just way too interested in my personal life." She shudders a little at the memory.

"That's creepy as fuck," I say. "I'm glad he's working with someone else—sounds like major stalker vibes."

She just shrugs and shoots me a look that says, "who knows."

I pull out my phone and see if I have any updates from Alyse about the venue. She told me earlier that people would start arriving at 7, but not to come before 7:30–8 o'clock so we're not bored. I glance at the car's clock, and it's almost 7.

"Can we stop at a liquor store before we go?" I ask Samaya without looking at her, already feeling my cheeks redden. I can literally feel her head looking at me. I glance over quickly to see her right eyebrow raise before returning her attention to the road.

"Pre-gaming for a women's get-together...?"

"I know, I know," I begin. "I just need a shot of courage, so I don't sit there silently while I'm supposed to be networking or whatever."

"As a therapist, I have to say that is a deeply unhealthy reason to drink alcohol," she begins, "but as your sister, let's definitely stop somewhere, cause I'm hella not ready to walk in this thang sober."

"That's my girl!" I say, reaching for my debit card and ID. We pull into the parking lot, and I bolt into the store. Luckily for my hair, the rain has stopped for a while. I look around for sodas, then remember that here in New York, there's no sodas at liquor stores, just the hard stuff. Missing California's looser liquor laws, I ask the clerk for four of the single shot-size bottles of Jack Daniels Honey.

Since the restaurant and bar we are going to for the event is right across the street, we pull in and park.

"Alright, what'd you get?" Samaya asks, turning off her headlights and removing her keys from the ignition. I pull the four bottles out, tossing two into her lap.

She raises her eyebrows. "Alrighty then!"

I laugh, unscrewing the top from my first mini-Jack. "These will have you hella smooth."

I look over to see my sister unscrewing her cap also. I wait for her fumbling fingers to finish and clink the neck of my bottle against hers.

"Cheers!" I say before throwing my head back and downing the bottle's contents in two swallows.

"Aagghhh!" Samaya exclaims, apparently having the same experience I am. "Damn, no chaser. That shit is intense." Her light brown cheeks reddened a little from the alcohol. She begins unscrewing the next bottle.

"Thug life ass!" I say, laughing. "Do you think we'll be good if we drink both now? I don't want to roll in here drunk."

She rolls her eyes and chugs the second bottle. "Amateur," she says, but almost chokes from the liquor. I can't help but giggle. I love my big sister and the fact that although she's very educated and very into healing, she can still be a little ratchet.

I take my second shot. This one definitely went down smoother, although you wouldn't know it judging by my face. Once I recover, I flip down the sun visor in front of me and check my reflection in the small mirror. I actually did my make-up today, so I am feeling extra cute. It felt good to get cute and prepare to go out with my girls. I look over at Samaya, and she is looking back at me, grinning.

"Ready?" she asks. "Let's do this."

CHAPTER FIVE

Seeing this many Black and brown female faces in one space in Suffolk County has my heart warm.

Yes! I think to myself. I have missed this so much. In California, when my girls and I hit Oakland or San Francisco, Black faces were everywhere: every shade, every age, and every style of dress. I immediately feel more comfortable, though it could've been the help I received from Gentleman Jack.

"Hi, ladies! *Welcome!*" A gorgeous, dark-skinned woman greets us warmly, handing us each a name tag sticker. Her hair is piled high in braids that look freshly done. She's dressed in a bright orange crop top and a loose, flowing brown and orange patterned skirt—very bohemian, but chic.

"Hi!!!" Samaya and I say nervously in unison. We fumble with our tags and put them on.

"On behalf of Black Female Collective, thank you for coming! Our group is over there by the fish tank and bar," she says, pointing toward the floor-to-ceiling aquarium. "First two drinks are on us." She winks at us, ushering us further into the restaurant.

"Do you think she smelled the liquor?" I half-whisper to Samaya. She shakes her head and laughs. We arrive at the group, and I scan the room for Alyse and spot her chatting up some twenty-somethings two tables over. She looks up and winks at me. I wave cheerfully and then flash her a thumbs-up on her hair. She went with a long ombre wig tonight, and she looks like a chocolate Barbie doll with a way better booty.

I turn toward Samaya, but she's already talking with a woman whose name tag reads Tina in blue Sharpie.

Ok, sis, I silently approve. I find an empty space at one of the larger rectangular tables and really take in the scene.

The lighting is dark, but not club dark, and there seems to be a bluish tint to the lighting, giving the space a jazz club feel. Drake is currently rapping about being *Mr. Right Now*, and the chatter of voices is rising. You can tell these women have been here for a while because the alcohol and camaraderie have loosened tongues. The short bartender is making major moves at the bar, shaking a drink and giving the woman in front of him a dazzling smile. I begin to relax even more.

"I'm so glad you guys are here!!!" Alyse says, running up to hug me. "I honestly thought you guys would flake."

She sits down at the table with me and takes inventory of the room.

"This is nice!" I tell her. "I'm loving the vibes, and the music is fire."

"See!" she squeals.

"What are you two up to?" asks Samaya as she approaches to take a seat with us. "Alyse! Hi babe! This is super cute—thanks for inviting me!"

"I was just telling Serenity that I am so happy y'all came!" Alyse says, giving Samaya a fierce hug. I love how well the two get along, they genuinely like each other.

"Where's the bathroom?" I ask Alyse, rising from my seat. She points vaguely to a far corner of the area. I begin walking in the direction of where she's pointed out.

I begin thinking about how relaxed Samaya looks and how happy that makes me. She's had so much to deal with in the past couple of years and somehow held down her private practice for her clients, only taking a month-long break when things got terrible. I knew I needed to get out more too. Seeing her thrive makes the little bit of anxiety worth it.

I enter the bathroom and select the cleanest-looking stall I can find. When I emerge to wash my hands, I see a woman exiting her stall as well. She's got caramel-colored skin and a sleek A-line hairstyle.

"Girl, *that dress!*" she says when she sees me. I smile brightly in appreciation.

"Thanks, girl! $18 at Forever 21," I blurt out. Why do I always feel the need to announce the cost of my outfit whenever I get a compliment about it?

I dry my hands with the air dryer before heading back into the restaurant. As I walk down the hallway, I text Jason to tell him I am actually out. I round the corner, but instead of a clear path, I run into someone, or something, hard. My phone goes flying, and mid-flight, my ID and credit card come flying out of the wallet thingy attached to the back of my phone case.

"I—I'm *so* sorry," I stammer, kneeling down to collect my items off the floor. As I begin to stand up, I hear the voice and see the face simultaneously.

"Are you ok?" asks the husky yet honey-smooth voice. The face, attached to the extraordinarily tall body, is friendly and concerned.

And fine as hell.

My throat catches. "Yes," I manage. His face goes from concern to a hint of amusement. With a face that looks like that, he must get this reaction a lot from women.

"That's a relief," he says. "I was worried you might come up swinging, you were walking so fast."

I'm blushing furiously as I take a better look at this beautiful man.

He's got to be at least 6'4, and his broad chest hovers directly in front of my face. Covering this epic chest is a button-down shirt donned with some light blue jeans that fit him… very well.

I swallow hard. We stare at each other for a second longer than casual.

"Well, I guess I should get back to the event," I say lamely, waving my hand in the general direction of the group.

"Ok, Serenity," he says with a smirk. My head snaps up.

"How do you know my name?" I ask.

He smiles. *Oh my God,* this man's smile is heavenly.

He points at the nametag where my name is scrawled. I blush even harder this time.

"Duh," I manage, laughing nervously.

I take a step to walk around him, and right as we are shoulder to shoulder, he leans down and whispers into my ear, "I'm Louis."

My entire body stiffens at the feeling of his warm breath near my bare neck and shoulder. His breath smells minty and fresh, and I immediately feel goosebumps arrive on my arm in his wake. I turn my head to get another look at his handsome face.

Damn.

"Nice to meet you, Louis," I say, not breaking eye contact. He smiles slowly with only the left side of his mouth. I finally tear my eyes away from that smile and walk back to the table where Alyse and Samaya are staring at me.

Great, I think to myself, *they saw that awkward exchange.*

I walk past them directly to the bar and order a Jack and Coke. I feel their approach on either side of me, and I start laughing.

"Oh my God, you guys don't miss shit, do you??"

"Girl," Alyse hisses not so discreetly into my ear, "that brotha was *fine,* fine!"

"He was so tall!" Samaya adds before ordering a Corona.

I think back to my brief encounter with Louis. It felt like so much longer, the few moments it lasted. I take a long swig of my drink and wince. It's strong.

"You guys, his name is Louis," I report.

"Did y'all exchange info???" asks Alyse giddily.

"No. We ran into each other as I was coming out of the bathroom — like literally ran into each other," I say, putting my face into my hands as I mentally relive the moment of impact.

"Mm-mmm-*mmm!*" Alyse says wistfully. "He could run into me any day of the week."

I slap her arm and then dare to peek over my shoulder to see if I can spot him again. I do, and he is staring directly at me from across the room. I whip my head back around so fast I almost gave myself and the women on either side of me whiplash. Samaya starts to turn around to see what I needed to peel my eyes away from.

"Do not turn around," I hiss.

As if on cue, they both immediately turn around and look. I again bury my face in my hands and moan, "I hate you guys, you know that, right?"

"Ooohhhh," Samaya says in a sing-song voice, "you don't want us to look because lovah boy is over there."

Now my face must be as pink as Alyse's hot pink pumps. As I inwardly die, I hear Samaya and Alyse giggling. I take a few more sips of my drink to try and wash away what just happened in my mind. I take a deep breath and slowly turn my head again to assess the damage. He's still there, but talking with one of the other two guys at his table.

Whew.

The girls and I get up to mingle with some of the other women.

In my mingling, I meet Angela, a nurse by day and a Pilates instructor by night. I also meet a woman old enough to be my mom who looked my age. She was one of the founding members of BFC, and her long, majestically graying dreads showed her age more than her face. A table of girls that looked my age gave Samaya and me side-eye anytime we mingled near them. They were giving off major, you can't sit with us vibes.

About an hour later, I feel my phone buzzing in my hand. It's Jason texting.

WYD?

I'm at the Bayport Inn, you gotta come, I text back.

I sway a little, the drinks definitely in full effect. It feels good to be out and a little drunk.

Bet, I'll be there in 10, Jason texts.

"Yay!!" I say to no one.

"Good news?" asks a voice that immediately makes my heart flutter.

Louis.

I whirl around. "Hey!" I say with a big smile. His eyes travel down to my smile and linger for a second before finding my eyes again. I begin to blush.

"Are you gonna turn red like that every time we see each other?" he asks, smirking and pointing at my cheeks. This, of course, only brings my face to yet another level of redness.

"Maybe?"

He laughs softly.

Damn. His laugh is just as good as his voice.

"So, Serenity, what's the news that made you squeal like that?"

"Oh! My friend Jason is coming to have a drink with my sister and me."

"Friend?" he says skeptically, raising an eyebrow. "Or boyfriend?"

"He's gay," I blurt out, then clamp my hand over my mouth, suddenly giggling. He watches me with genuine interest and amusement. "I'm sorry, but I just meant he's definitely not my boyfriend."

His face brightens just enough for me to notice. I can't help but beam up at him stupidly. He is *so* damn attractive. Plus, the drinks have made me less self-conscious.

"You're cute," he decides. "And I am glad you don't have a boyfriend."

"Oh, yeah?" I ask playfully, my liquid courage in full effect now. "You're not so bad yourself."

Alyse bounds over, practically dragging Samaya behind her by her hand.

I cringe because Sam is *way* past buzzed—homegirl is drunk. Her eyes dart between Louis and me mischievously.

"Hi, Louis," Alyse says boldly. He shoots a look at me that seems to say, *how does your friend already know my name?* I shrug and smile up at him.

"Hi…?" He trails off, looking at me for introductions. I realize I am still staring up at him, smiling. I snap out of my apparent trance.

"This is my best friend, Alyse," I begin, gesturing to my roommate, "and this is my big sister, Samaya."

Samaya reaches out, all business, and shakes his hand. "Nice to meet you, Louis."

He looks between us. "I can definitely tell y'all are related," he says as he shakes her hand. Samaya catches my eye and gives me the slightest nod of approval. I smile even wider. I feel Louis' hand on the small of my back, and electricity shoots through my body.

He leans down and whispers, "I gotta get back to my boys, so they don't think I ditched them trying to join girl's night out." Feeling his warm breath on my neck again is almost enough to make me weak in the knees.

I turn and face him. "Of course," I say, "have fun with the guys. It was really nice to meet you tonight."

"You too, ma'am," he says, and I can tell he means it. He begins to walk away, then stops abruptly and pauses for a moment as if calculating his next move. He turns to look at me, and time seems to stop. I notice Alyse and Samaya out of the corner of my eye, watching. He walks the three steps back to me and sighs.

"Ok, I know we just met in a bar, and this is so cliché, but I'd love to connect with you again." Now it's his turn to seem unsteady and nervous. I smile inwardly, enjoying seeing his humanity. His eyes finally find mine, and I almost melt.

Sheesh. He is handsome.

"Do you always get numbers from random girls in bars?" I joke.

"I knew you were gonna ask me that," he chuckles, shaking his head. "I normally don't, but I mean, you did run into me, so maybe I can get your number just to make sure you make it home ok?"

He pulls out his phone, unlocks it, and hands it to me. I go to his contacts and select "Add new contact" to add my information. I hand him back his phone and smile.

He looks pleased. We say our goodbyes, and when I turn back to the girls, Jason has joined the group at some point while I was googly-eyeing Louis.

"That man is perfect," Jason says, almost drooling. I laugh and look at the girls, who are grinning so hard, their cheeks must be hurting. Jason waves his credit card and points back to the bar. Apparently, this place turns into a low-key club situation after 11 p.m. Now that Jason, aka "the life of the party," has arrived, it's going to be a long night.

CHAPTER SIX

By the time we walk out of the Bayport Inn, it's nearly 1 a.m. Louis and his friend, Jamal, walk out with Samaya and me. Jamal and Samaya laugh about something he is whispering into her ear, and I smile. It's been so lovely to see her laughing and relaxing, especially in the presence of a male.

I turn my head over my shoulder to seek out Alyse. I see that she is just exiting the restaurant talking with Sabrina, one of the BFC founders, no doubt networking her ass off. Always the entrepreneur.

When I turn my attention back to Louis, I am surprised to see him staring right at me with a slight smile curling across his lips.

Those beautiful, full lips.

I smile back at him and ask, "what's that look for?"

He reaches out and pulls me into a tentative hug. "I like you, Serenity," he says simply. I hug him back, equally as uncertain.

As soon as our bodies connect, my head automatically lies on his chest as if it belonged there. His hands slowly and rhythmically rub my back, and I can feel his heart beating under his shirt. I close my eyes, wanting to memorize this moment. This hug is heaven—not sexual at all, but not brotherly either. It feels safe and strong, yet gentle and tender at the same time.

We'd spent most of the evening talking and laughing. And although I have two left feet and zero rhythm, we even danced a little. The conversation was light but comfortable, not just because of the alcohol. We talked about work and family. I found out that Louis is a writer and currently works at a start-up company doing all their press releases, blog posts, and social media content. He also has some freelance clients in the city. I learned that his parents are still married and that his family was originally from Louisiana, but they moved to the East Coast when he was twelve. I found out that he played basketball in college, but he didn't pursue anything professionally due to a career-ending knee injury.

He learned that my father left when I was young and that my mom might as well have been gone due to her constant struggles with addiction. I admitted to him that I didn't know what I wanted to do professionally long-term, that I just knew I wanted to help women somehow. He didn't make me feel silly or less-than for that. This is probably my favorite thing so far about him—I felt comfortable being myself around him. This was partly because of his openness and palpable kindness, but partly because, after my last situation, I refuse to ever put on an act or a show for a guy I like.

And I *definitely* like Louis.

I reluctantly pull away from our embrace and look up at him. His eyes look like two pools of Crown Royal: brown, deep, and liquid. We stand there like this for what seems like an eternity. I turn to look for my companions. Samaya is lip-locked with Jamal, fiercely and shamelessly kissing him like there's no tomorrow.

"Oh shit!" I say with a laugh. "Well, they definitely hit it off." I scan the parking lot, looking for where we parked. I spot Sam's car and begin to turn back to Louis, then I see a silver Lexus, and I freeze.

It's the same exact model as David's. I look closer, and I see a figure in the car. Because the person is looking at his phone, the light brightens his face just enough for me to make out the features.

It *is* David.

I tear away from Louis, leaving him stunned, and stride over to Samaya. I try to remain as calm as possible in hopes that David won't realize that I recognized him. I tug on Sam's arm, and she whirls around looking sheepish.

"Hey, girl—" she begins.

"David is here!" I hiss into her ears. Her eyes go wide, and I can almost hear her heart begin to pound, but maybe it's my heart beating out of control. "We need to go, *NOW.*"

She pulls away from Jamal, frantically scanning the parking lot, then sees his car, now idling, and headlights on. She looks at me with a mixture of terror and panic. We both look back towards David's car and see it is backing out of its spot.

By now, the guys are next to us.

"What just happened?" asked a perplexed but concerned Louis. Right then, we hear the screeching of tires and see David peeling off and speeding off into the night. I let out an audible sigh of relief. I turn back to Samaya, searching her face for how she wants to answer his questions.

"Are you ok?" I ask her, pulling her into my arms. She is crying now, the alcohol making her unusually open with her emotions.

"Oh-oh my God, girl," she whispers into my ear. "What the fuck was he doing here?"

All four of us are huddled together now. Alyse runs over from her car. "Was that David?!" she asks in disbelief. She wraps her arms around Samaya.

"Who is David?" asks Jamal. "And what the fuck just happened?"

Samaya and Alyse untangle, and the three of us girls exchange a glance as if to ask *how much do we tell these guys we just met?* Samaya nods.

I sigh. "David is… Samaya's ex-husband." I can feel Jamal stiffen as his eyes go wide. "I don't know why he was here or how he even knew we were here, so it's a little weird, to say the least."

"He's a nut," says Samaya, now hiccupping and wiping away the last remaining tears from her face. "I need to go."

"I'll drive you," I say quickly. I turn to Louis and see the look of concern covering his face. "I am so sorry about all of this…" I trail off, looking away.

I reach to get Sam's keys from her and feel a gentle hand on my wrist. My eyes fill with tears. This is the worst ending to an otherwise epic night.

He pulls me towards him and wraps his long, muscular arms around me, more fiercely than the first time. He plants a quick kiss on the top of my head before whispering, "Please text me when you get there safely." I relax into his arms for a second before pulling away.

"I will." I turn to see Jamal and Alyse walking Sam to her car. I jog over to meet them, unlocking the car so we can pile in. I get in and start the engine as my sister gets in next to me. Jamal looks shaken, but gives her a quick kiss and murmurs something to her, and she nods.

"I'm gonna meet y'all there," calls Alyse over her shoulder as she scurries to her own car. I take one last glance over at Louis, and he is still standing there, stoic, eyes locked on us. I give a little wave and pull out into the dark night.

CHAPTER SEVEN

My anxiety heightens as we pull into Samaya's neighborhood. I decide to circle her block once to see if David's silver Lexus is here.

"Where are you going?" she asks when I drive past her house instead of pulling into her driveway. I continue to scan both sides of the street carefully, squinting to attempt to see better in the dark.

"Making sure David's car isn't parked anywhere on your block," I say. I see her shiver as I look out her window in my peripheral vision. I round the last corner of her block, and since I don't see his car anywhere, I pull into her driveway. I open the garage so I can park the car in there.

Once we get inside, Samaya goes around the house to close all of her blinds and curtains while I lock up the front door before heading to the back door to ensure that is locked too. When I get back to the living room, Samaya walks over and sinks into the couch, her face in her hands.

For a while, we just sit there, stunned, probably both replaying the events of the night since we are both now definitely shocked into sobriety.

There's a knock at the door, and we both jump. Samaya looks at me with eyes that probably mirror my deer-in-the-headlights look. My phone alerts me to an incoming text, and

I look down at the phone face up on the couch, seeing Alyse's name.

It's just me.

"It's Alyse," I tell Samaya, my voice full of relief. I jump up from the couch and peer through the peephole in the door — one can never be too sure. I see Alyse there, looking nervously about her. I open the door and usher her inside. She immediately kicks her heels off and rushes to Samaya's side on the couch.

"Girl, *what the fuck*," she says. "Are you ok? Why was David there?"

"I have no idea how he even knew where I was, Alyse—I am just as shocked as you are."

"Are you guys, like, beefin' or something?" Alyse asks, looking from Samaya to me. "I know y'all are separated, but did something happen?"

Samaya sighs and sinks deeper into the couch. She looks like she wants to descend so far into it that she just disappears. "He's been on a rampage lately, sending me texts and calling me to blame me for what's happening in his life."

My mind begins to reel. The part that concerns me the most is that David somehow knew we'd be there.

"Do you think he's tracking your car?" I ask as my mind reaches for possible scenarios. I saw an episode of Criminal Minds where a woman had installed a GPS on her boyfriend's car to catch him cheating on her.

"We still have the same Verizon phone plan," Samaya says. "Can he track me somehow that way?"

"No, sweetie," I say gently, "you'd have to share your location with him."

"Where's your phone?" Alyse asks her.

Samaya looks around for her purse and sees that it's on the center island in the kitchen. She gets up and walks over to grab it, rummaging around for her phone as she returns to her burrow on the couch. Before handing it over to Alyse, she looks at something on it and then gasps at what she sees.

"What?" I ask. But she continues reading whatever it is she is reading. Alyse and I exchange a glance, and she shrugs. Samaya tosses the phone toward me and buries her face in her hands.

"I hate him," she mumbles into her palms.

I grab her phone and read the text message — well, messages. They are all from David.

WHORE!

We aren't even divorced and you're already hooking up with random guys.

Fucking bitch.

I can't believe this.

Although there are several more in his string of insulting texts, I stop reading. I've seen enough.

Too much.

I drop the phone onto the coffee table before me and sit next to Samaya, rubbing her back. Alyse grabs the phone and reads the messages to herself.

As I rub Samaya's back, I can feel her shaking. What a dick.

"Oh my God, girl, this man is crazy as hell," Alyse says, clearly disgusted. "You guys aren't even together anymore, so where does he get off talking to you like that?"

"That's exactly the problem. David does get off on talking to me like that."

I glance at her phone just to check the time. It's almost 2:30 a.m., and I'm exhausted. Emotionally and physically, although I doubt I'll get much sleep. I look at Samaya. She has her knees pulled up into her chest as she stares off into the air in front of her.

"Look," I begin. "I'm going to stay here tonight. You should try and get some rest tonight — if you stay up, all you're gonna do is stress out about this shit."

"Serenity, you don't need—"

I cut her off. "I'm staying," I say firmly.

"I'm staying too," Alyse echoes.

I stand, putting my hand out in front of Sam. She looks up, sighs, and grabs my hand. I help her up and lead her to the foot of the stairs. I turn to see Alyse right behind me. I raise an eyebrow.

"I'm not staying down here by myself, the fuck!" she says, clearly shaken. I don't blame her. I grab her hand with my free hand, and we walk upstairs, hands linked like a human chain.

I wake with a start. I sit straight up, momentarily confused, until I remember where I am.

Crash!

It's thunder, I realize after a terrifying second. I place my hand over my pounding heart. *Get a grip, girl.*

I look over at Alyse, sleeping soundly on the other side of the queen-sized bed in Samaya's guest bedroom. Taking a deep breath, I get up gently to not wake her up. Once I am safely off the bed, I walk towards the door and slowly open it to make my way down to grab some water from the kitchen. After all those Jack Daniels drinks, my head is pounding, and my mouth feels like I slept with a cotton ball in it.

The floorboard in the hallway creaks loudly, and I pause. Then I hear something downstairs. It's slight, so I listen more intently as I stand in the darkness, trying to hear over my jackhammering heart.

It sounds like a soft whooshing, like feet moving quickly over carpet downstairs. I hold my breath, hoping I'm trippin' and the events of last night just have me imagining things. I stand completely still and hear it again. I slowly begin backing up towards the guest bedroom door, my heart beating so hard now that I can hear it in my head.

The next thing I hear makes my heart almost stop. The front door creaks shut and then latches softly. I gasp, running into the guest room and closing and locking the door. I shake Alyse awake in full-on panic mode.

"What?" she says groggily before sitting straight up on her side of the bed. She takes one look at my face in the dim light. "What happened, girl? You look spooked!"

"Girl!" I hiss, breathless, "someone was downstairs in the house. I heard the front door close too!" My hands are shaking so uncontrollably at this point that I have to put them between my thighs just to steady them. Alyse's already wide eyes become owlish.

"What. The. *Fuck,*" are her only words. She looks towards the door. "Maybe it was Sam?"

I look at the digital clock on the nightstand next to the bed. 4 a.m. Samaya has zero reason to be up, let alone sneaking around her own house. I tell Alyse this, and she nods shakily.

"I have to go check on her," I say, rising from the bed. Alyse joins me, and we exchange a terrified look before creeping back into the hallway.

CHAPTER EIGHT

We enter the hall cautiously and pause in the darkness to listen for additional sounds anywhere else in the house. I slink cat-like toward Samaya's room a few feet away. When we reach her door, I open it slowly.

It's completely dark save for the soft glow of a dim salt lamp in the far corner of her room on her desk. I look closely at her bed and see her dark form there.

"Sam?" I whisper. When she doesn't respond, I say her name a little louder.

Still nothing.

My heart starts to pound again. I walk over to Sam's bed and peer down at her. I can see her chest rising and falling with breath. I let out a long sigh of relief. I reach over to turn on her bedside lamp, and she groans softly in protest, squeezing her eyelids together at the sudden assault of light. I shake her shoulder until she wakes up.

"Somebody was just in the house!" Alyse blurts out from behind me as she rushes over to the other side of Samaya's bed and sits down. Now it's Sam's turn to sit straight up in bed. She looks around confused and panicked, eyes bloodshot from tears a few hours ago.

"What?" she says, trying to wrap her still-groggy mind around Alyse's words. Samaya looks at me in hopeful bewilderment, hoping I have more details for her.

I take a deep breath, trying hard to steady myself. "I was gonna go downstairs to get some water," I begin, "but when I got to the hall, I swore I could hear footsteps downstairs, then I heard the front door open, and the latch closed—that's when I knew someone had been inside." The words tumble out as I recall the memory.

Samaya looks horrified and stunned. Her hand flies to her mouth. "Oh my God," she whispers.

"We need to call the police," Alyse says, glancing around for Samaya's cell phone. I spot it on the nightstand and pick it up with trembling fingers.

I dial the numbers 9-1-1 and wait for the dispatch to pick up the phone.

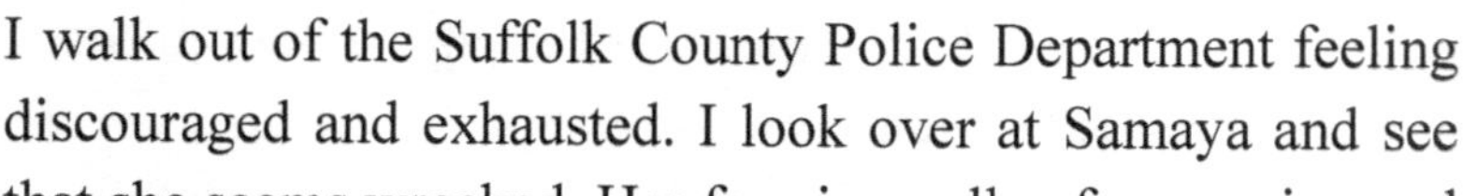

I walk out of the Suffolk County Police Department feeling discouraged and exhausted. I look over at Samaya and see that she seems wrecked. Her face is swollen from crying and the lack of sleep. We are both silent as we approach her car.

"I'll drive," I say, and she tosses me her keys and walks around to the passenger side. We climb in, and as I start the engine, I hear her let out a tired sigh.

"Well, that was a joke," she says. "I mean, I knew that cops are a joke, but I thought maybe they would do more than that."

An officer, Detective Markovich, had called us in and asked Sam a few questions, but when they found out that whoever came in obviously had a key and hadn't stolen anything, this was more a domestic issue and suggested we come down to the station to make our statements.

"Do you know who had access to your house key?" Officer Markovich had asked her. Samaya told him that she thought it was most likely her soon-to-be ex-husband. Markovich scribbled something in his notepad as she spoke.

"He showed up at an event that my sister and her roommate invited me to, at the Bayport Inn."

"Did you tell—what's your husband's name?" he asked.

"David."

"Had you mentioned to David where you all were supposed to be last night?"

"No, definitely not. We aren't on great terms."

"Then how did he know you were there?"

Samaya and I exchange a look.

"I don't know, that's why all of this is so alarming," Samaya said, a hint of frustration in her voice. Her distrust in police seeped into her tone of voice.

I don't blame her and have similar feelings. Chris Robinson, a friend she'd gone to high school with, had been shot by the Marin County Police Department six years ago for the simple fact that he was a Black man in a dark hoodie. The officer alleged that he thought Chris was a "credible threat." Somehow, that statement justified the killing of otherwise innocent men.

Markovich must've sensed her frustration. "Ma'am, I know you're shaken up, but I just want to get all the facts," he says softly.

She dropped her shoulders a little. "I have no idea how David knew that we were there, but he was there when we left the event around 1 a.m."

"What time did you hear the intruder in the home?"

"It was a little after 4 a.m.," I'd chimed in. "I was the one who heard the footsteps downstairs and the front door closing."

More notes in the impossibly small notepad.

"Did you see anyone?"

"No, it was completely dark."

"Is there anything you'd like to add?" Markovich was looking expectantly at Alyse now. She swallowed uncomfortably and cleared her throat.

"Um, no, sir. I just woke up, and Serenity told me someone had been in the house, then we went to check on Samaya and let her know what was happening."

Officer Markovich gave Alyse a once-over, lingering just a little too long on her robust bustline. I rolled my eyes in disgust. Uniform or not, men are just men. Luckily her eyes were already back in her lap, and she didn't catch him admiring her tits.

"Alright, ladies," he said, "I'm going to go over this information with my partner, and then I will come to get you guys—just go ahead and wait back in the lobby."

We filed out wordlessly and sat in the hard plastic chairs that make up the lobby of the police station. After about ten minutes, Markovich walked out of the conference room with a short Latino man whose badge read Garcia. Garcia cleared his throat and glanced at Markovich before addressing us.

"Good morning, ladies. Firstly, I am so sorry about what has occurred—it sounds like you had a traumatic evening last night," he'd said. "Unfortunately, since nothing was stolen and we aren't sure who was in the home, we don't have much to go on."

My jaw dropped, and I looked at Samaya. She looked more exhausted than shocked.

"What do you mean? He followed her to the Bayport Inn. Can't you use stalking or something?" I ask.

"Well, he was at a public establishment—it could've been coincidental," Garcia said.

"But what about the menacing texts he'd sent?"

Markovich sighs. "The law is a tricky thing, ma'am. We'd have to be able to prove he was there for her—had he approached her at the establishment, we possibly could've used that to at least go knock on his door. Right now, we have nothing."

I shake my head, incredulous. "Wow," I said under my breath.

"So, what do you suggest I do, officer? Wait until he comes into my home and kills me?" asks Samaya. Markovich's face turns red.

"Of course not, ma'am. Look, I know this is frustrating. I will suggest that you change the locks in your home and maybe invest in an alarm system."

And that had been that.

I pull onto the highway, and we drive in silence for a while. We head to my apartment so Samaya can drop me off before she runs to Home Depot to get all new locks and deadbolts for her house. I tried to come with her, but she refused, saying she wanted to be alone. While I don't particularly like the idea of her being alone right now, I know my sister, and I know her need for space during stressful times. She is a Scorpio to a T, retreating into the depths when things become uncertain or feel "too big." Being a Pisces, a fellow water sign, I understand her intense connection and commitment to processing her emotions.

"Please call me if anything happens or if you want me to come over. Seriously, Sam."

"I will, babe. Thanks for everything, sister," she says wearily as she climbs into the driver seat. I watch as she drives off, and I say a silent prayer:

God, please be with my sister.

CHAPTER NINE

When I wake up, I have three new text alerts. I smile when I see the first one is from Louis.

Good morning, beautiful

The next is from Alyse from late last night, presumably when she got home, asking if I have any tampons. I assume she figured that out since the text was sent over six hours ago. The subsequent text immediately makes my stomach turn.

I miss you

It's from my ex, Dre. I'm immediately annoyed. What is it about guys reaching out as soon as you meet or start talking to someone new; it's like they can sense you're on the cusp of moving on, and their fuck-boy Spidey senses kick in. They reach out with the *WYD* or *I miss what we had* bullshit. I wonder if he's still talking to what's-her-name or if he's just out fucking anything and everything in his newfound freedom.

I exit out of his message and return to my good morning text from Louis.

Good morning sir, I type.

Sending *Handsome* feels like I'm doing too much too soon, so I opt for a smiley face emoji. It feels strange to text a guy I don't really know, but it also feels exciting. My heart beats a little faster when I see that he's responding.

I just wanted to check on you. I know it's been a crazy couple of days for ya.

Aww, thanks. Feeling a little more like myself today, I text back.

His response is quick.

Good. I know we just met, but if you need to talk I'm here.

My heart swells. So, the other night wasn't an act—he might just genuinely be a nice guy. Before I toss my phone down and get ready for my day, I text Alyse to see if she's home. I wait a few minutes, lying in bed, mentally going over my day.

No response. It's only 8 a.m. She's probably still asleep. I decide to sit down to meditate, something I do every now and then. I'd taken some yoga classes in the Bay Area, and they help with my anxiety. The problem is that I'm just not consistent with it.

I settle down on the floor, situating my body in a comfortable seated position. I roll my shoulders back and down, then roll my neck to the right. It pops so loud I can't help but laugh. My neck is tight, and understandably so. It's been a crazy week. Closing my eyes again, I begin to deepen my breath, inhaling deeply all the way down into my belly. I hold my breath for a count and then exhale slowly through my mouth the way Jennifer, my previous yoga teacher, showed us in class.

After a few deep breaths, I focus my awareness on my body and notice that my shoulders are almost up to my ears. I soften there, allowing them to relax down to their intended position.

I reach upward with the crown of my head and try to really get grounded, allowing myself to focus on the feeling of my butt rooted to the floor. My breathing becomes rhythmic, and my mind softens as the meditation does what it's intended to do.

I don't know how much time has passed when my phone rings. I take a deep inhale through my nose and exhale it out through my mouth, silently thanking the universe for these moments of peace. When I get up and look at my phone, I see it's Samaya.

"Hey, girl!" I say into the phone. "How are you?"

"Better today. Do you work today? Let's do something. I need to get out of this house. It's creeping me out since all that mess happened Friday night."

"I do work, but it's a short shift—only 12 to 4 today," I say.

"Ok, cool, let's do Cheesecake Factory when you get off," she says. "I'm craving their herb-crusted salmon."

I laugh. "I'm down, girl. Let's meet at 4:30."

We hang up, and I look at my clock. I head into the bathroom to shower and get ready for work. I need to leave early to stop by the Safelight place to quote my busted windshield.

I think back over the last few days as I wash my hair. First, I hit the bird with my car, then all the shit with Samaya and David. Maybe hitting that bird really is bringing me bad luck. But I also met Louis, and that is most definitely a positive.

I smile at the thought of Louis, the one shiny bright thing this weekend. I immediately think about Dre and his slimy ways. He seemed nice in the beginning—not this nice, but nice nonetheless.

I sigh and rinse my hair. I know you're not supposed to take the energy of your past relationships into your new prospects and relationships, but Dre's actions were so blatant, and still to this day, I cannot get the image of him eating that girl out off my mind.

I rinse off and step out of the shower, reaching for my towel. I grab my lotion and apply it absentmindedly to my neck and shoulders. My mind drifts back to Louis, more specifically to the hug we shared in the parking lot and how good he smelled. It's been months since I've had sex or even been touched by a man.

I let my towel drop to the floor and gaze at my naked body in the mirror. I lightly trace my right pointer finger up my stomach, then graze my breast. I imagine that it's Louis' hand, and my right nipple immediately stiffens as my finger passes over it. I feel that faint, familiar tingle in my core.

It's been so long.

I close my eyes and allow my mind to wander, imagining Louis standing behind me, gently exploring my body with his strong hand. I trail my hand down my waist again, imagining that it's his, and I let it trail all the way down to my clit. It's so sensitive with the anticipation of touch that I moan when my fingers press against it gently. My whole body shivers.

God, I need to get laid.

I wrap my towel around myself and head back into my room to get dressed.

CHAPTER TEN

"**C**heers!"

We clink glasses and giggle. I take a big gulp of my lemon drop martini and watch Sam wipe her lips after sipping her white wine. We've barely sat down and already ordered our food. I lean back and turn toward her.

"So," I say, "how are you? How was your first night in the house with all the new locks?"

She takes another sip before answering. "For the low, low price of $500, a woman can feel safe and secure in her own home again." She says it in a perfect suburban white-girl voice. "I slept so much better though, girl I can't even lie. I just could've spent that money in so many other ways."

"I feel you, sis, but peace of mind is priceless."

She nods hard. "Fuck yes. Minor financial setback for peace of mind? I'll take that. It's just frustrating because it's yet another thing David has stolen from me."

I wince. I know exactly what she means. "Have you heard more from him?"

"Girl, yes. He kept calling me yesterday wishing I catch an STD for 'cheating on him.' I'm like... bro... we've been separated for months. I finally blocked his crazy ass."

"Good," I say, stirring my drink.

"I'm just so ready to move on with my life. That man has done nothing but drag me down since the day we met. I refuse to give him anything else — especially my energy."

Our food arrives. My tomato basil pasta looks divine. You'd think working at Mario's all day would kill my appetite for Italian food, but no. This California girl is ready for all the carbs.

Next to me, Samaya moans into her forkful of herb-crusted salmon like she's been spiritually reunited with happiness. Her eyes roll back dramatically. I laugh and dig into my pasta.

"You girls want another drink?" the waitress asks. She looks like a Grey's Anatomy character whose name I cannot remember to save my life.

My glass is basically empty. My mouth is full of pasta, so I nod wildly with a thumbs-up. She smiles like she knows my soul and also thinks I'm a mess.

My phone pings. I glance down and see Louis' name. Sam leans in with her nosey self.

"Oooooh! Is that dude from the other night??"

I nod and open the message.

Thinking of you. How's your day going?

My stomach does that ridiculous little flip.

Hi! It's going good, grabbing food and drinks with my sister. WBU?

Nice. Day off today. At Smithhaven mall with my boy.

I squeal and show Samaya. "Girl. He's HERE. IN THE MALL."

"Tell him to meet up with us!" she says. "I owe him an apology for the other night… Jesus. What a shit-show."

I glance down at my outfit like a coward. Sam catches me and rolls her eyes. "You look fine."

That's crazy! We're actually in the Cheesecake Factory here, I text.

His response comes instantly:

Want some company? Don't wanna intrude tho.

My heart jumps.

Come thru

I stand so fast Samaya's head whips around like she's searching for David. I grab her shoulders.

"I'm just going to the bathroom to make sure I don't look a mess. I just got off work."

Her body relaxes. She smiles softly. "You look beautiful, sister."

I speed-walk toward the restroom. Almost trip over a server. Apologize with frantic eyebrow movements. Continue my mini-sprint.

Inside, I immediately have to pee. Anxiety = bladder betrayal.

After, I check myself in the mirror. Not bad. Cute, even. I fluff my curls and tug my black shirt into place. I do a little half-turn to check my booty — she's giving pasta-fueled plump. My "lil booty," as the aunties would say, is definitely lil but also definitely sitting.

Also, Louis saw it the other night and did not run. So.

My phone buzzes. It's Sam:

They're here, and his boy is Jamal!!!!!!!

I smile at myself like a lovesick idiot. Perfect. Literally perfect.

I take a steadying breath and walk out.

As I approach our section, I see Samaya laughing with Jamal and Louis. Louis has his back to me, and even like that he's taking up half the restaurant's energy. Hoodie, jeans, hat — casual but fine as hell.

Samaya sees me first. Her smile widens in a *yo, your man is here* kind of way.

Louis turns.

His eyes lock onto mine instantly.

"Hey," Samaya sings, eyebrows bouncing between us. Louis and I still haven't looked away from each other.

"Hey," I manage, finally glancing at Jamal. He pulls me into a bear hug.

"What up, lil sis?" he says. I'd forgotten how animated he is. *Okay Suave Jr.*

I pull away and look at Louis again. "Hi, Louis."

"Hi, Serenity," he says in that honey-warm voice I've been replaying in my head for days. He pulls me in for a quick hug—firm, intentional, like he means it.

I slide into the booth next to Samaya. Louis sits across from me with Jamal beside him.

"Did y'all order yet?" I ask. The waitress magically appears and takes their orders.

When she leaves, Jamal jumps right in.

"So, what happened on Friday night?"

Samaya shifts, uncomfortable.

"Just some old family drama," I say quickly.

"My ex-husband showed up," Samaya adds quietly. "Completely unexpected."

Jamal's eyes widen.

"We've been separated for months," she adds quickly, and he relaxes.

"Is he stalking you?" he asks.

"No. I don't think so," she says. "He's just struggling with the fact that it's over."

"I'm sorry you're dealing with that," Louis says softly.

Thankfully the conversation lightens when our drinks come. And Jamal — Lord. He is younger, and it shows. But in a fun way. Samaya looks… alive. Playful. It makes me warm to see her like this.

Throughout the meal, Louis keeps catching my eye. Not in a creepy way — in a quiet interest way. His energy is different. Calmer. Grounded. Attractive in a grown-man way.

Eventually Samaya glances at her phone and gasps. "Oh shit, I gotta go. I have an early client tomorrow."

"I could help you with that," Jamal says, smooth as hell.

The silent eye conversation between the two of them says everything. Neither of us has had sex in months. This is the universe working overtime.

"Alright," she says softly.

I look at Louis, and he just smiles like I know your sister's about to get her back blown out.

We pay our bill and head outside.

Louis scratches the back of his neck. "So… I came with Jamal, and now he's heading over to your sister's…" He trails off.

I laugh. "Do you need a ride home? I can take you."

I probably sound too eager. I don't care.

His smile is pure relief. "Cool. Thanks."

We say our goodbyes and walk to my car.

When he settles into the passenger seat, I have to look over just to process the moment.

This fine-ass man is in my car.

He smiles at me.

I smile back.

"Ready?" he asks.

God help me.

"Yes."

CHAPTER ELEVEN

As soon as he unlocks the door to his apartment, my nerves kick in again. The drive over is full of easy conversation about my playlist and my musical preferences, but now that I'm standing in the threshold of his place, suddenly everything feels too real. My chest tightens, and a single thought flashes through my mind:

What am I doing here?

Louis steps inside and turns toward me, lifting his arm in a gentle come on in motion. He tosses his keys into a bowl on a small wooden table near the door. Organized, I think, mentally taking note.

The living room is neat. A black couch—clean, simple, surprisingly comfortable-looking—sits in the center of the space. A wooden coffee table anchors the room. A tall lamp stands in the corner. When he turns it on, warm light spills through the space, revealing a small kitchen and two closed doors that must lead to the bedroom and bathroom.

I wander toward the kitchen—really just an extension of the living room. It's spotless except for a single bowl and spoon in the sink.

He joins me. "Want something to drink? I've got water and a couple beers, I think."

He opens the fridge, bends his tall frame down to look inside.

"Um… I'll take a beer," I say.

Louis hands me a Corona after popping the cap off. He grabs one for himself and two glasses of water. Always thoughtful, apparently.

"Would you like the grand tour?" he asks, giving a half-grin. "Although full disclaimer, it's not that grand. It's just a one-bedroom."

That smile. The one that makes my knees threaten to give out.

"I'd love a tour."

He leads me to the first door and pushes it open. "Bathroom," he says unnecessarily.

I peek inside. "It's so clean!"

He smirks. "What did you expect—piss all over the seats or something?"

I laugh. "Trust me, I've seen some thangs."

"Oh, I believe you," he says, chuckling. "Why do you think I no longer have roommates? And it ain't because the cost of living is cheap."

We move on to the next door. He just taps it. "Laundry."

Then the last door. He opens it and flicks on the light.

"This is me," he says.

His room feels like him—simple, warm, masculine. A writing desk sits in the corner with his laptop open from some ongoing project. A basketball rests beside a rolled-up yoga mat.

"You do yoga?" I ask, eyebrows raised.

He shrugs, smiling sheepishly. "I try."

I slow-walk past him and peer into his open closet. Stacks and stacks of shoeboxes line the wall. Jordans, Nikes—most of the classic ones.

I glance back at him, raising a brow. He shrugs with a grin.

"I'm a basketball player and a sneakerhead at heart."

"I'm not mad at it," I say, lifting my hands in mock surrender.

I drift toward his desk and peek at his open laptop. Microsoft Word is pulled up with several paragraphs written. "What are you working on?" I ask, curious.

He steps beside me in two strides, suddenly shy.

"It's… a short story. I'm thinking about submitting it to Writer's Digest for their competition."

"A short story?" I ask, excited. "I didn't know you wrote fiction too. What's it about?"

He hesitates. "You really wanna know?"

"Of course."

He takes a breath, then smiles. "It's a horror story. The main character is a Black kid from Harlem who moves down south. He starts getting haunted by the ghost of a slave owner. So it's scary, but also about how racism still shows up in modern America."

I pause, impressed. "Sounds very Jordan Peele. I like it." I gesture to the laptop. "Can I read it?"

He closes the laptop gently.

Or not.

"When it's ready, you can read it. It still needs some work."

"I'm going to hold you to that," I say playfully.

He gives me that sexy, slow smile again, and my stomach flips.

We head back into the living room, and I take a seat on the couch. Louis dims the lights, sets our waters on the table, and settles in beside me.

"So, Serenity," he says, voice low and warm, "now that I've finally got you all alone, I wanna know who you are."

Well. Damn. Diving right in, sir?

I swallow, automatically twirling a curl between my fingers—my signature anxious tell. He chuckles softly. I take a swig of beer to steady myself.

"What do you want to know?" I ask.

"Well, let's start with what brought you out here."

Here it is. The question I was hoping to dodge.

Dre.

"It's a long story," I say, exhaling. "But I've been here since the summer, and so far, it's pretty cool."

He squints at me gently. "Did you and your sister move at the same time?"

"Oh no, she's been here for years—she went to college in the city."

"Got it." He nods. "So what about you? What made you move here?"

I counter quickly. "What made you move to Long Island?"

He leans back, thinking. "The city is too hectic for my artist soul."

My heart melts.

Not just because he said "artist soul," but because he said it without irony.

"I like it here," he continues. "Still close to the city, but peaceful. A little more space."

He looks at me again. "But you still didn't answer the original question."

"I know…" I sigh. "It's just… a lot."

He shifts closer, wraps an arm around my shoulders, and gently pulls me against him. The second my head rests on his chest, something inside me softens. His cologne, his warmth, his quiet steadiness—it's all grounding.

"It's a depressing story," I whisper.

"Bring it on," he says. "I don't scare easy."

So I tell him.

All of it.

Everything about Dre, the betrayal, the way it broke something inside me. He listens—truly listens—without interrupting. His hand rubs my arm when I get to the worst parts. By the time I finish, I feel emotionally wrung out.

"Got anything stronger than beer?" I ask, voice small.

He cups my cheeks gently and turns my face toward him. His eyes are warm and sincere, and something in me cracks a little.

"I'm sorry that happened to you," he says softly. "You didn't deserve that. He's a piece of shit."

I blink fast—too fast—and one rogue tear escapes anyway. *Dammit.*

He tilts my chin up again. "Serenity… don't hide that. You're allowed to be hurt. What he did was fucked up."

My body moves before my mind catches up—I wrap my arms around his neck and collapse into his chest. He hugs me tightly, one arm around my waist, the other moving slow circles on my back.

We sit like that for a long, long time. Breathing together. Quiet.

Eventually he lets me go and stands. "It's close to midnight," he says with a soft grin. "I don't have shit to do tomorrow, but I don't want to mess up your day."

"You kicking me out?" I ask dramatically.

"Hell nah." He opens his freezer. "I got Honey Jack. If you still want that drink."

He holds up the bottle. I grin and throw both thumbs up.

"My favorite."

He laughs and grabs two red Solo cups.

"*Aye!* Party cups!" I giggle.

He mixes the drinks. I take a huge swig—and almost choke.

"No soda??"

"It's Honey Jack," he says, confused. "You don't drink it straight?"

I cough. "I have—I just wasn't expecting it."

He laughs. "We thuggin' it today, baby. All I got is coconut milk or orange juice."

I cringe. "Yeah… this is fine."

He takes my hand and leads me to his bedroom. My heart tries to sprint out of my chest, but I follow.

Inside, he closes the door gently. The blue LED lights glow against the walls, mixing with the soft overhead light. It's warm. Sexy. Calming. All at once.

"I love your lights," I say.

"It's a vibe," he agrees, dropping onto the bed and patting the space beside him. I sit.

He watches me for a long moment—long enough for my knees to go weak even though I'm sitting. Then he reaches over and brushes a curl away from my eye.

"You're so beautiful, Serenity," he whispers.

The way he says my name… *God.*

"Thank you," I whisper back.

His eyes drop to my lips. My breath catches. I lean in at the exact moment he does, and when his mouth touches mine, everything else fades. His kiss is slow at first—soft, curious. Then deeper. Hotter. His hands slide to the back of my neck, pulling me closer.

I climb onto his lap, straddling him, kissing him harder. Our breaths get louder. His body heat wraps around me like a blanket.

When we finally separate, both of us are breathless.

"Damn," he murmurs.

I lay my head on his shoulder, smiling into his neck.

"Damn is right."

He laughs lightly. "Wanna watch a movie?"

I nod. He holds onto my thighs, refusing to let me get up until he kisses my forehead, then each cheek.

"Okay," he says softly, "now you can get up."

He returns with snacks—Skittles, Honey Buns, Doritos—like a giant child.

"Diabetes much?" I tease.

"You know you want these Honey Buns," he says in a fake southern drawl.

"I do," I admit, grabbing one. "And some Doritos."

"My kinda girl."

We crawl under the plaid throw blanket and he turns on the TV.

"Candyman?" he asks, excited.

"Which one?"

"The new one, *duh*."

"I love scary movies, but I can't watch them alone."

"You're not gonna go in the bathroom and say his name three times, right?"

I snort. "I'm only half white, bro."

He cracks up.

We settle in. About ten minutes later, I'm curled against his chest, half-asleep, feeling the safest I've felt in months.

And that's how the night ends.

With snacks, blue lights, his arm around me—

—and me drifting off on his heartbeat.

CHAPTER TWELVE

When I wake up, I immediately feel something warm beside me. Sunlight slices through the window straight into my eyes, so I squint and roll over fast to escape the glare. The first thing I see is Louis' sleeping face.

I prop my head up on my hand and just… study him. His lashes are long and thick—unfairly so. His lips are slightly parted, breath soft and steady. He looks peaceful in a way that makes my chest melt a little.

I ease myself out of the bed, moving slowly so I don't wake him. He stirs but doesn't wake.

Whew.

I tiptoe into the bathroom. After I pee, I step up to the mirror, bracing myself for the hair disaster I'm expecting. I wasn't planning on falling asleep here, so I didn't do the nightly pineapple ponytail situation. But when I finally take in my reflection, I'm pleasantly surprised—my curls are a little frizzy, sure, but nowhere near the usual level of chaos that comes from sleeping recklessly without protection.

I wash the sleep from my eyes and scan the counter for toothpaste. When I spot it, I squeeze a dot onto my finger and brush my teeth the old-fashioned hood-girl way. It'll have to do.

Back in the bedroom, Louis is still asleep. I reach down to the floor on the side I slept on, grab my phone, and check the time. Almost 9:30 a.m. I slide back under the blankets, and not even ten seconds later, he wakes—eyes blinking open slowly as a smile spreads across his lips.

"Good morning, sleepyhead," I say.

"Hey, beautiful."

My God. His morning voice should be illegal.

He yawns and stretches, then sits up. As he swings his legs over the opposite side of the bed, the sun hits his back—and that's when I notice the tattoos. His whole back is covered. And somehow that just makes him even finer, especially because he's not that typical "I'm tatted so I'm a bad boy" type. He turns and catches me blatantly staring.

"What?" he asks, smiling like he already knows.

I blush instantly and shake my head.

"Uh oh," he teases. "The blushing is back."

I throw a pillow at him, and he laughs, dodging it easily.

"Hungry?" he asks.

I nod. "I can grab something on the way home th—"

He frowns at me like I just said something offensive. "Or you can eat here. I'll cook us breakfast."

He gets up and walks out. I sit there stunned, sinking back into the pillow with a huge stupid grin. No man has ever cooked for me in my twenty-nine years of existence.

It's almost noon by the time I'm rushing home to change and get to the auto glass place. If I'd known I was spending the night away from home, I would've packed clothes. Rain smacks against my windshield, and people are driving like they've never seen weather before. I glance at the clock and force myself to relax. I still have a little time.

At the next light, I call Sam. If I know my sister, there's a good chance things got spicy last night with Jamal.

Her voicemail picks up instantly.

No ring.

That's… odd.

She never has her phone off.

Unless—

No. I decide to assume the fun option: she got laid and forgot to charge it.

At the light, I text her:

Long night? Call me back!!

The rain thickens. My wipers work overtime. I swear I hit every red light between the mall and the apartment complex.

When I finally pull in, I have maybe thirty minutes to shower, change, and head right back out.

Alyse is waiting the second I open the door. "Where've you been?"

"Walk with me," I say, sprinting to my room. "I'm running late."

She hustles behind me, breathless. *"Well??"*

"Girl. I went to Louis' house after drinks."

Her eyes nearly fall out of her head. "Oh my GOD! The guys from Friday?!"

I grin while pushing past her to start the shower.

"Did y'all… you know?" she asks, narrowing her eyes.

"Fuck?" I say. "No. I'm not ready for all that yet."

I shoo her from the bathroom, shower quickly—making sure to keep my curls dry—and pull my hair into the messiest bun known to man. Hoodie, jeans, two hair ties for safety, and I'm out the door.

"I want full details when you get home!" Alyse calls after me.

"I'll be back in two hours!"

On the drive to the windshield repair shop, I call Sam again. Straight to voicemail again.

A strange unease hits my chest. She did say she had an early client this morning… but even then, she'd never turn her phone off.

At Safelite, the paperwork is easy. The wait time isn't. Over an hour. I sit down and call Sam again.

Nothing.

The longer her phone stays off, the more my anxiety ratchets up.

Trying to distract myself, I call Louis.

Partly because I'm bored. Partly because I need reassurance.

And partly because Jamal was with Sam last night.

He answers on the second ring. "Did you miss me already?"

I smile. "Maybe."

"What's up?"

"I'm stuck at the auto glass place for over an hour, but also… I can't get a hold of Sam. Her phone is off. It's never off."

"Didn't she say she had a client today?" he asks. "Maybe she turned it off for work?"

He doesn't know her. Sam doesn't turn her phone off for anything.

"I don't know. Have you talked to Jamal?"

"Nah. Want me to call him?"

I hesitate. Am I overreacting? She's an adult. She's fine. But something in me is vibrating with dread.

"Could you? Please?"

"Of course."

While he calls, I stare out the huge window. Rain sheets down the glass. Cars inch through the Walmart parking lot. Somewhere behind me, the coffee machine sputters—heavy, burnt-smelling, the exact scent from the AA meetings Mom used to drag me to.

My phone rings.

"Hey," Louis says. "Jamal said he left around two. She told him she was going to bed."

I chew my bottom lip, staring out at the rain.

"Okay," I say quietly. "I'm gonna call you back."

"You sure? Want me to come meet you?"

"Let me call you right back."

I hang up and call Sam again.

Again—straight to voicemail.

My stomach twists.

My palms sweat.

My shoulders crawl toward my ears.

I drop them consciously. Roll my neck. Try to breathe.

When I ask the woman at the front desk about wait time, she sighs like I've ruined her life, then reluctantly checks. When she returns, her tone has softened.

"It'll be a couple more hours, sweetie. One of our guys had to pick up a tool from another location. Tim says he's so sorry."

"A couple *hours?*" I repeat. "So… four p.m.?"

She tries to sound sympathetic but only manages to look blotchy and irritated. "Yes. We'll call if it's going to be later."

They won't. I know they won't.

"Thanks," I say, heading back to my seat.

I text Louis:

Please come get me. It'll be here until at least 4 p.m.

His reply is instant:

On my way.

Relief hits me hard. Outside, the storm is relentless. Sirens wail somewhere in the distance. Cars tread carefully through the waterlogged lot.

But underneath all of that, one thought pulses through my mind:

What the hell is going on with Samaya?

Everything in me wants to believe she overslept or forgot her charger or turned her phone off by mistake. But my gut— the same gut that woke me up at 4 a.m. the other night—won't settle.

Just as the panic threatens to spiral, I see Louis through the rain, jogging up to the front door.

I jump up and hurry toward him.

"Please call me when the car is ready!" I say to the woman at the desk as I grab my purse and umbrella.

Louis pulls me into a hug under the awning.

"Hey," he says, warm and steady

"Hi," I whisper into his chest, overwhelmed. I pull back, breath shaky. "Thank you for coming—can you take me to my sister's?"

CHAPTER THIRTEEN

As soon as we round the corner onto Samaya's street, my stomach tightens. My already through-the-roof anxiety spikes even higher.

"It's the grey house on the right," I tell Louis, pointing. He slows as we get closer.

Her car sits in the driveway, and before I even register the thought, I notice her front door is slightly open. My heart starts pounding. I'm out of the car before Louis even has it in park.

"Ser—" he starts, but I'm already gone. My legs tremble, but somehow they carry me to her car. I cup my hands around my face and peer through the windows. Empty. Louis appears beside me, and I shake my head.

Something is definitely wrong. I can feel it.

I walk slowly to the front door, Louis close behind. It creaks when I push it open. I crane my neck into the entryway and living room. Empty. Normal. Too normal.

We step inside. I take only a few steps before Louis speaks behind me.

"What the *fuck.*"

I turn. His hand is still on the doorknob, but his eyes are locked on the top half of the door.

Blood.

A bloody, hand-shaped stain smears across the door. I gasp, hand flying to my mouth. Louis jerks his hand off the knob and pulls me back outside.

"We need to call the police. Now," he says, eyes wide as two full moons.

I just stand there, frozen in shock.

"Now," he repeats, sharper this time.

My fingers fumble through my hoodie pocket, finally closing around my phone. I dial. Everything feels slow and distant. Louis paces in front of me, hands dragging down his cheeks, then up over his head in his own version of panic.

The dispatcher tells me to get somewhere safe and wait for officers in case someone is still inside. I hear myself answering, "Okay." My phone slips from my hand and lands in the wet grass. I drop beside it, pulling my knees to my chest and staring at nothing.

Louis crouches in front of me. I blink back into myself. He offers his hand, and I take it. When he pulls me up, he wraps me into his arms—my body stiff at first, then melting against him.

"What'd they say?" he asks gently.

"They're sending an officer," I manage.

"Okay. Good."

"I need to go inside," I say, stepping back. His grip tightens.

"We can't go in, Serenity. There's blood, and it's obviously a crime scene."

Something hot flares in my chest. "My sister could be in there."

His face falls. "We need to wait for the police," he says, but even he sounds unsure.

I pull away and run for the house. He follows.

"I'm going in," I say flatly.

He nods—and doesn't try to stop me.

I ease the door open and step inside. Louis stays right behind me.

"I'm not letting you go in this house alone," he says quietly. "We don't know who's here or what happened."

Together, we walk through the living room and into the kitchen. I stop cold.

Two bloody smears streak across the white walls—one near the entry to the kitchen, one beside the knife block. I look at Louis. His face is ashen.

I bolt toward the stairs and see bloody handprints trailing up the railing.

"We need to get the fuck out of here," Louis says firmly.

I start to shake my head, but he grips my shoulders and forces my gaze to his.

"Serenity, there is blood everywhere in this house. Something went down. And I am a Black man in a very white, very Republican part of the country. If police come in hot and see me standing over a crime scene, they will shoot first and ask questions later."

His words hit hard. I blink as they sink in, then nod.

We step back outside to wait for the police.

Sirens approach within minutes. Louis stiffens beside me.

Two detectives step out of the first vehicle—Garcia and Markovich. A second patrol car pulls up behind them.

Markovich's eyes widen when he sees me. "Serenity," he says, genuinely surprised.

"Hi, Detective. Thanks for getting here so quickly."

"What's happened?" he asks, pulling out his little notepad.

"I haven't heard from my sister since last night, and that's not like her. Her phone's been off all day," I say, the words pouring out fast. "My, um, friend came to pick me up from my appointment so we could check on her. We went inside to look for her." I gesture toward Louis.

"That's when we saw the blood," Louis adds.

"What's your name?" Markovich asks, looking up.

"Louis—Louis Carter."

"We didn't go upstairs," I say, glancing at Louis again. "But there's blood on the railing leading up."

The detectives exchange looks. Garcia steps forward.

"Ma'am, I know you're worried about your sister. We're going to check the house. This is Officer Scott." He gestures to the newly arrived uniformed officer. "She'll wait out here with you and ask a few more questions."

I nod, shaking all over now as the gravity of everything presses down.

Louis pulls me into his chest and rubs slow, steady circles along my back. I bury my face in his shirt.

All I can think—all I can feel—is that something is very, *very* wrong with Samaya.

CHAPTER FOURTEEN

The Suffolk County Police station is freezing and tiny, but I barely notice because I'm already numb.

After searching the house, the officers confirmed Samaya wasn't there. This is now officially a missing person case. They instructed us to follow them to the station to make formal statements about the days and hours leading up to this morning.

Samaya's bedroom told an even more disturbing story than the blood downstairs. Large bloodstains covered her carpet and bed. The sheets had been stripped, and two massive stains soaked into the mattress. Bloody handprints and splatters marked the wall above her headboard.

The officers said they could smell blood, and that some stains looked different, as if someone had started to clean but suddenly stopped. They feared she might be deceased, but perhaps whoever tried to clean had been interrupted. The bloody footprints going down the stairs suggested she may have escaped. Maybe—hopefully—she's still alive somewhere.

Since Jamal seems to be the last known person to see her, he's on his way to the station too. When Louis called him and explained what happened, the disbelief—and fear—hit his face instantly.

The door to the station bangs open, and Jamal bursts in looking exhausted, worn down, and scared as hell.

"Bro, what the fuck is going on?" he demands, ignoring the raised eyebrow of the woman behind the receptionist's glass. Louis pulls him to the far corner and fills him in. Jamal collapses into a chair, burying his face in his hands.

"No. *No.*" He repeats the word over and over, shaking his head. "I was there till like two!" His eyes bulge. "They don't think I had something to do with this, do they?"

Detective Markovich emerges from the back.

"Jamal?"

Jamal straightens, stands, and sticks out his hand. "Yes, sir."

They shake hands. His hand is visibly trembling. He follows Markovich into the conference room to make his statement. Once they disappear, I turn to Louis. He looks almost as anxious as I feel.

"This is crazy," he says, catching me staring at him.

"I know. I don't know what to think, but I have a sick feeling that something awful happened to Sam." Tears burn behind my eyes. He puts his arm around me.

"I know this is not looking good," he murmurs. "But we gotta trust that it's going to be ok. They gonna find your sister."

His use of we makes something inside me unclench just a little. I'm so used to walking through hard shit alone—or with Sam—that having someone beside me feels strange and oddly comforting. The tears spill over, and I let them. I lean into his shoulder, letting the weight of all of this hit me.

My phone rings. A Long Island number. I consider ignoring it—but it could be Sam.

"Hello?" I ask, hopeful.

"Hi, this is Karen from Safelight. Is this Serenity Jones?"

I completely forgot my car was still at the auto glass shop.

"This is she."

"Hi, Serenity, your car is all ready for pickup."

I hang up and tell Louis. He walks to the receptionist and speaks with her quietly. I don't want to leave the station, but I also don't want to be without my car. If Sam calls, I need to be able to go immediately.

When Louis returns, he looks concerned—and tired. He drags his hands down his face.

"I didn't really want to leave before Jamal got done."

"I can Uber," I say quickly. Honestly, I could use a few minutes alone.

"No." His tone is firm. "I'll drop you off and then come back."

"I'll meet you back here," I counter.

We walk to his car in silence. His energy feels heavy, thoughtful.

And how could it not? His friend is being questioned about a possible murder. They've been dragged into this mess because of me—and because of David. I can't shake the certainty that David is behind everything.

"Look, Louis," I say softly, "I'm so sorry you guys are even involved in this. This is a whole ass mess."

He whips his head toward me. "Don't do that."

I blink. "Do what?"

"Blame yourself or feel bad about what's happening. Yeah, it sucks, and it's scary as fuck, but I don't blame you or your sister. And Jamal doesn't either. If anything, I'm worried as fuck."

I look away, vision blurring. I'm grateful for him but terrified. Overwhelmed. Lost.

Where are you, Samaya?

At Safelight, I quickly pay Karen. Seeing my car restored—crack-free—gives me the smallest sliver of relief.

I start the drive back to the police station. Traffic is thick. Everyone heading home from their normal-ass workday. I wish I were doing the same. I wish Sam weren't missing. I wish today were just… normal.

My mind spirals while my car crawls along the highway. I hope the detectives have called David in. Everything points to him. He's been harassing her for months. Getting increasingly irrational. And didn't he tell her he was going to "make her pay"?

When I pull into the parking lot, I barely remember the drive.

Inside, I breathe a tiny sigh of relief when I see Jamal talking to Detective Garcia. He looks far better than he did when they first pulled him back.

I scan the room for Louis. When I don't immediately see him, panic crawls up my spine. Jamal notices instantly, cuts off his conversation with Garcia, and walks over.

"Hey. Louis is answering some questions about the night at the women's event," he says, squeezing my arm. "I told the officer how weird it was that Samaya's ex showed up even though she didn't tell him she'd be there."

I nod.

"I hope that's okay," he adds. "We talked about it last night while we were hanging out. She seemed pretty freaked about it."

"No—totally ok. I was thinking about that the whole drive here. I can't believe I didn't mention it."

"You got a lot on your mind."

I smile weakly, suddenly feeling dizzy. I drop onto a hard plastic chair behind me. It feels like shock, but somehow I'm fully aware of everything.

Then the sickness hits again.

"You good, ma?" Jamal asks quietly.

"Yeah. I mean—no. I don't know," I whisper. Of course I'm not good. My fucking sister is missing.

A door opens. I snap my head toward it.

Louis.

I jump up and practically run to him. His face, his presence, grounds me. He pulls me into a hard embrace, and I cling to him.

"Serenity?" Detective Garcia calls. I turn toward him.

"I just want to update you. We've been trying to reach David but haven't made contact. Do you know where he may be or how we can reach him?"

"All I know is he lives in some apartments near the University with some guy named Rob," I say. "Officer, I know he took her. He was just in her house the other night."

"We've put an APB out for him and contacted his family. We're tracking Samaya's phone and bank accounts. We notified everyone in her office building to call us if they hear from her."

"Do you have a team out looking for David?" My voice rises without permission. "He could be anywhere with her!"

He shifts, uncomfortable. "Ma'am, we're doing everything we can. I'll call you personally when we find anything—about Samaya or David."

My breath catches. I can feel myself unraveling.

"I just need y'all to find my sister," I whisper.

Officer Garcia puts a tentative hand on my shoulder, meeting my eyes. "We will. And we'll notify you the moment we know anything."

I nod and back away. I grab my purse and walk outside into the drizzly grey evening. It's almost dark—fitting, really. My mood matches the sky.

What the fuck is happening?

Louis jogs outside, Jamal behind him. We say goodbye to Jamal and watch him climb into his Jeep. Louis tells me he has writing to do but that I can come by if I want. I tell him I'll meet him later.

When he drives away, I head to my own car and collapse into the seat.

The only thing I can do now is go home, tell Alyse everything, and wait.

And pray Samaya shows up at my house.

CHAPTER FIFTEEN

As soon as I walk into my apartment, Alyse ushers me inside and wraps me in a hug. We sit on our tiny couch, and I start telling her the tale of this very long day. She listens intently, only interjecting a few times for extra details and clarification. When I finally finish, she leans back into the couch, taking it all in. Her face looks concerned, but thoughtful.

"So David is mysteriously nowhere to be found?" she asks.

I shake my head. "Nope."

She twists a lock of her hair, still thinking. I sigh and stand, wandering into our kitchen—which is technically still part of our living room. Before I even open the fridge, I say a silent prayer that there's wine or something in there.

No such luck.

I check the freezer, digging through frozen Amy's meals and a god-knows-how-old bag of ice.

Jackpot. A half-full bottle of Sky vodka.

I grab a glass and pour just a small amount. I don't want to get tipsy when the police could call at any moment, and I might have to leave fast. I pull the Simply Orange out of the fridge and add a splash.

I flop back on the couch and take a long swallow. Alyse gives me a sympathetic glance.

"Girl, I can't even imagine how you must be feeling… what your mind must be thinking," she says. "What can I do?" Her eyes look sad and pleading as they search mine with genuine concern.

I don't even know how I'm feeling.

I'm numb and scared and worried. I feel angry because I know David had something to do with this. But because I can't prove it with tangible evidence, it's like: too bad, so sad.

As a woman of color who grows up in Hunters Point—probably the blackest area of San Francisco—I know good and well the justice system isn't built for us. But realizing it also isn't built for women, or victims in general, makes me feel physically sick.

"The system is *fucked,* girl," Alyse says, like she can read my mind. "You always see those Dateline shows and shit talking about what the cops should've done, but now the victim is dead, and it's all this shoulda, coulda, woulda mess."

She catches my face and grimaces. "Sorry girl, I'm not saying your sister is dead. I'm just saying it's fucked up how they do women."

"No, I get it. Trust me, you ain't telling me nothing I didn't already know."

"It's just frustrating because we know David was involved… I mean clearly he's MIA now, and the cops haven't already busted his door down? Get the fuck outta here." Her hands fly as she talks.

My mind swims with possibilities. I know David was pissed when he sees Samaya kissing Jamal. And knowing

David, I know that triggers him beyond belief. Plus, he's in her house the other night, looking for something. Maybe he realizes she isn't home alone and backs off because we're all still there. But Sam changes all the locks, didn't she? Did Jamal leave the door unlocked when he leaves?

Too many questions.

I need to sleep.

"I think I'm gonna try to get some sleep," I tell Alyse, rubbing my temples with both hands. "Otherwise I'll sit here running possible scenarios over and over and be delirious by tomorrow."

She jumps up and sticks her hand out. I take it, letting her pull me up. "Yes, try to get some sleep. I know it'll be hard. Do you want one of my sleeping gummies?"

I consider one of her THC gummies, then hesitate. "I don't want to get paranoid. I'm already trippin'," I say ruefully.

"You right, you right." She giggles softly and shakes her head. "You and weed… sometimes don't get along."

I smile weakly and walk into my room. Alyse stays in the doorway as I sink onto my bed. She leans her head against the door frame.

"If you need anything, please don't hesitate to wake me up. Seriously," she says.

"I will, babe. Thank you."

The moment she closes my door, I grab my phone. Three missed calls from a blocked number. No voicemail. I frown. The police would've left a message, right?

I see a text from Louis telling me to call if I need anything. I smile.

The next notification is from Stella—Mario's wife—saying the same and telling me not to worry about work this week.

I think about calling Louis, but text him instead.

Just seeing your text. Thank you so much. Gonna get some sleep now, but wanted to say good night.

I stand and grab sweatpants from my dresser. I peel off my pants and pull on the baggy gray sweats. When I climb back into bed, Louis has already responded.

Hey, beautiful. Good night. Please keep me posted. I'm here for u.

The message gives my heart a tiny bit of warmth, and I drift off way easier than I expect.

When I wake up, reality hits instantly. I sit straight up and glance out the window. Still dark. I dig for my phone, buried somewhere in the comforter, and check for updates.

Nothing.

It's almost 7 a.m.

I flop back down with a sigh. Staring at the ceiling, my mind starts moving again. I wonder if the police find David yet. I know he has a large family on Long Island, and more in the city. Maybe he's hiding out there.

I dig through my memory for his cousin's name in Nassau County—was it John? Jeff?

He has so many damn cousins.

Back when we first meet, we tease each other about who has more cousins: black people or Italians. David's argument is that his cousins are real, while ours are just "play cousins." He has a point. Most of the "cousins" we grow up with are just kids of our parents' friends or auntie's friends, not actual blood cousins.

I pick up my phone and call Samaya. Straight to voicemail. I don't even know why I call.

I get up because there's no point lying here waiting for the inevitable.

Samaya isn't going to call me.

Samaya is gone. And maybe something worse.

So the best thing I can do is get up and get ready for this day.

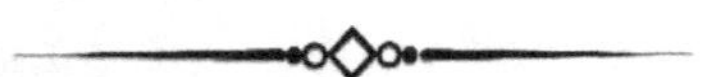

"We picked up David at a relative's house in Nassau County," Garcia says as I sit in this conference room again, stunned and sick with disbelief. "We're interrogating him now."

I'm getting way too familiar with this room. Garcia called to say they found David, and I rush over immediately. For an update. And if we're being honest, to watch him get arrested.

I nod, still processing. "This is good, right?"

Garcia sighs. "It's good if we have enough to hold him on. Right now he's claiming he was out with friends and hasn't spoken to Samaya since the texts a few nights ago."

"But he's lying. He's a pathological liar *and* an alcoholic."

"Our guys are working on him. I think we can get him to break—especially since he hasn't had a drink in a while. He's already getting agitated, and there are a few physical concerns."

"Physical concerns?"

Garcia shifts like he doesn't want to go further. "Yes. There are scratches on his forearms that seem… concerning."

My heart speeds up. Scratches? I swallow hard, searching his eyes.

"Serenity, I don't want you assuming they're from an attack. He's saying they're from his cousin's cat, which could be true. But with everything going on and his recent behavior toward your sister, we're taking it seriously."

"Cat scratches. Convenient timing." I scoff, anger and disbelief rising. "What about his record? He's been arrested for domestic violence while they were married and living together!"

"We're looking into all of that," he says.

It doesn't feel reassuring.

"What about the blood? At her house? Has it been identified or tested?" I ask.

"It's being tested in our forensics lab as we speak."

I realize this police stuff is just a giant wait-and-see game. I get it—I watch true crime too. But it hits different when the victim is your sister.

"How long is the interrogation gonna take? How long before you arrest him?"

"If we have something to hold him on, we'll arrest him today," Garcia says. "But most likely we'll need a warrant for his place to search it. The questioning could take hours. So far, he's not giving much. We confiscated his phone too, and we should have call and text records within a week or so."

I nod slowly. They're working. We'll have answers soon. Something real.

I thank Garcia, then drift to a row of seats by the large tinted window. The rain has slowed to a drizzle, but the sky is still dark and heavy. David could be in there for hours. I don't want to stay here, but I don't want to go home either.

I tell the woman at the desk I'm leaving and ask her to please have Detective Garcia call me with any updates. Then I walk out into the misty afternoon, jog to my car, and fumble to open the door with slick hands. When I dive inside, I let out a long breath.

I start the car and turn down the air while I wait for it to warm. I pull my phone from my purse.

A text from Jason checking in. A missed call from Louis.

I shoot Jason a quick reply: *I'm shaken, but as ok as I can be.*

Once my phone connects to Bluetooth, I call Louis back.

"Hey, love," he says in that honey-dripped voice that somehow still makes my breath catch, even now. "How are you? Any updates?"

"Sort of. They found David. He's in there being questioned now. I'm leaving the station."

I hear him exhale in relief. "I know that at least is a small relief for you."

"It is. I still feel all over the place and freaked out," I admit.

"Have you eaten anything today?"

I blink. It's the first time I've even thought about food.

Shit. I'm starving.

"I don't remember the last time I ate."

"Ok. Let me buy you lunch," he says. "Least I can do to distract you from everything going on in your world."

"Just name the place," I say, too drained to argue or decide. Seeing him would help. Food would help. Even if only a little.

We meet at Rhum, a little Caribbean place near Sam's house. The second I walk in, I see him. Mostly because he's the only black face in the place—but also because that face is so damn handsome.

He stands immediately, that half-smile already on his mouth. He folds me into a hug—the kind that makes you feel protected from everything and everyone, even when you're falling apart.

"Hey," he murmurs into my hair. "You smell so good."

I feel his heartbeat under my ear. I close my eyes, wanting to stay right there.

"Hey."

We pull back. His face is full of concern. "How are you?"

"A wreck," I say, sliding into the booth across from him. "But food is a great start. I seriously don't remember when I ate last."

I rub my belly like it needs proof. I skim the menu, and because I'm me, I already know what I want: fish tacos.

After we order and our drinks arrive, I lean back and close my eyes for a second. When I open them, Louis is watching me. I blush and lift my glass.

"I'm sorry I'm so distracted," I say.

He frowns. "Um, yeah. As you should be. You're dealing with a lot." His voice softens. "I just want to feed you and support you however I can right now."

"You're helping a lot. The last thing I wanted to do was go home. And since I can't go to Samaya's because they're wiping it clean for evidence... I literally have nowhere else to be."

He takes a sip of his drink, still holding my eyes.

"How about after we eat, you come over to my place and just hang out? We can watch a movie or something."

I nod slowly, exhaustion crashing into me all at once.

All I want is to lay down for a while and forget that any of this is real.

CHAPTER SIXTEEN

Being in Louis' apartment feels oddly familiar, considering I have only been here once. He takes my coat and hangs it near the front door in the closet.

I shiver. *It is freezing in here.* Like he notices—or maybe he is cold too—he walks over and turns on the heat using the thermostat on the opposite wall.

"Sorry," he says, apologetic. "It gets so cold in here."

He disappears into his room and comes back with a red-and-black flannel blanket. He wraps it around my shoulders.

"Thanks," I say, walking over to his couch and curling up. I tuck my legs under me so the small throw blanket covers me completely. Louis sits beside me and rubs my back in brisk circles, trying to warm me up. We sit like this for a few quiet moments.

My mind is all over the place, and I feel numb and wound up at the same time. Each time I start to relax or my thoughts drift somewhere else, Samaya flashes back into my head, and with her come the disturbing possibilities of what may have happened to her.

What if she is alive and trapped somewhere?

I shiver again, but this time it is my thoughts, not the cold.

"Still cold? The heater should be warming things up by now," Louis says.

"I feel it." I rub my arms. "I'm sorry, I just can't stop thinking about Sam and what happened to her. I keep picturing her out in the cold or maybe locked in some basement somewhere. I just want to know she's ok."

"I get it. I can't imagine how you must be feeling, and I think it's totally normal for your mind to go to worst-case scenarios," he says, rubbing slow, comforting circles on my back now.

"I can't bring myself to think that she might be somewhere… dead." My voice cracks hard on the last word.

"Shhh…" he says softly. "Let's not go there. Let's assume David just took her somewhere and she's going to be ok. Maybe she got away and is hiding out somewhere. We really don't know yet, Serenity."

I shake my head. "No. She wouldn't go into hiding, and she definitely wouldn't just run away from her life without telling me. She loves her work and her life here. Well, except for the drama with David. But we all assume he'll get over it and move on, you know?"

Louis nods, but he looks like he's considering something.

"What?" I ask.

"Well, didn't you say she's a psychiatrist?"

"Sort of. But I think she just does, like… talk therapy," I say.

"Did she ever talk about any problem patients? Or anyone especially disturbed?"

I comb my mind for stories she shares. She usually can't say much because of HIPAA, but we've still had conversations about a few clients. The other night she tells me about the boy whose parents might be abusing him, but nothing about that situation makes me think he would be a danger to her.

My mind circles back to the other story she tells me that night about the guy she sees at the coffee shop. She does say she feels uneasy, and it definitely gives stalker vibes. But would he kidnap her? And why? I don't know. Somehow it still feels far-fetched.

And what about David? With his latest pop-up at the women's event the other night, I can absolutely see him being the culprit in Samaya's disappearance. Between the texts, the drinking, and his all-around belligerent behavior, he is the only person who makes sense.

I glance over at Louis, and he is watching me.

Shit.

I've been lost in my thoughts and completely fail to answer his question. I flash him a weak smile.

"My bad. I kind of got lost there."

He cuts me off gently. "Please stop apologizing. You're in the middle of a crisis. You have every right to be a little tripped out and off."

I'm blown away again by how kind this man is. I can't even get Dre to acknowledge me enthusiastically when I ask how I look, let alone be naturally considerate like this.

Great, I think. *I am comparing Dre to Louis.*

Why do we always compare what we had to what we have? Especially when there is no comparison. Louis and Dre are as different as night and day. I look at this man who has been nothing but kind and respectful to me, and I smile at him.

"Louis, thank you."

He smiles faintly, caught off guard. "What'd I do?" he asks.

"You are one of the kindest men I know. I mean, I know we barely know each other, but since the moment I met you, you've been nothing but sweet and genuinely supportive."

"You mean since the day you collided into me in the bathrooms in that bar?" He smirks.

I blush. "Yeah. I guess so."

"You aren't used to men being nice to you? I can't imagine that."

"Well, imagine it. My ex was a real piece of work." I shake my head. Louis looks genuinely perplexed.

"What?" I ask.

"You're just so beautiful and sweet. I can't imagine a man not feeling like the luckiest man on earth to even be your man," he says.

"See!" I say, exasperated. "How are you real?"

He laughs and stands. "Want anything from the kitchen?"

"That depends on what you got in there," I say, standing to join him.

I follow him into the kitchen. He opens the fridge, bending down to assess the contents. I peek over his shoulder and see there isn't much to choose from. I eat at RHUM, but not much, and I'm already hungry again.

"Well, it's not looking good, ma'am," he says, straightening up.

I laugh. "Yeah, I saw."

"Hey, hey now." He raises his hands in mock defense. "I'm a busy single man."

I hop up onto the counter, swinging my legs. "I'm actually getting hungry. I know we just ate, but I barely touch mine and I'm pretty sure I leave my to-go box at RHUM. But I also don't want to go back out into the cold right now."

He takes two steps toward me until he's standing directly in front of me. "So what should we do, Ms. Jones?"

He's close enough that I smell his cologne. I swallow hard. He watches me, his eyes dropping to my lips and then lifting back to mine. My heart starts beating harder, and I wonder if he can see it through my shirt.

We just look at each other for what feels like forever. Then he lifts his right hand and cups my cheek.

"I want to kiss you," he says quietly, "but I know you have so much on your mind, and I don't want you to think I brought you over just to make out."

My body goes warm with anticipation.

"So then kiss me," I breathe.

And in an instant, his lips are on mine, devouring me. The kiss is needy, like he's been waiting for weeks. Like he's been craving this exact moment. I moan beneath his mouth and soften into him as he pulls me closer.

When our lips finally separate, we stare at each other, breathing raggedly.

"I've been thinking about doing that since the first time we kissed," he admits.

All I can do is nod, locked in his brown eyes. This man does something to me. It's physical, yes, but it also feels safe. Like coming home for the first time in my life.

He rubs his hands up and down my arms, still gazing at me. "You're hella dope, Serenity."

"Aye, picking up my Bay Area lingo, I see," I joke. He smiles and shakes his head.

"Let's get you some food, woman."

By the time we finish eating, it's after 10:00 p.m. We order McDonald's from DoorDash because I want a strawberry shake. Louis is reluctant to eat trash food, but he obliges—and even gets a Big Mac for himself.

I look around for my phone. When I check my messages, I see two missed calls: one from Alyse, the other from a blocked number.

Shit.

"I think I miss a call from the police," I say, panic rising. Maybe they leave a voicemail.

Sure enough, there's a new one.

"Hello, this is Officer Markovich with the Suffolk County Police Department calling for Ms. Serenity Jones. I just wanted to let you know that we have finished our interrogation with David Esposito. If you have any questions about the matter, please feel free to call me back. Thank you."

I pull the phone away from my ear.

What the fuck does that mean?

"What happened?" Louis asks.

"That was one of the officers from my sister's case," I say. "But all he says is that they finish their interrogation. He doesn't say David is in jail, or what happened, or anything."

"Hmm. That is weird for sure. I can't imagine them not arresting him though."

"Right. Same. But wouldn't they say that?"

"Just call him," Louis says. "That way you know for sure and can get an update on what he says."

I nod, scrolling through my recent calls to find the precinct number. My hands are shaking, and for some reason I have a sick feeling about what I'm about to hear.

"Suffolk County Police Department," a female voice answers.

"Hi, um, I need to speak with Detective Markovich. I just got a voicemail from him."

"Please hold."

I say ok and look at Louis. He's looking right back at me, his rich brown eyes expectant but calming. I mouth I'm on hold, and he nods.

"Hello, ma'am?" the woman says.

"I'm here."

"Detective Markovich is off duty right now. Can I get you to someone else? And what is the case number you're calling about?"

I tell her I don't know the case number, then give my sister's name and a quick rundown. She puts me on hold again—forever long—until she transfers me to Officer Garcia.

"Detective Garcia speaking," he says, distracted.

"Hi. It's Serenity. Samaya's sister? I'm trying to get an update. Detective Markovich left me a message saying you finish David's interrogation, and I'm wondering if he's in custody and how it went. Does he know where my sister is?"

The words spill out in one fast, desperate jumble.

"Serenity, hi," Garcia says. "Yes, we speak with him. Unfortunately, since he has a cousin corroborating his whereabouts on the night your sister goes missing, there isn't much we can do except wait and see."

"Wait and see?" I repeat, incredulous. "What does that even mean? That doesn't make sense. There is no one else who would take my sister!" My voice climbs into something sharp and shrill.

"I completely understand why you're upset. And I agree, he's the most likely suspect. But we can't keep him in custody unless we have proof. Something that places him with your sister the night she disappears."

"What about the scratches? Did you even check his phone records?"

"We are trying to get the transcripts from his phone. This takes time, Serenity. I know this isn't what you want to hear, but we are doing everything we can. We look at his phone and there are no messages to and from Samaya in the past couple weeks—"

"That's *bullshit!* He's texting her the other night. I see the messages with my own eyes!" I cry, not caring that I sound hysterical. This is insane. How do they just accept what he says?

"Which is why we request his phone records from T-Mobile," Garcia says, calm and practiced. "It shouldn't be more than another couple days before we have those here."

My eyes fill. Tears spill as I shake my head.

"I just want you to find my sister," I say quietly.

"We are doing everything we can, Serenity."

I thank him and hang up. I toss my phone onto the couch and look up at Louis, shaking my head. He opens his arms, and I collapse into them, laying my head on his chest and stretching my legs out along the couch.

"What did they say?" he asks after a beat.

I sigh. "Basically, they have to let him go because they don't have enough to hold him. And now they're waiting on the real phone records, and it may be a few days or even a week."

"That's so frustrating. I'm so sorry. I know that's not what you want to hear."

"Definitely not. And he deletes all his messages from Sam, so obviously he's hiding something," I say. "All I know is time is of the essence. The longer this goes, the less likely they are to find her. And I know he has something to do with this. I just know it."

CHAPTER SEVENTEEN

I am *exhausted*.

Beyond exhausted, really.

Between the news of David's continued freedom and the fact that I haven't gotten real sleep over the past few nights, I am completely burnt out. We've also had a couple more drinks, so that definitely doesn't help.

"You should stay," Louis says, idly playing with one of my curls between his fingertips.

I look at my phone and see it's now approaching 12:45 a.m. I groan.

"Shit. How did it get so late?" I whine. Louis just smiles.

"Listen," he begins, "I'm going to go get my bed made up for you, and I'll sleep on the couch. I know you're exhausted, and I really think you should stay and get some sleep."

I consider it for all of two seconds. The answer is simple. "Yes, please. I would love that."

Louis looks visibly relieved. He nods and stands, heading down the hall—probably to grab blankets from the closet. I lean back into the couch and close my eyes. I could fall asleep right here, right now.

Not wanting to, I get up and wander down the hall toward where he goes.

"Hey, you," I say, leaning against the doorframe of his bedroom.

He straightens fast like I scare him. I giggle.

"You can't be sneaking up on me like that," he says, shaking his head while laughing.

"My bad."

We head back into the living room, and he starts making up the couch with the bedding he's pulled from his closet. Watching him do all this makes me realize how silly it is. I mean, I already sleep next to this man once, and I really do not want to spend a night on this couch. I need real sleep tonight.

"So… I know you just got all those blankets out for me," I say slowly, "but I'm thinking I should just… you know, sleep with you?"

The second it leaves my mouth, I cringe. "I mean sleep in the bed with you."

He laughs sheepishly, and I feel immediate relief—but I'm still blushing.

"I know what you meant."

"It just sounded so wrong when it came out of my mouth," I mutter, shaking my head.

Louis gathers up the now-useless blankets and walks toward his room. He pauses and looks back at me over his shoulder, expectant. I follow him quickly, suddenly nervous.

He tucks the bedding away in his closet and turns to me.

"You're going to need something to sleep in," he says, looking me up and down.

I glance at what I'm wearing and realize these jeans are absolutely not happening in bed.

"Do you have a T-shirt I can borrow?"

He crosses to his dresser and rummages through a drawer. When he straightens up, he tosses me a red shirt. I hold it up and read the front.

I Love NY is scrawled across it in bold white letters.

I cock an eyebrow and shoot him a look.

"I don't know how much I'm loving New York right about now," I say dryly.

He gives me a half-smile and a small shrug like yeah, I feel you. Then he leaves the room.

I strip quickly and pull the shirt over my head. I fluff my curls in the mirror, hoping they still look respectable.

When he steps back into the room, his eyes widen.

"What?" I ask, suddenly self-conscious.

"Nothing." He pauses, then grins. "Well, actually two things. Red is definitely your color. And you look hot as fuck in my T-shirt."

I give him a shy smile and shrug. "Thanks for the shirt."

He peels back the blankets, and we climb into bed.

He looks at me like there are a million things he wants to say, but all he says is, "All good. Anytime."

His eyes don't leave mine, and I can't pull mine from his. He leans closer, and I meet him halfway. We kiss, soft and sweet.

And then guilt hits me like a wave. I pull my face away.

His eyes search mine with concern.

"Are you ok?" he asks quietly, brushing a stray curl from my face.

"I just feel bad. And scared." My voice cracks, and then I start crying.

He doesn't say anything right away. He just wraps his arms around me and holds me tight, letting me fall apart.

"Serenity, I got you," he murmurs after a beat.

"It's not that I'm not into you," I say through tears. "I just have a lot on my mind."

His face falls slightly, but his voice stays steady. "Please know there is never any pressure on you to do or be anything other than yourself."

His eyes are so sincere. He kisses my forehead gently while I wipe my tears.

"Thank you," I whisper, finally easing into his chest.

He's quiet for a moment.

"I know this is going to sound cliché," he says slowly, "but I'm not like most men—and I am definitely *not* your ex. I really like you, and I believe we come into each other's lives right now for a reason. Let me be here for you, Serenity."

I nod against him, and my whole body softens. I lift myself onto my elbow and look into his liquid brown eyes. He meets my gaze without flinching.

When I kiss him again, he's tentative at first—soft, grounding, comforting. But within seconds his hands are in my hair, and we are full-on making out, hungry for each other like we've been starving.

I break the kiss only to climb on top of him. The need to be closer overwhelms me. I hear him groan beneath me as my warm center presses against his hardening dick. I moan back when I feel his bulge throb against my clit. Wet is an understatement as I grind against him.

When I open my eyes, he's looking at me with a piercing intensity that makes my heartbeat stutter and then race even faster.

"Serenity," he starts. Even hard as a rock beneath me, he's still checking in.

I lean down and graze his ear with my lips. "I want you," I whisper.

His hands clamp onto my thighs as he starts moving with me, matching my rhythm.

"I want you too. So bad." His voice is strained, barely above a murmur.

I kiss him again, even needier now, tasting his desire on my tongue. I reach down to guide him inside me, and he catches my wrist.

"Wait," he breathes. "I need to taste you."

Before I can even register it, his arm wraps around my back and he flips us smoothly so he's above me and I'm on my back. I stare up at him, stunned and breathless.

He smiles slow and lazy, then shifts down until his head is between my thighs. When I hear him sigh at what he sees, I squeeze my eyes shut—half embarrassed, half desperate.

First he kisses my right thigh. Then my left.

Then his warm tongue flicks over my clit, tentative and slow, and I gasp.

Holy shit.

He takes his time at first, tasting me like he's learning the shape of me, and then he gets more fervent. His breathing deepens. The strokes of his tongue get hungrier, more sure. I moan, helpless, eyes rolling back as pleasure takes over my whole body.

When I feel the orgasm building, my legs start shaking. I reach down, trying to push him away, but he catches my wrist and holds it, not stopping for a second.

He keeps licking me exactly how I need it.

"Oh God," I cry out.

And then I come. *Hard.*

He climbs back up, bracing his hands on either side of my head.

"Holy shit," I breathe, still trembling.

He smirks, then kisses me deep.

"You taste so good," he murmurs against my lips, and I can't help the smile that slips out with my blush.

"I want you," I pant. "Inside me. Now."

He drags himself against my slick wetness, slow and deliberate, teasing me with the head before he finally starts to sink into me. I moan as his width stretches me open, every inch making my breath catch.

"Oh shit," he mutters, voice low and rough, like he's fighting for control.

His hands grip my hips, and the pressure of his fingers grounds me even as pleasure ripples up my spine. We move slowly together at first, inch by inch, like he's learning me—memorizing the way I breathe, the way my body reacts to him.

My mouth falls open when he slides deeper, the fullness hitting me in a way that steals the air right out of my lungs. I close my eyes and let myself take him, my whole body pulsing around him as I surrender to every inch.

"Serenity…" he breathes, the sound almost reverent.

He pulls out slightly, then pushes back in with a slow, controlled thrust that makes my toes curl. His forehead drops to mine, his breath mixing with mine, his body warm and solid above me.

I wrap my legs around his waist, pulling him closer, deeper.

"Fuck," he groans, the sound vibrating through my chest.

He kisses me—hard, hungry—and the rhythm between us builds, still slow but heavier now, more intentional. Each thrust sends a wave through me, lighting up every nerve, tightening everything low in my belly.

My nails dig into his shoulders as I arch into him.

"Right there," I whisper against his mouth. *"Please…Louis…"*

He adjusts his angle just slightly, and the sensation knocks a gasp out of me. His hand slides up my thigh, fingers brushing my hip as he holds me steady and pushes deeper, slow and deep, slow and deep, like he wants me to feel all of him.

"Look at me," he says quietly.

I open my eyes, and the way he's looking at me—intense, focused, like he's as wrecked as I am—makes something inside me break open.

A soft cry escapes my throat as my body shudders beneath him.

"Yeah," he whispers against my skin. "That's it. I got you."

His words, his voice, his body—all of it crashes over me, drawing me right to the edge as he thrusts, slow but devastating.

And I fall into him completely.

CHAPTER EIGHTEEN

When I leave Louis', I go directly to Mario's to grab my check and see if Jason is working. Pulling in feels strange, and I feel like I haven't been here in forever, even though it's been a week. I let out a long breath and turn off the car. I check my reflection in the rearview mirror.

I look tired.

Like bone-deep tired, the kind you can't cover with lip gloss or pretend away.

"Serenity! It's so good to see you!" exclaims Margaret, one of the girls who started around the same time that I did.

"Hey, girl," I say. "It has been a minute! How are you?"

"I heard what happened to your sister," she says, ignoring my question. "I am so sorry…"

I swallow hard. "It's a scary time for sure."

I immediately regret my decision to come into the restaurant. What I thought would be a quick pick-up and conversation with Jason, I realize now is going to be a long line of people asking all the questions I don't want to answer.

"Hey, is Jason around?" I ask. "Or maybe Stella?" I look around, looking for anyone who can get me out of this conversation. I want to get my check and talk to Jason and then get the fuck out of here.

"Uh, yes, I think he's around here somewhere."

I give her a quick, half-hearted hug and book it down to where the kitchen is. I keep my head down as I reach into the back pocket of my jeans and pull my phone out so I can text Jason.

Where are you?

I wait for a response.

Nothing.

I peek my head into the break room in the back and see it's deserted. Where is he? He said he'd be here today.

I decide to order some food since I am starving and the food will be discounted. I scan the restaurant for a free table and spot a small nook by the window that looks secluded.

I slide into the booth. I lay my phone screen-side up on the table in front of me. Margaret approaches tentatively with a menu and a sheepish smile. "Staying awhile?"

"Yea, I just realized I haven't eaten yet, so I might as well grab something here."

She nods and lays the menu in front of me. She gives my shoulder a reassuring squeeze and leaves me alone to decide on food.

I scan the menu, not sure what I want to order. I set it down and pick up my phone to check for Jason's response.

Nothing yet.

I lean forward and put my head in my hands. The last few days feel like a bad dream that I just want to wake up from. But this is really happening. Samaya is really gone, and there's nothing I can do except wait for the police to provide us with an update.

Suddenly I feel overwhelmed. My stomach is in knots, and my body feels hot all over. Tears prick my eyes, and I try my best to fight them back.

Pull it together, Serenity, I think to myself. This is not the place for a breakdown.

I take three slow deep breaths. The kind that go all the way down into my belly, just like the ones I learned in Yoga class. I try to focus all of my scattered attention on my breathing.

Inhale. Exhale.

Inhale. Exhale.

I place my hands on my thighs, palms facing down. I remember the Yoga teacher saying placing your hands somewhere on the body can help ground you. I take a huge breath, one so deep that it takes a while to finish, and then I slowly blow the breath out of my mouth. I feel my shoulders drop. I feel my stomach unclenching ever so slightly.

I slowly open my eyes, but keep my gaze downcast. I feel… better. Well, at least my anxiety has subsided enough for me to not feel like I need to run out of this restaurant like it's on fire. So that's a big, little win right now.

I look up finally and see Stella, Mario's wife approaching me. Her eyes look red as if she's been crying. I take a deep breath, trying not to lose it again.

She slides into the seat across from me, and wordlessly reaches out and takes my hands into hers.

"I'd ask how you are, but I feel like that's almost rude. You must be a wreck," she says.

"Hey, Stella," I begin. "Yes, things have been super tough."

She nods sympathetically, "I can't even imagine. Please know Mario and I are here for you. Whatever you need. Seriously." She squeezes my hands at this, and I know she means it. I feel that tell-tale lump in my throat, signaling tears are just around the corner, and I swallow hard.

"Thank you," I whisper around the boulder in my throat, "You guys have been so understanding this past week. I know I've missed a few shifts, and I'm really sorry, I—"

"Shh, shh," she puts a hand up, cutting me off in her thick New York accent, "The last thing you need to be worried about is coming into this old place." She stops and looks around, ensuring our privacy. Stella leans in and whispers, "If you need any help financially, don't be afraid to talk to me about an advance—whatever you need, seriously."

The tears come now, unbidden; I withdraw my hands and cover my face, shoulders shuddering now.

"Oh, honey." And she's up in a second, sliding into the booth next to me, wrapping her arms around me. I surrender, leaning into her, allowing the motherly comfort I so desperately need right now. She slowly rubs my arm and I allow myself to cry.

"Oh, baby girl!" I hear a familiar voice say in dismay.

Jason.

"Now's not a good time," Stella says in an annoyed voice. She and Jason are constantly butting heads.

"No, Stella, it's ok," I sniff. I wipe my nose on the napkin. "I wanted to talk to Jason, and I knew he was working today."

I see Jason give her a triumphant yet indignant look. "Yes, Stella, I am here to support my best friend," but he says Friend like Frannnn in his dramatic drawl. I shoot him a look, and he shrugs as if to say, "What'd I do?"

Stella stands and ignores Jason, turning to me. "Remember what I said, Serenity. Anything at all." She gave my shoulder one last squeeze before walking away.

Jason is seated across from me with an expectant look on his face. "Bestie! What is happening? Are you ok?"

"What do you think?" I ask. "Samaya is gone. I know David has something to do with it, but the cops can't do shit without proof." I do air quotes when I say proof.

"Fuck them fuckin' police," Jason says too loudly, causing an older white couple to turn their whole heads in our direction to see who made such a statement. "They so quick to shoot us down in the street for nothing, but when some real shit happens, it's always some technicality bullshit."

I don't disagree, but I also know this isn't the time or place for this kind of conversation.

"David lied about contacting Sam in the days leading up to her disappearance," I say, diverting his attention back to the matter at hand. "He must've deleted the messages because the cops didn't see them. He was saying some pretty harsh shit."

"The night y'all saw him at that event?"

"Yes. So now the detective is waiting for the transcript from the carrier, which could take days or even weeks.

Meanwhile, my sister is gone, and David is sitting at home chillin'." I feel myself getting angry. Anger feels better than despair, though, so I welcome it.

"Have you tried calling David yourself?" he asks.

"Hell no! Why would I call him?"

"Well, sweetie, you know him better than those police. Also, he's always liked you, so maybe he'll spill more to you than to the cops. And if you can call him when you know he's most likely going to be drunk—bingo! I bet you he'll say something to incriminate himself."

I sit there, stunned. Why hadn't I thought about contacting David myself?

"Do you really think he'd tell me what happened? Especially since he already talked to the cops and told his side of things?"

"I think it's worth a try," he shrugs, starting to stand up. "I gotta go. Stella is always on my ass about getting back late from lunch." He rolls his impossibly big brown eyes, giving him an almost cartoonish look.

I stand up too. "Thanks for being here for me, Jay," I say. I give him a big hug, and he returns the embrace fiercely.

"I fuckin' love you, sis! Always here for you. Please keep me posted and let me know after you talk to David."

I promise him that I will and sneak out the door before anyone can stop me to talk.

"So, you think with everything going on, you should call this crazy-ass dude?"

Alyse has different feelings about Jason's suggestion about calling David. She stands before me, hands on her hips and head cocked to the left like a puppy who's just gotten a command it does not understand, one eyebrow lifted.

"Well, yes. I think it couldn't hurt," I say. "It's not like I'm gonna meet him for dinner or something."

She shakes her head in disbelief, "I don't know, girl. It just feels like stirring the pot."

"I can't just sit here and do nothing, Alyse! The police say they are doing everything they can, but time is passing, and we have no new leads or information. I am losing my mind just waiting around!" My eyes fill with tears for the third time today.

Her demeanor visibly softens. "I know, babe. I just want you to be safe. And smart."

"I get it. But I honestly think the worst-case scenario would be that he tells me nothing."

She stares at me and considers this for a beat. After a while, she nods.

"Ok, I only have one request."

"What is it?"

"I wanna be there when you make the call—just so we both hear what he's saying. If he makes any threats, we need to go straight to the cops."

"Yes!" I cry. "And, having you there would make me feel so much better too."

She sits down beside me on the bed and hugs me tight. "Of course."

I pick up my phone with shaking hands, mentally preparing myself to dial David's number. When I get to his name in my contacts, I feel the cold, heavy lump in the pit of my stomach grow even heavier, creating a flurry of anxiety throughout my entire body. As I press call, I hear Alyse take a sharp intake of breath. I meet her eyes, and she nods at me as if to say, "I got you."

"Hello?" His familiar voice says. My throat catches, and I momentarily lose my voice.

"H-hello?" I say. "David?"

Silence.

"Who is this?" His voice is gruff. Anxious.

"It's me, Serenity," I say, trying to sound normal, but knowing my voice sounds tight.

There's a long pause on the other end, and I can hear his ragged breathing as he calculates his response.

"I already told the police I didn't fucking see her that night," he growls.

Ah, I think to myself. *He's drunk.*

I take a deep breath and let it out slowly between pursed lips.

"Right," I say coolly, "except I know about the texts you sent after the event the other night. You know, the ones you conveniently deleted before you went and spoke with the cops." I didn't mean this to come out so accusatory, but here we are. I glance over at Alyse, and her eyes are as wide as saucers. Apparently, she is as shocked as I am at my sudden bravery.

David laughs, "Yea? So what? You can't prove shit."

"Well, I can't, but once they get the phone records, you're fucked. So just tell me what you know about the night Samaya went missing."

"My cousin wiped that phone clean, little girl," he snarls. "So, good luck."

"Just tell me what you did with my sister, you fucking asshole!"

"You stupid bitch. You're as bad as your whore of a sister."

I feel my breath getting shallow as my anger surges so intensely my whole body overheats in an instant.

"Don't you dare talk about my sister that way, you piece of shit," I hiss through clenched teeth. My blood is boiling, and I can feel my face redden with pure fury. My entire body shakes in anger.

"You think you're mad? You don't even know anger until you have the person you gave everything to throw it all away," he says bitterly, a slight slur to his words. I hear him swallow hard, no doubt taking a swig of whatever his choice of liquor is tonight. "That bitch took everything from me. I'm sure she got what she had coming to her."

Yea, because you did it, I think.

"You are so fucking delusional, David. You killed your own daughter because of your drinking! Have you ever thought about that? That is your problem—you can't ever take responsibility for your own actions."

He laughs, like an actual deep belly laugh at this.

"Do you think I don't know I killed my own fucking daughter? You don't think Sam reminded me every day of my fucking life of this fact?" His voice is loose with liquor, emotion taking over fully now.

"You're useless," I mutter, disgusted by the conversation, "I hope you burn in hell for everything you've done to my sister." I say this last sentence like a sacred prayer, meaning every single word.

It's quiet for a beat, and then I hear his heavy breathing on the other end. For the first time in several moments, I remember that I am not alone in the room, and I glance over at Alyse, whose cocoa-colored face looks a new shade of gray. I shake my head.

"Hello?"

I hear a long inhale on the other side of the phone. "Don't ever call me again," I hear, and then the call is disconnected. I let the phone slip from my hands and onto the bed beside me.

My hands shake. My chest heaves from the energy of the conversation and the emotion that built up during. Although I didn't get any definite answers from the call, I did know one thing for sure.

I hate this man.

With every cell in my body.

And now I'm even more sure—it was him.

CHAPTER NINETEEN

"I told you it wasn't a good idea to call him," Alyse says, handing me a glass of water.

My hands are still shaking violently with emotion. I can hardly hold the glass without the water sloshing over the sides of it. The tremor feels like it's in my bones, like my whole nervous system is buzzing and refusing to come down.

"I know, I know," I say, taking a long swallow of the cool liquid. "I should've known he'd be useless." I put the cup down on the nightstand and put my face in my hands. Talking to David makes me feel ten times worse than I did twenty minutes ago. Like I just opened a wound that was already bleeding and poked it on purpose.

"What was he saying? He sounded pissed."

I close my eyes and rub the bridge of my nose with my first finger and thumb. My head feels tight, like there's a rubber band around my skull. "Long story short, he didn't have much to say besides insults about my sister. He is such a dick." The understatement of the century, but I don't have the energy for more right now.

When my eyes meet Alyse's, she looks upset but cautious. I don't want to give a play-by-play of the conversation and she senses that. She knows when to press and when to just sit with me, and I love her a little extra for that.

"I'm sorry, Serenity," she says quietly. "I know you were hoping to get some answers about Samaya."

I groan loudly. "I think I'm going to go lay down. I don't want to think anymore." I want my brain to shut off like a light switch. I want quiet.

She nods and embraces me before heading into her room. I stare blankly in front of me for a moment, still tasting David's voice in my ear, still hearing the way he said her name like a curse. Then I pull myself up from the couch and slump into my room to lay down.

I sit on the edge of my bed and run my hands over my face. I feel exhausted, but it's mostly emotionally. The kind of tired where even your eyelashes feel heavy. Alyse was right. Calling David *was not* a good idea.

But I'm desperate for answers.

Desperate enough to keep doing dumb shit if it means I might find her.

I scoot back and lean against the wall, tucking my knees beneath me as I look around my room. The air feels too still, like the whole apartment is holding its breath with me. My eyes land on Sam's laptop that the police had returned to me the other day.

Standing, I cross the small bedroom to pick up the laptop and return to my nest of a bed. Once I have my furry white blanket tucked in all around me, more for comfort than warmth, I open the laptop and power it on. It starts up surprisingly fast. But the first screen that shows up asks for a password.

Well, shit.

My first thought is to use my late niece's birthdate. I hesitantly type in the numbers, but am alerted that it's incorrect. I groan. Of course it's not that simple. Nothing about her life ever is.

Most devices only give you a few chances to enter an incorrect password before it locks you out. I let my gaze drift to my dresser, where a framed photo of Sam and I sits. We're smiling so hard in it, like the world hasn't started breaking apart yet.

"What's the password, babe?" I ask as if she will answer me from whatever abyss she's in.

I try my birthdate. Presumptuous, maybe, but we are closer than most siblings. We share everything. Or we did.

No luck.

I try three more options and am locked out after my fifth attempt. I close the laptop and slide it over on the bed. The hollow click of it closing feels like a door shutting in my face.

I lie back, placing my hands behind my head and staring at the ceiling. I've looked around her house for clues, but found nothing that gave me a clue to her whereabouts or who might've hurt her. Everything points to David. Every trail, every gut feeling, every second of silence.

I sigh, rolling over to my side, and hope to fall into sleep easily. Maybe a nap will be good for my tired brain. Maybe sleep will be the only place I get a break.

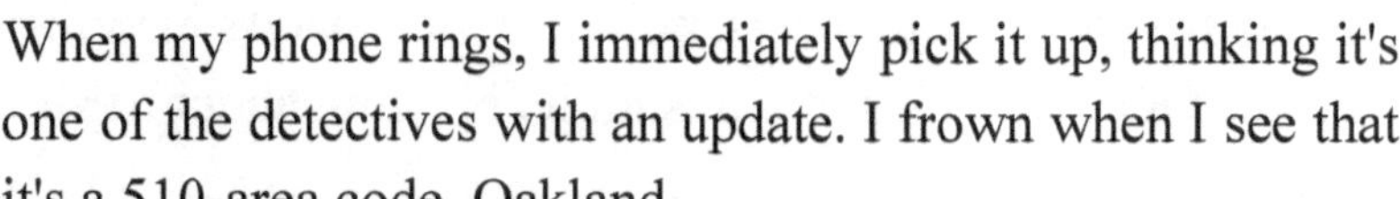

When my phone rings, I immediately pick it up, thinking it's one of the detectives with an update. I frown when I see that it's a 510-area code. Oakland.

The number stares back at me like a ghost.

I immediately think of Dre, who lives in Oakland. I consider ignoring the call, but decide to answer it after a few rings.

"Hello?"

"Hi, this is Keisha calling from Highland Hospital here in Oakland," a young voice says, "Is this Serenity Jones?"

My pulse quickens, "Yes, how can I help you?" Did Samaya somehow end up back home in the Bay? My mind jumps too fast to keep up with itself.

"Hi, thanks. I am calling because we have you listed on the emergency contact sheet for Alexis Proctor. You're her daughter, right?"

I let out a long, slow exhale. "Yes. What's happened? Is she ok?"

"Your mother has suffered a massive heart attack," she says in a measured tone.

I feel my insides turn to stone.

No. Not now. Not with everything going on. My whole body goes cold, like I just stepped into a freezer.

"She's stable now, but because of the lack of blood flow to her brain when her heart stopped, she's in a coma."

I feel a small sense of relief, but also rising panic. Relief because she's alive. Panic because coma is its own kind of cliff.

"Will she be ok?"

There's a long pause on the other end and my heart sinks. That was not a reassuring pause.

"I think you should alert the family and come visit as soon as you can. With comas like this, there's no guarantee that she will wake up, and based on the scans we've done and the length of time she lost blood flow to her brain, the doctors believe that there could be a significant loss of brain function."

"You mean, she could be brain dead?"

"That's a possibility we are worried about," the woman says, "but we won't know until she wakes up."

A single tear streams down my cheek. This cannot be happening. Not stacked on top of Samaya. Not like a cruel little bonus tragedy.

"Are you able to come in today? I also see there is a Samaya Jones listed on the paperwork. I haven't been able to reach her, though. You two are the only ones listed on her emergency contacts. I would suggest contacting any other immediate relatives and having them come in to visit–just in case things progress."

Her words hit me one by one, like someone dropping bricks onto my chest.

Emergency contact.

Visit.

Just in case.

It all folds in on itself in my mind, collapsing into a single, awful meaning. My ears start ringing—an electric, high-pitched hum that eats up all the silence between us. My mind swims, and I feel as if I am hearing the words, but it's like I'm underwater, and everything is muffled and warped and far away. Like my ears are stuffed with cotton and my brain can't grab onto anything solid enough to hold onto.

I can feel my pulse hammering in my neck, in my wrists, in my teeth. The room tilts, just slightly, like the floor is shifting under me.

"Ms. Jones?"

Her voice sounds like it's coming through a tunnel.

"Yes," I whisper, my mouth dry, "I can't be there today. I—we—live in New York now, so I would have to book a flight."

As I say the words, the reality of the distance hits me like another blow. She is across the country. She is alone. I am here.

I hear the heater kick on in my room, a low hum that somehow feels too loud. I hear the rain hitting my window in soft, steady taps. Tiny sounds that suddenly feel enormous, like the world is paying extra attention just because mine is falling apart.

Everything feels like it's happening in slow motion.

Like someone hit pause on real life but forgot to pause my heart.

It keeps pounding, panicked, frantic, clueless about what to do with all this pain.

"I know this is a lot, miss," she says, her tone softening, becoming less robotic, less detached. "Please save this number and let me know when you've made your travel plans. I'll be sure to call if there are any changes or updates."

"Thanks," I say in an almost inaudible whisper.

I end the call and stare into the empty air in front of me. My phone feels heavy in my hand, like a brick. I am numb and overwhelmed all at once. My mind feels blank, like I know what the woman told me but it's not sinking in, not settling anywhere. My brain is a white screen, no loading bar, no spinning wheel—just nothing.

I stand up robotically, like someone else is moving my body for me, and walk to my bedroom door. I hear music coming from Alyse's room, something upbeat and careless and wrong for the moment. I open her door without knocking.

She turns, startled, wearing a bra and sweatpants, but the second she sees my face, she rushes toward me.

"What happened?"

Suddenly, everything hits me all at once.

Samaya's gone.

My mother is in a coma.

And I need to leave New York to see her if she doesn't pull through.

The weight of it buckles me. I lean my back against her wall, suddenly needing something solid to keep me upright.

My shoulders slump, and I begin to sob. It's not a gentle cry—it's the kind that shakes your whole rib cage, the kind you can't swallow down even if you try. I slide down the wall until I am seated next to Alyse's door, a puddle of tears and hurt, collapsing into myself. The kind of ache that makes your chest feel hollow and crushed at the same time.

"Oh babe," she says, dropping down beside me, rubbing my back, "what happened? What is happening, Serenity? Did they find Samaya?"

This only makes me cry harder. My face sinks between my knees, and snot is everywhere—on my hands, on my pants, on my shirt. I'm too broken to care.

"N-n-no," I whimper. "It's my mom."

"Oh, shit…"

"She had a heart attack. She's in a coma—the hospital just called me and said we need to see her… in case she doesn't pull through."

My mind is reeling. My heart is breaking.

Grief and fear sit on my chest like twin weights.

And I don't even know which pain to hold first.

CHAPTER TWENTY

I can hear Alyse talking as she clicks away on her laptop, but my mind is a million miles away—floating somewhere between dread and exhaustion, between everything that's falling apart and everything I'm pretending I can still hold together.

I don't know what I would do without her. After my breakdown in her room, she helped me up, made me tea, tucked me into bed like a kid having a nightmare. And honestly, everything since has felt like a nightmare—one of those long, disorienting ones where no matter how much you try to wake up, you just fall deeper.

I sit wrapped in my white furry blanket, holding her favorite holiday mug. It's basically Santa's face—except this Santa is Black, has a wide smile, and a single gold tooth. My hands tremble around it, but the warmth helps keep me from shaking apart completely.

"Ok! I found a flight that leaves Friday at 9:30 a.m. I can take you to the airport in Queens that morning before work," she says, clicking one last time for emphasis.

"How much is it?" I ask, feeling my stomach twist. Missing work, windshield repairs… and now flights. My bank account is probably crying in a corner somewhere.

"It's $229 for a round trip. And it's a straight shot. No layovers."

I put the mug down and press my hand to my forehead. This is all so much. Too much. And somehow, despite everything with my mom, I feel like I can't leave New York. Not now. Not with Samaya missing. Not with everything still… unanswered.

"Girl, I just feel like I can't leave. Sam is missing. Flying across the country doesn't seem like the best idea right now."

Alyse considers this slowly, the way she does when she's weighing all the emotional math in real time. I swear I can almost see the gears turning behind her eyes.

"Well, yes," she says carefully, "but this is your mother. And I know from experience that if something happens to her—God forbid—you will feel all kinds of fucked up that you didn't go and say what could possibly be your goodbyes."

Her words slice straight through the fog of my panic. My mom. My complicated, messy, painful relationship with her. The last several years flood into my mind like a montage I never asked to watch. Addiction, relapses, promises she never kept. My sister and I trying to help her, only for her to fall back again. My own name—Serenity—a cruel reminder of sobriety she could never reach.

How do you name your child after the Serenity Prayer, then never make even one real attempt at choosing serenity?

Suddenly, I feel angry. Anger is easier than grief. Anger feels like something I can hold.

"Why should I go see her?" I snap, pacing now. "Do you know how many things of mine she missed because she was too strung out to show up? Or worse—how many events she did show up to, high or drunk out of her mind? And now I'm supposed to drop everything and fly across the damn country to see a woman who loved drugs more than she loved her daughters?"

Alyse's eyes drop to her hands. When she looks back up, they're shimmering—not with judgment, but with sympathy, quiet and heavy.

"It's totally your call, girl," she says softly, her voice gentler now, careful like she's placing something fragile into my hands. "But the reality is… we don't know where Samaya is or when she'll turn up. We do know your mother is dying. And I know she wasn't the best mother to y'all. But regret is real."

The words don't just land. They sink—heavy, slow, like stones dropped into deep water. My shoulders slump under their weight, my chest tightening around a truth I've been trying to outrun. Her voice doesn't judge or push; it simply holds up the truth in a way I can't look away from.

I stand up because sitting still hurts, because if I don't move, I might actually break. I walk to my window and stare out into the storm. The rain is coming down in sheets now— loud, relentless, almost angry. It blurs the world outside, stretching the streetlights into long golden smears across the wet pavement. Everything looks hazy and distorted, like the whole world is crying with me.

A car pulls into the lot below. A woman jumps out, holding a jacket over her head as she sprints to the back door. She opens it, and instantly two tiny arms reach for her, desperate and instinctive. The little girl folds into her mother like she belongs there, burying her sleepy face in her mother's neck. The mom lifts her effortlessly, the child's legs curling automatically around her waist—clinging to her like a koala in a storm.

That image breaks something inside me. Not loudly—just quietly, like a thin thread snapping. It hits me in a place I don't usually let myself feel: that ache, that longing, that hollow missing piece of what motherhood could have been for us.

My eyes fill with tears, hot and immediate, but I blink them back before they can fall. I know what's coming if I let even one slip. I steady myself against the cold window frame and force myself not to look away, not to retreat into the familiar comfort of anger. Anger is easy. Anger is armor. But the truth—the real truth—is raw and tender and hurts in a quieter, deeper way.

My mother wasn't always the woman she became. Before the addiction. Before the grief. Before trauma carved pieces out of her she never got back. She was a young girl once. A girl who survived things she never had language for. A girl who never had therapy or community or safety. A girl carrying invisible wounds with no tools to treat them. Her own brutal childhood—the violence, the neglect, the absence of love— dragged her into darkness long before drugs ever did. The darkness she kept falling into wasn't because she didn't love us. It was because she didn't know how to climb out.

It wasn't a lack of love. It was a lack of help. A lack of healing. A lack of a single damn person ever choosing her before the world broke her.

I swallow hard, chest tight, emotions swirling so thick I can barely breathe. When I finally turn back around, Alyse is still sitting on the edge of my bed, her laptop in her lap. And the look she gives me—*God.* It's so full of compassion and recognition and steady presence that it makes my heart ache in a different way. She looks at me like someone who refuses to let me fall apart alone.

And it hits me that meeting her was one of the greatest gifts of moving to New York. One of the first soft places I've ever had to land. One of the first times in my life I've had someone who feels like chosen family. Someone who stays. Someone who sees me. Someone who holds space for the versions of me I don't even know how to hold.

"Book it," I finally say, crossing the room to grab my credit card.

She nods with a small, relieved smile.

A few moments later, the flights are booked. Official. Real. My stomach drops. My phone vibrates on the bed next to me. I dig through my blanket and grab it, answering without checking the caller ID.

"Hello," says the voice I didn't even know I needed to hear.

Louis.

"Oh Louis," I whisper—and immediately start crying. I am a wreck today. A full, messy, unraveling wreck.

"What happened? Are you ok?" He sounds alarmed.

"No. I am not ok." I choke on the words. "My mom is in the hospital back in Cali. Sh-she had a heart attack."

"Oh no… Serenity, I'm so sorry. Is she…?" His voice trails off, like he's afraid to finish the sentence.

I take a breath that doesn't feel like enough air. "She's in the hospital in a coma. They think there's some brain damage, but they're not sure how much. I'm flying out on Friday to go see her, just in case she…" My voice breaks before I can say dies.

Louis is quiet for a beat. I can hear his deep breaths. Like he's absorbing the news with me. Like he's holding part of the weight.

"God, Serenity," he says finally, voice low and steady. "I don't know what to say. What can I do? Are you ok?"

"I'm still processing it," I say, rubbing my forehead. "Alyse booked the flights for me. Louis… I feel like my world is falling apart."

"I know," he murmurs. "I can't imagine how overwhelmed you feel right now."

I look around my room, feeling claustrophobic. Suffocated. Everything feels surreal—like I'm standing on the edge of something, watching my own life crumble in slow motion.

"Hey…" he says softly when I go quiet again. "I'm here."

I swallow hard. "Can you come get me? I mean… if you're free."

"Of course," he says instantly. "Text me the address. I'm on my way."

CHAPTER TWENTY-ONE

I groan as the intrusive sound of my iPhone alarm sounds. Not ready to open my eyes yet, I blindly run my hands over the blankets in search of it. My hand discovers its sleek plastic case, and I fumble to end the sound.

Silence.

I open my left eye to see the time. It's time. Today I fly across the country to see my mom. The last two days have been a foggy blur. I still have mixed feelings about making this trip, but I know that I am making the right decision by going. And I know Samaya would want me to be there with Mom.

The weight of her name presses onto my chest.

Where are you, Sam?

Markovich and Garcia assured me that they would call me with any updates. They also said that they should have the contents of David's cell phone by the end of the day today. This information gave me a little bit of hope.

As the days go on, the more I'm beginning to lose hope. I haven't admitted this to Louis, Alyse, or anyone, but it has been chipping away at me internally. So much so that now I feel a hollowing feeling inside me that the outcome for Sam isn't good. A kind of slow, sinking certainty I keep trying to outrun.

I need to get up.

Swinging my legs over the side of the bed, I sit up and stretch. My neck pops, and I immediately feel the tightness there. I turn on my bedside lamp and scan the room, seeing my carry-on suitcase. I silently thank Past Me for having enough clarity to pack my stuff last night.

My phone pings with an incoming message, and I frown. It's not even 6 a.m. Who would be texting me this early? I smile when I see Louis' name on the screen.

Good morning, beautiful. I just wanted to wish you safe travels. Please let me know when you make it to the airport

This man doesn't miss a beat.

Good morning. Thank you and I will.

I duck down to glance into the mirror above my dresser and wince.

It's time to get my life together so I don't look like death on this flight.

The airport feels colder than it should. I shift my backpack on my back to grab my luggage out of the overhead bin. The line ahead of me is finally thinning, and I am beyond excited to get off this airplane.

The five-hour flight felt longer because I was so anxious about what I left behind and even more anxious about what I am about to walk into. I have a phone full of messages and a head full of thoughts. Not to mention that I'm exhausted.

Sleep eluded me on this long flight due to the toddler who decided to throw four separate tantrums.

By tantrum number three, I nearly had one myself.

I murmur a quick thanks to the flight crew as I exit the airplane and make my way down the makeshift hallway into the airport. I scan my surroundings to look for a restaurant and spot one with a bar.

Perfect.

I have about an hour before my cousin, Jess, gets here to pick me up. As soon as I posted in my stories on Instagram that I was at JFK heading home, I received a flood of DM's asking a million questions. When I saw Jessica had responded, I was immediately excited.

She is from my dad's side of the family, the Jones' side. I didn't know my dad very well, so I value the few people I do have a relationship with on his side of the family. Jess is my aunt Janet's daughter and three years younger than me. When she saw I was flying in, she immediately offered to pick me up and said I could stay with her and her son, Chance.

I'm not really a kid person, although, I would consider children with the right person. Honestly, the thought of staying with a four-year-old for three days with everything going on right now makes me wince, but the hotel prices made me wince worse, so I was grateful that she offered.

I tuck my luggage beneath the bar and take a seat. Looking to my left, I see an older woman looking at her phone. The bartender is serving a beautiful mimosa to a young man to my right. The music is low, which I am grateful for after the loud flight. I sigh and pick up my menu, suddenly famished.

After I order, I finally look at my phone to sift through the messages. I text Alyse and Louis, letting them know that I am safe and sound in San Francisco.

Then I see a voicemail from an unknown number and frown.

I press play.

"Hi Serenity, this is Detective Markovich. I have some news for you in your sister's case. I know you're traveling today, so please call me when you have some time to talk."

My heartbeat quickens.

We have some news in your sister's case.

The sentence repeats in my mind, over and over, until it feels like someone is tapping it onto the inside of my skull.

I glance around me, wondering if I should do this here. I spot an empty table in the corner of the tiny eating area. I quickly gather my stuff and make a beeline for the table.

Once seated, I pull out my phone and call Markovich's number.

"Hello, you've reached Detective John Markovich, please leave me a brief message, and I will get right back to you as soon as I can. Thanks."

I sigh. "Hey, it's Serenity. I got your voicemail. Just calling to see what the updates are. Please call me back as soon as you can."

I know my voice sounds high-pitched and frantic, but I don't care. My nerves are shot.

My drink arrives, and I gratefully order some fish tacos from the sweet server. I take a long sip of the lemon drop martini, and its warmth is comforting to my nerves. My phone rings, and I snatch it up, thinking it's Markovich. I frown when I see a 510-area code number that I don't recognize.

"Serenity?" I hear a familiar voice say. My back stiffens.

It's Dre.

"I saw that you're in the Bay, and I heard about what happened to Samaya. Are you ok?"

His voice equally weirdly comforts me and makes me angry simultaneously.

"Dre, hi..." I trail off, not knowing what to say or how to feel.

"I know I'm probably the last person you wanna talk to right now, and trust me, I fully understand why. But I do love you, and I just want you to know if you need anything while you're out here, just holla, fa' real."

His smooth Oakland lilt melts through my defenses and my eyes tear up.

"Thank you, Dre," I say, voice shaking. "I really appreciate that."

"Can I see you? Take you out for some food or somethin'?"

I consider this. "I don't know, Dre."

"Just think about it, aight?"

"Ok."

The waitress walks up with my food. "I've got to go."

We hang up, and I stare at my tacos, feeling more confused than hungry.

What just happened?

My phone rings again, and I look at it wearily. When I see it's a private number, I snatch the phone up.

"Serenity? It's Detective Markovich."

"Hi," I say breathlessly. My voice comes out thinner than I intend, like it's squeezing past something lodged in my throat.

"I have a few updates. Are you in a place where you can talk—are you alone?"

"Yes, I'm fine, please just tell me what's happening," I say, my heart rate already picking up. It spikes so fast it feels like my pulse is trying to climb up into my ears.

I hear him take a long, low inhale. The kind that usually comes before bad news on TV. But this is real. This is mine.

"We found some… items—personal items that we believe belong to your sister. We found what we believe to be her purse and a jacket. It was found at the beach about twelve miles from her home. Based on the condition of the items, we believe that Samaya may have been attacked, and then whoever attacked her dumped her into the water. We are going to begin looking at this as a homicide investigation. I am so sorry, Serenity."

For a second, everything goes silent.

Not quiet—*silent.*

Like someone pulled a plug on the world.

Even the clinking of glasses at the bar fades, the background chatter evaporates. I feel the edges of my vision blur like a vignette tightening around me.

I hear the words.

I feel my heart drumming so loudly that I briefly wonder if the whole restaurant can hear it.

My mind knows what the detective is saying, but simultaneously can't process what he's just told me.

Items by the water?

A homicide investigation?

My mind swims as if it's also underwater and carried out by the current. A sickening sway. A drowning sensation. Like a wave rises inside me and drags my breath under.

"...We have a team out combing the water near the beach. The problem is since so much time has passed, if she was left there the night she went missing, her body was most likely carried out to sea by the currents."

My hands shake as I hold the phone to my ear. My heart beats quicker still, like it's trying to escape my body. My skin prickles hot and cold at the same time, like I might faint or vomit or both.

"...again, I am so sorry, Serenity..."

I hear him speaking.

I know what he's saying.

But my mind is rejecting it — like a tennis racket swatting away the meaning.

"...if you have any questions for me, ok?"

I see the waitress serving a drink to the men at the table in front of me like everything is ordinary, like the cops didn't just tell me my sister might have been thrown into an ocean.

The world keeps moving.

People keep eating.

No one notices my entire life tipping sideways.

"Serenity? Serenity, are you there?"

My focus snaps back. "What are you saying?" My voice cracks so sharply it hurts.

But I know what he is saying.

He says words that mean my sister is dead, her body washed away into an ocean three thousand miles from here.

A flash of memory hits me — her laughing in her kitchen, her saying she loved her new job, her asking if I wanted tea. I feel it like a punch.

"I know this is a lot to process, and I am so sorry to be telling you this while you are in California visiting your mother, but I wanted you to be the first to hear about this—"

I cut him off. "What items did you find? What makes you think there was an attack?" My mind is starting to work a little better, but everything feels like it's sliding around inside my skull. Like thoughts have no walls to cling to.

"We found a jacket and her purse. The ID in her wallet confirmed that it belonged to her. The jacket was ripped, and there was blood on both items, which we are running tests right now to identify whose blood it is."

My mind races. My eyes sting with impending tears. I blink hard to keep them from spilling, not ready for the world to see me crack open.

"What about David's phone?"

"Well, that's the other update," he says. "We've put a warrant out for his arrest."

I gasp, and my hand flies to my mouth. I feel my stomach clench tight, like my body already knows what this means.

"There were text messages between him and Samaya that were pretty incriminating," he continues. "I saw the messages you mentioned in our first interview, the ones after the women's event you all went to. But there are messages between the two of them the night she went missing; from what the messages said, it sounds like he's been stalking her when she goes out in the evenings, and we believe he may have seen her that night."

I knew it.

The certainty hits my chest like a lead weight. Rage flashes hot under my ribs, tangled with grief, tangled with fear.

"Wow," I say breathlessly, taking it all in. "This is a lot."

"Yes, it is. Again, I am so sorry to have to tell you this while you are on the other side of the country. I will let you know what we find by the beach, if anything, and I will also keep you in the loop on what happens with David—we are hoping to have him in custody before the end of the weekend."

I end the call and stare blankly at the food before me, suddenly too stunned to eat.

Samaya is dead?

Samaya is dead.

Those words feel so strange in my mind, like someone telling me the sky is green or that grass is pink. It doesn't compute. It doesn't land.

It just floats there, heavy and impossible, refusing to settle, refusing to be real.

Like it is hovering just outside my body, waiting for permission to sink in, and I can't. I won't. I refuse to let it.

A buzzing starts in my ears.

That faint, high-pitched sound trauma makes when the world becomes too loud, too sharp, too bright. I stare down at the table, at the untouched tacos, at the lemon drop sweating in its glass, and everything feels surreal. It is like I am watching myself from somewhere above, disconnected and suspended.

I think back to the day we were in her kitchen talking about David's latest shenanigans. She had looked genuinely concerned, scared even, and I totally downplayed it.

I can see it so clearly now. Her eyes flickering. Her fingers twisting the hem of her shirt. That uneasy laugh she did when she didn't want to worry me. I brushed it off. I told her he was just being dramatic. I told her she was fine.

I should have taken this more seriously. This is the same man who pushed her down some stairs while she was pregnant. This is the same man who gave her a black eye after she threw away his hidden liquor bottles.

The memory slams into me, violent and sudden.

Her bruised face.

The way her voice shook when she told me she was done.

The way she went back anyway because leaving an abuser is never simple, never safe, never clean.

Guilt twists low in my stomach, sharp and stabbing. It spreads through my chest, hot and nauseating, like something boiling underneath my ribs.

I put my elbows on the table and put my face in my hands.

The pressure does nothing. It doesn't stop the ache. It doesn't stop the replay of every moment I could have done more. Every sign I minimized. Every fear she hid behind a brave face that now feels like a warning I ignored.

I can't help but wonder if I should have handled things differently.

The thought hits me like a confession and a curse at once.

If I had listened harder.

If I had pushed more.

If I had shown up that night.

If I had done anything differently. The word repeats in my mind like a punishment.

My breath shakes.

My hands tremble.

My whole body feels like it is folding in on itself.

Because how do you live with the thought that maybe, just maybe, you could have saved your sister?

CHAPTER TWENTY-TWO

Jess' apartment is cute, made cuter by the fact that her son, Chance, is at his dad's until Sunday night. With everything going on, the last thing I have the bandwidth to deal with right now is a never-ending-question-asking four-year-old.

Jess has good taste, and I am impressed by what she's been able to do with the small space on her single mama budget. The couch is sandy-colored, but somehow not stained by Chance. The hardwood floor is worn, but covered here and there with brightly colored rugs. It's cozy and comfortable, and the couch pulls out into a bed, so I am happy to be here.

Jess joins me on the couch. "Babe! What can I do? What do you need? I don't work until nine tonight."

Jess bartends at a lounge in Oakland some weekends for extra cash. She's finishing up her bachelor's at San Francisco State University. While she has a decent day job, being a student and a single mother whose baby daddy does not pay much in child support means the extra money is a huge help. Plus, she's drop-dead gorgeous, so I know she is getting some fire tips.

I look at her, really taking her in. She looks so much like my dad's side of the family: the athletic build, the distinct jawline, the lips that look like they belong in every family photo. She seems so adult now, even though it's only been eight or nine months since I've seen her. Something about the set of her shoulders, the slight weariness in her eyes, the grounded energy. Life changed her too.

She notices me staring and tucks a lock of her straightened hair behind one ear. "What's up?" she asks with a shy smile.

"You just look so much like your mom, and I can't believe how mature you look now. You done grown up on me," I say with a smile.

She laughs and shrugs. "Motherhood will do that to you. But seriously, Renny, can I do anything to help?"

I forgot about this childhood nickname that only like three people could ever get away with calling me. Serenity was such a hard name to pronounce for my younger cousins, so a few of them started calling me Renny, and it just stuck. Hearing it now hits me right in the chest. Something warm. Something familiar in a way I didn't realize I needed.

I think for a moment. If she's going to work later, I will need a car. I remember the $500 Mario and Stella sent me on Venmo last night when I told them about my trip to see my mother.

"Need to rent a car," I say. "Can you just drop me off at a place? I'll find one close by."

She nods, eager to be of some kind of service, and I pull out my phone to find the nearest, cheapest rental car place.

By the time I find parking in the hospital's massive and damn near full parking lot, it's almost six. This gives me about an hour to spend with my mom. With the fragile mental state I am in, though, that's probably all the time I could handle anyway.

My stomach knots as I take the long walk toward the entrance. I have no idea what I am walking into other than knowing she is in a coma. I haven't seen Mom in almost nine months. When I tried to reach out and let her know I was leaving for New York, her phone was disconnected. This wasn't unusual for her. She often struggled with having enough money to pay her bills.

The automatic doors whoosh open, and the sterile smell of hospital air hits me immediately. Antiseptic. Old sheets. Something metallic. Something human. My chest tightens.

I glance around the entryway to the main hospital entrance and spot the information desk.

"Where can I direct you, sweetie?" asks a kind-faced older man. His white hair and a name tag that reads *VOLUNTEER* in bold but shaky print tell his age and status here.

"Um, I'm looking for room 22C?" I say, looking at the tiny slip of paper where I wrote my mother's room information during my call with her nurse the other day.

He directs me to the fourth floor, and I head to the elevator.

I notice the tremor in my hands as I press the "four" button and am instantly glad I am solo on this elevator. I close my eyes and try to steady my breath, not wanting to bring this manic energy into my mom's room and space. My shoulders have crept almost to my ears. I lower them and count backward from ten.

My eyes fly open with the opening of the elevator door. I step out slowly, scanning both directions like I'm five again and about to cross the street. The hallway smells like old people, cleaning supplies, and something unidentifiable that sits heavy in the air. I move down the hall quietly, reading room numbers while deliberately avoiding making eye contact with any patients inside.

I spot 22C, and my heart begins to drum again.

I peek my head in and see the curtain drawn around the bed. On the whiteboard, I see her name written in neat handwriting with notes from the nurse. That simple confirmation hits me harder than expected.

I tiptoe around the curtained bed and look in at my mother.

She lies completely still. She looks tiny and strangely frail for her fifty-nine years. There is a ventilator, and the machine appears to be breathing for her. The quiet whoosh of air in and out fills the small room.

A deep sadness crashes over me so fast it almost knocks the air from my lungs. Seeing Mom like this forces me to think of my sister. Loss layered on loss.

I pull the little plastic chair from behind me and place it next to the bed. I sit down and look at this woman; this complicated woman who did so many things wrong in her lifetime but also so many things right. The woman who gave me life. The woman who broke pieces of me she never meant to break. The woman whose pain shaped mine. The woman I still love in some quiet, aching way.

I glance at her hands. They are lying on her belly, rising and falling gently with the machine's rhythm. I reach out and rub the back of her hand with the back of mine, feeling the papery texture of her skin. I assume her hands are aged more from drugs and alcohol than from actual years lived.

I take her hand in mine. No response. Just the steady rise and fall.

"Mommy." My voice cracks. I swallow and try again. "Mommy, I am so sorry. I don't know if you can tell that I am here, but I am here." I say it earnestly, like I can will her to know it.

We sit like this for several moments. I watch her breathe.

Something inside me breaks open.

Maybe because everything else in my life is falling apart.

Maybe because this is the first time in decades she cannot interrupt.

Maybe because seeing her like this bypasses every defense I have ever built.

Words spill out of me.

I tell her about Sam being gone and that she's now presumed dead. My voice shakes on the word gone. I tell her about my job and how kind Stella is. I tell her about Louis and Jason and Alyse. I pour my life into the air, into the space between us, into the version of her that maybe still listens beneath the coma.

When I am done talking, I release her hand and lean my head against her shoulder. And I weep.

I cry for my mother and our strained relationship. I cry for Samaya and the life she should be living. I cry for her daughter, Samantha, whose life was cut so short, but also tears of bittersweet joy that they could be together in heaven. I cry even harder as I think of Mom joining them soon and leaving me here. And finally, I cry for myself and for the great many losses I have faced in the thirty years of my existence. I cry for all of us.

"Ma'am?"

My head snaps up at the soft voice of the nurse. I wipe my eyes and glance at my phone.

Shit.

"I'm sorry," I say as I gather my stuff. "I didn't realize the time."

Her face softens. "I understand, dear." She wheels in what looks like a blood pressure machine. "I'm here to take her vitals."

I wipe my eyes and slowly stand. I give my mother's hand one last squeeze and turn to walk out. When I reach the doorway, I turn back to look over my shoulder at the woman who raised me. The woman who failed me. The woman who loved me the only way she knew how.

I say a silent goodbye.

Then I walk out.

A cold feeling rises from the pit of my stomach and fills me like an icy mist, along with a deep, palpable sadness, because I know in my heart that this might be the last time I will see my mother.

CHAPTER TWENTY-THREE

I sit in my car outside of the Jaded Lounge, Jess's job, my fingers still gripping the steering wheel even though the engine is off. I can't tell if I'm debating going inside or just procrastinating having to feel anything. I'm exhausted in that bone-deep, soul-worn way, and I can't tell which choice is better: stepping into a dim bar full of strangers or sitting alone in Jess's quiet apartment with too many thoughts.

I think I'll just go in and feel it out. I have to go inside anyway to grab the key I forgot earlier.

I take a quick glance in the car mirror and fluff my curls half-heartedly. They look like curls with a long, dramatic backstory.

I sigh. This will have to do for now.

When I get inside, I see that it's pretty dead—it's still early. The crowds don't really start piling in until after ten. The first thing I smell is the sweet, sticky, sour scent of marijuana lingering in the air like it pays rent here.

Ah, California. It's good to be home.

I think I'll stay. With the way I feel, I don't really want to sit in Jess's apartment by myself until she gets home at one. Being alone with my thoughts feels dangerous tonight.

I approach the bar and order a Blue Moon beer. I turn and lean my back against the bar, surveying the room from behind the safety of my bottle.

The lighting is dim, which I am grateful for after the hours of crying earlier. The tables on the far side are tall, with burgundy velvet seat bottoms that look like they belong in some retro hip-hop movie. The artwork takes the cake, though.

Multiple poster-sized pieces line the walls: various celebrities and musicians smoking weed. My eyes scan over them slowly, taking them in. They range from G-Eazy to Tupac. The colors are vivid, the smoke almost ghostly in the dim light.

I decide that the one of Nipsey Hussle is my favorite. He's younger in this photo, his hair parted perfectly down the middle, slicked down and braided into his famous pigtail-style braids, blunt smoke curling in front of his face like an aura.

"Hey! You're here!"

I turn my head to see Jess rushing up to me. She wraps me in a hard hug, grounding me for a moment. She pulls away but keeps her hands planted on my shoulders like she's physically holding me together.

"How'd it go? You know, at the hospital with your mom?" Her eyes search mine.

I swallow hard. My throat is still raw from crying.

"It was… not good. She looked so thin. Like crazy thin. She wasn't even breathing on her own. The machine thingy was breathing for her. It was hard to see, especially with everything else going on."

Jess's eyes glisten with unshed tears as she nods. "A lot is going on, Ren. I can't imagine how you must be feeling… with the news about Samaya and your mom. Just know that I am here for you. Whatever you need. Seriously."

She pulls me in for another hug, and this time I let myself cry on her shoulder. The second I feel someone hold me, the pain rises like a tide I can't stop.

Before Jess leaves, she slips something into my purse and kisses my cheek. I look at her, puzzled, but she gives me one last bear hug and hurries back to her shift.

I take a long swig of my beer, draining it. When I open my purse, I see what she left for me: a little pink wristband that says *VIP – STAFF* and a plastic tube. I open the cap and the strong smell of weed assaults my senses.

A pre-rolled joint.

Well, that explains the strong smell when I walked in.

I smile and shake my head, closing the cap and tucking it deep in my bag. I slide the wristband across the bar toward the pretty young woman making drinks.

"What does this get me?" I ask.

She glances down and grins. "Oh girl, you drinking *free* tonight. Unlimited."

I attach the band to my wrist. "Well, in that case, can you make me a Hennessy and Sprite?"

She gets to work, hips swaying slightly as she eyeballs a generous amount of Hennessy into the glass. The first sip is heaven; the warmth hits my sternum like a tiny, temporary miracle.

I text Jess a quick thanks.

Then I see it: a text from a number I don't recognize.

It's from Dre.

Hey, just checking on you…

I consider ignoring it, but loneliness creeps in like fog. My heart is already raw and frayed.

I appreciate that.

His reply is almost immediate.

Can I see you?

I stare at my drink, take another long gulp.

I'm at Jaded Lounge.

Dre: *You gon be there for a min?*

Me: *Yes.*

I put my phone down and stir my drink. The idea of seeing him shouldn't feel comforting… but it does, in a broken, familiar way. Grief makes you reach for anything that feels like home, even old habits disguised as people.

The lounge is fuller now. I finish my drink and decide to step outside to call Alyse. Then I remember the joint and turn back to the bartender.

"You wouldn't happen to have a light, would you?"

She grins wickedly. "Here you go, boo. Just bring it back. Ima need it for my dinner break." She mimes smoking.

"I got you," I say, weaving through the crowd toward the exit.

Outside, the cool night air hits me in the face and I breathe deep. My mind feels jumbled and fuzzy, like someone shook a snow globe inside my skull. The time difference makes everything slower, heavier.

I search the block for a place to light the joint. I haven't smoked since leaving the Bay months ago, so I'm both nervous and excited.

I round the corner and find a secluded spot.

That'll do.

I'm sitting across from Dre inside the Jaded Lounge, feeling a little nervous and extremely stoned. He looks exactly like I remember. Short but muscular, full of Oakland swagger. There's a hopeful look on his face that makes my chest twist.

"It's good to see you. I know the circumstances are not great... Are you ok?"

I look down at my drink. "Yea, shit's been crazy, Dre."

"Sounds like it."

We sit in silence. It stretches, awkward and too loud in my head.

I take another big swig of my drink. When I look up, he's texting, barely engaged.

Classic Dre. Half-present, half-distracted.

He looks up when he hears me sigh. "It's my mom, girl. Don't trip."

I nod and finish my drink. My head feels buzzy, my body warm and heavy. I look around for Jess, hoping to anchor myself. No Jess in sight.

"So, how you been?" I ask to fill the space. The longer we sit here, the more obvious it becomes that we never had much depth together.

"I been good, girl. Just coolin'. Working with my cousin driving trucks."

He keeps talking, but his voice blurs. The liquor hits harder, mixing with the weed. I feel a little dizzy. I need air.

"Hey, can we go outside for a little? I need some air."

He agrees instantly, almost relieved.

As soon as we step outside, the night air gives me a sliver of clarity. I breathe it in like medicine.

"You still got some tree?" he asks.

I frown, remembering the joint. I dig through my purse until I find the plastic tube. He pulls out his own lighter and flashes me a smile before lighting the joint and taking a long pull.

He hands it to me. I inhale—gently—but it hits me like fire. I choke, coughing so hard tears fall.

"They ain't got the good shit over in New York, huh?" he teases.

I giggle despite myself. I am incredibly and undeniably stoned.

Then suddenly his arms are around me and we're chest to chest. I look up at him, too emotionally wrecked to trust my judgment.

His lips graze mine.

Then we're kissing. Hard. Familiar. *Wrong.* Comfort wrapped in chaos.

His hands grip my waist, my ass, pulling me in. His mouth moves against mine with the confidence of someone who remembers exactly how I taste.

"Come on," he says, breath warm. He leads me around the corner.

We stop at his black Chevy Tahoe. The car chirps open.

"Dre, I—"

He cuts me off. "Shh. Get in."

And I do. I'm too gone to fight myself.

Inside, he strokes my cheek, eyes softening.

"I miss you, Serenity. I really do."

I hiccup, nodding. He pulls me into another kiss. It grows deeper fast. Desperate. I climb onto his lap, wanting to forget everything for five seconds.

Then I feel the bulge beneath me.

"Dre!" I gasp.

He smirks. "You see what you do to me, baby?"

Instant nausea hits me. Everything clears.

Reality slams back into my body.

What the fuck am I doing?

I scramble off his lap.

"What the fuck?" he snaps, annoyed.

"I-I need to go. I'm sorry. I shouldn't have come here."

"Wow," is all he says at first. Then:

"What a bitch."

The kindness he faked evaporates instantly.

"I knew I shouldn't have come to see your crazy ass."

Fresh tears rise. I back away fast.

He keeps throwing insults as I turn and run back toward the bar.

I push past the crowd, vision blurred with tears. My body is buzzing with weed, alcohol, fear, shame, grief — all of it tangling together in my chest.

Once inside the lounge, I find a quiet corner and sink into it, trembling.

What the fuck was I thinking?

CHAPTER TWENTY-FOUR

The headache slams into me as soon as my eyes open. I squeeze them shut again as if I might get a wake-up do-over.

No such luck.

I roll over to my back, eyes still closed, gently squeezing the bridge of my nose with my first finger and thumb. The pressure seems to help a tiny bit, but not enough to peel my eyes open yet. My mind is fuzzy, but clear enough to bring forth mental screenshots of the night before. Not just the images, but the feeling of them too. The way everything blurred and sharpened at the same time. The way I kept reaching for anything that felt like a lifeboat.

I hooked up with Dre.

What the fuck.

The words don't sit right in my head. They feel foreign, like I'm reading someone else's memories. But the ache in my body tells me I'm not imagining it. I cover my face with my hands now and roll over to my side. My stomach twists in that slow, nauseating way that isn't just hangover. It's shame. It's grief. It's the sick reminder that I am still human enough to make messy choices even when my life is on fire.

What was I thinking? The guy is a dog and really showed it last night. I replay how he yelled at me after I pulled away and pushed him off of me. The anger and the apparent resentment. He's not used to not getting his way with women, especially me. I know it hurts his ego, but it is not my responsibility to mitigate his emotions for him.

And yet I still feel dirty. Not because of what happened, but because of the way it happened. Because of how fast it went from comfort to entitlement. Because I let myself lean into the familiarity like it was a blanket instead of a trap. I should not have smoked that weed, and more importantly, I should've known better than to agree to see him. I was in the most fragile state of mind.

As I internally beat myself up, everything comes flooding back. The shocking sense of sobriety I feel, mixed with an unruly incoming hangover, has me feeling emotionally raw. Like my nerves are exposed. Like I'm walking around without skin.

I roll over to my side, assuming the fetal position, squeezing my eyes shut, hard. With so much shit happening, hooking up with Dre makes me feel stupid and weak. It makes me feel like I betrayed myself. Like I betrayed Sam too, somehow, even though that doesn't make sense. Nothing makes sense right now.

I want to call Sam so she can tell me it's ok and that we all have made these kinds of decisions in moments of weakness. She'd say to me that yea, I'm a dumbass, but also she'd have some comforting story from her own past that would make me feel less like a weak woman and more like an ordinary, human woman navigating the complex world of men.

The thought lands and then breaks me. Because I can hear her voice so clearly in my head, almost like she's right here, and that's exactly what makes my chest cave in. The thoughts of Samaya combined with the worsening headache make me cry. I try to keep quiet as I hear one of the doors open in the hall, but the sound of me falling apart has a way of leaking out anyway. Grief is loud even when you whisper it.

"Oh, Ren, boo!" Jess is rubbing her eyes and rushing over to me, wrapped in a silk floral robe, "Honey, are you ok?"

I cry even harder. I think I was in shock for the past twenty-four hours, and it's all hitting me now. My head hurts, my heart hurts, and I feel like everything is falling apart in front of me. Jess seems to sense my overwhelm and just lays down behind me, wrapping her arms around me from behind, stroking my arms, and quietly murmuring, "I got you, love, it's ok." Her few years as a mother, serving even me now.

We lay like this for a long time, me sobbing, soaking the pillow beneath me, and her holding me tightly and murmuring loving words into my hair. My body shakes with it, the kind of crying that makes you feel hollowed out after. I don't even know what I'm crying for first. My sister. My mother. The version of me that shouldn't have walked into Dre's Tahoe. The version of me that wants to rewind my entire life about ten steps.

"I fucked up last night," I say finally, sitting up and wiping my eyes. "I hooked up with my ex outside of the bar."

Jess had stood to go grab something from the other room, but when she heard what I said, she turns over her shoulder to look at me, eyebrows raised, *"Dre?!"*

I nod, ashamed. My face feels hot. My whole body feels like it's braced for impact.

She disappears and returns with a box of Kleenex. I gratefully take one and wipe my snotty nose and wet face. I blow my nose and wipe my face. Taking a deep breath, I tell Jess what happened. I tell her about the weed. The kissing. The Tahoe. The switch in his voice. The way my brain finally snapped back to me.

"Are you fucking serious?" she asks, voice disgusted. She stands up and begins pacing around the small living room. "He is such an asshole! Like, who does that, knowing what you're going through?"

I sigh. "That's just who Dre is, girl. That's exactly why we broke up. All he cares about is getting his and what's best for him." Placing my elbows on my knees, I cover my face with my hands. "And that's why I feel like such a fuckin' dummy. What was I thinking?"

"This is not on you! He took advantage of the fact that you were grieving and thought he could weasel his way into your pants!"

"Yes, I'm sure you're right, but I'm just mad at myself for even agreeing to see him. I should've known this was his plan and should have known that I am in no state of mind to be around him."

Because Jess is right. But I'm right too. Both things can be true. He took advantage, and I walked into the room anyway. I let grief turn into carelessness. I let loneliness tell me comfort was the same as safety. And now I'm stuck with the fallout of something I didn't even want once I came back to myself.

"Fair," she says. "But I still blame him one hundred percent. You just found out your sister is…" she can't bring herself to say the word, "not ok. And your mother is dying. That's a lot, girl. Please don't put so much pressure on yourself right now. It's gotta be hard enough just getting through the day, let alone navigate his manipulation."

I snort bitterly, "Am I even making it through the day, though?" My head's pounding becomes more apparent again, "Do you have any Tylenol?"

"Yes!" She jumps up, happy to help.

While she's gone, I find my phone and look at my messages. I expect to see messages from Dre, but then I remember that I drunkenly blocked him last night.

Well, at least I made one decent decision last night, I think to myself.

I see two texts from Louis, the first one asking how it went with my mom. The second message is more concerned.

Hey, sorry to hit you again, but please let me know if you're ok.

I begin to text him back and then throw my phone down on the bed.

What do I even say? *"Hey, things suck. Not only is my sister dead, but my mom is probably dying at any time. Oh! And I hooked up with my cheating ex last night."*

I pick up my phone again and stare at the screen. Here is this beautiful man, inside and out, and he could be in New York doing anything, and he is checking on my broken ass. And I don't even deserve his sweetness right now. Not with the way I feel. Not with the way I'm afraid I'm already ruining something good before it even has a name.

Sorry for the delay. My mom is not doing well. I'll call you after I go to see her today.

I feel like such a fraud. Like I'm handing him only the parts of me that feel acceptable, and hiding the rest like a stain.

Jess returns, shaking the bottle of Excedrin in front of me like a rattle. She tosses it to me, and I miraculously catch the bottle. I reach for the bottled water next to me and down two extra-strength pills.

Let's hope this helps me get rid of this massive headache before I head to see my mom in an hour.

I walk out of the hospital feeling a strange sense of peace. And not just because my hangover seems to be gone.

I spent three hours with mom today and I'm so glad I decided to come back. I told her how I've felt over the many years that were distant between us. I told her how much I love her and how much Sam loved her. I even told her about what happened with Dre last night.

The entire time I spoke to her, she was still and unresponsive. She didn't move or blink. But somehow, I had never felt so connected to her. There were long periods of silence where I just gazed at her face as if to memorize every single line and feature on it. I reveled at how much she looked like Samaya. Well, how much Samaya had looked like mom, I guess.

I didn't expect that. I didn't expect my body to loosen, my chest to unclench, the words to pour out of me like a confession I'd been holding since I was a kid. I didn't expect to feel like she heard me even if she didn't move. Like whatever part of her spirit was still hovering in there knew I was sitting by her side.

When I felt like there was nothing else that I needed to say to my mother, I was startled by how much time had actually passed. It'd felt like an hour or so at most, definitely not three hours. I stood and kissed my mother, knowing that I would probably never see this woman again while she was earth-side. And I felt almost relieved.

My mother has had a hard life, from birth till death. I felt a sense of ease for her that she wouldn't have to battle addiction and the feelings of worthlessness that I knew she'd struggled with for the 59 years of her life. I felt relief that I wouldn't have to live with the nagging guilt that came with having a mother who needed your help, but you couldn't help because of newfound, healthier boundaries. Although I knew having boundaries protected me and allowed me to have a healthy relationship with her, I never really got over the feelings of guilt that came with enforcing them.

I also felt a sense of peace. Even though I haven't fully processed that Samaya is no longer alive, the only solace I have is that they may be together soon.

My phone vibrates in my bag, and I reach into the passenger seat to retrieve it.

It's Louis. I consider letting it go to voicemail, but decide I will not be in better shape to speak with him later, and there's no time like the present. I'd told him I would call after I left the visit with my mother, and I am amazed at his call time.

"Hey," I say. "I'm just leaving the hospital."

"How is she? How are you?"

"She's not responsive. The doctors don't think that she'll wake up."

"I'm so sorry, Serenity. How are you holding up?"

"Not good," I say numbly, "I just really want to come home. I can't think straight here. It's been really strange being home."

"That's understandable—you have a lot going on."

I wince at his kindness towards me. If only he knew how close I'd come to fucking my ex last night, he'd be less sympathetic.

"Thanks for understanding." I consider telling him, but can't deal with that right now. I will tell him when I see him and let the chips fall where they may. "How are you?"

"I'm good, working on a new project for a company in the city. The pay is really good, so I'm happy. Plus, it's keeping me from moping around my apartment because I miss you so much. I've been worried about you."

"I know, and I'm sorry I haven't been in communication," I say sincerely.

"Don't worry about it. I just can't wait to see you."

My face burns with shame, "I miss you too." And I mean it. I miss him so much my core aches. I just also feel incredibly guilty for the mishap last night.

We talk for a few more minutes before ending the call. I lean back in my rental's seat and close my eyes. I let out a long breath then start the car. I need to get to Jess's house to get some rest. All I want to do now is go home.

CHAPTER TWENTY-FIVE

I look for Alyse's car and spot her pulling into the arrivals area for JetBlue. I wave frantically, rolling my luggage behind me. The cold air nips at my cheeks, that sharp New York breeze that always feels personal, like the city welcoming you back by slapping you in the face.

"Keep it going, keep it moving," a very New York-ish sounding voice barks at the car ahead of her. Typical airport chaos. I shoot him a grateful smile anyway, pointing to Alyse's car like some frantic mime.

She pops the trunk, and I quickly toss my things inside, then scurry to the passenger side and climb in.

"Baaaaaabe!" she squeals as she checks her rearview mirror for oncoming traffic. A car honks—loud and aggressively—and she fires back a string of curse words before flooring it back into traffic. I've never felt so happy to see someone.

"Girl, thank you so much for picking me up."

"The fuck?" She gives me a sideways glance. "You weren't taking no fucking train."

The warmth in my chest catches me off guard, and suddenly I'm fighting tears again. "Everything is messed up. Alyse," I moan as I cover my face with my hands.

"Tell me everything. Have the cops given you any more updates about the search?"

My mind reels as I prepare to answer, already feeling that pressure in my throat that means crying is seconds away. "So much has happened, girl. I haven't spoken to the cops since they called me the other day and told me that they think Sam is dead."

"I still can't believe they told you that over the phone. And how are they so sure that she's dead? Just because they found her purse does not mean she's dead."

"I don't know." My voice sounds thin. "My mind has played out every possible scenario too. But it's been weeks, so it kind of makes sense."

Detective Markovich had texted me last night and said they would continue searching the beach until tonight. He also said that once he contacts me with the final report, I should start the process of planning her funeral if that's something I want to do for her. Funereal. Final. Permanent. The words sit like stones in my stomach.

I can't fathom planning my sister's funeral. With there being no body, she doesn't even feel dead. She feels missing, paused, suspended in some awful space I can't reach.

"I am just so sorry, sis. You have so much going on right now, and I just feel so bad. I don't even wanna ask, but I have to… how's your mom?"

She says it tentatively, her voice softening, that concern tightening every syllable.

I tell her about the visit with my mother. The machines. The stillness. The way grief felt like it had hands around my throat. While she looks straight ahead at the road, I can tell she is fully with me, every word landing. She shoots me a sympathetic smile, her eyes warm even in the dim morning light.

"So, I need your advice," I say after we finish talking about my mom. My chest tightens because I know what comes next. I figure we have another thirty minutes of driving until we hit Long Island—might as well tell her everything now.

I look over at her, and she glances back at me, expectantly.

"I kind of made out with my ex," I begin. "And I feel like shit about it."

"Wait, you hooked up with Dre? The dude who cheated?"

My cheeks burn with embarrassment, and I cover my face with my hands. "Yes, that's the one," I say through my fingers, wanting to disappear into the seat.

"Where? When? And *why?*"

I try to cover everything at once, my words tumbling out. "Um, in Oakland outside of my cousin's job in Dre's Tahoe. When—Friday night. And I don't know why! He asked if he could come see me when I was at my cousin's job—the lounge downtown. She gave me a joint, and I smoked, so I wasn't thinking clearly. And with everything going on, I just lost my head."

"Wait, you got *high?*" She looks shocked. "You ain't allowed to go to California no more by yourself."

"I know, I know. I was a hot mess, girl. When he asked if we could connect, I felt like it'd be nice to see a familiar face, you know? But then the next thing I knew, I was on top of him in his car, and his hand was up my shirt."

"Sounds kind of hot," she says, glancing in the rearview mirror to merge onto the highway.

"Stop," I moan. "You're supposed to be telling me that I'm trippin' and that he's gross. I caught this man eating another woman's pussy on our couch earlier this year. There should have been no making out."

"You right. I will say just don't beat yourself up about it. It's not like you fucked him." She glances over at me. "Did you?"

I shake my head vigorously. "God no. As soon as I felt him get hard underneath me, I came to my senses. And all I could think about was Louis…" My voice trails off, the guilt crawling back in.

We drive in silence for a beat. The hum of the car fills the space. My mind feels too full but also empty in a weird way— all swirling thoughts and none of them landing.

"Should I tell him?" I whisper finally. "Louis, I mean. Should I tell him what happened?"

She considers this for a moment. "Are y'all officially together?"

"No, we haven't even talked about it, but we are having sex and spending a lot of time together."

"Then no." She says it with firm finality. "If y'all are not officially in a relationship, then you aren't required to tell him."

I look out the passenger side window at the passing trees, soaking in the blur of green and gray. The rest of the drive is quiet, and I'm okay with that. My body feels heavy. My spirit feels heavier.

All I want to do is get home and lie down. I have never felt so overwhelmed in my life.

CHAPTER TWENTY-SIX

The sound of my cell phone ringing pulls me from my thoughts, and I jump, startled. I reach for the phone and see that it's a private number.

This better not be Dre.

"Hello?" I say groggily, rubbing my eyes with my free hand. My throat feels dry, my voice thick with sleep, and for a split second I think maybe this is just a wrong number and I can go back to pretending last night never happened.

"Good morning, Serenity. It's Detective Markovich. I'm sorry to wake you—I know it's early."

I immediately sit straight up in bed. My heart kicks hard, like it's slamming against the inside of my ribs. "Yes, no worries. Were you able to arrest David?"

There is a long pause on the other end, and my heart sinks. It drops so violently that I press a hand to my chest, bracing.

"Well, that's why I'm calling. We found David's body in his home when we went in with the arrest warrant–"

I cut him off, "wait, *what?!*" The word rips out of me sharper than I intend.

"His body was discovered late last night. Based on the condition of the home and the body, we are treating this as a homicide. We'll need you to come in for an interview later today if possible."

I am in complete shock. My breath stutters out of me, shallow and fast, and it feels like the room tilts for a moment.

"How?" I ask finally. "How was he killed?"

"You can discuss that with Detective Adams when you come in."

"Detective Adams...?"

"Yes, sorry. He's the homicide detective that will be handling this case. You will be meeting with both of us today to discuss what happened and what this means for your sister's case."

My breathing feels restricted. How can this be? The words blur around the edges like they're too big to fit into my brain.

I glance down at the time on my phone, "I can be there in thirty minutes," I say quickly. "Thank you for calling me."

I sit there stunned after ending the call. The silence in my room feels unnaturally loud, like the air itself is listening.

What the fuck.

I jump up and wrap my robe around myself. My hands fumble with the fabric because they're trembling too hard to cooperate. When I leave my room, I go straight to Alyse's door and open it, not bothering to knock. She's sound asleep on her bed. She must've worked late last night.

"Alyse!" I hiss in a loud whisper. When she doesn't budge, I walk over and shake her shoulder gently. Her eyes fly open immediately, and she looks confused but surprisingly awake. She looks around the room and sees me standing there shaking.

"What's happening?" she asks, sitting up quickly.

I sit at the edge of her bed next to her, my entire body shaking with shock, "They found David. He's been murdered!"

Her eyes go wide, and her hand flies to her chest, "What the hell! *How?*"

"I don't know, they wouldn't tell me over the phone. The police found him at his house when they went to serve the warrant last night."

She sits there, processing the information I've just relayed to her. I stood up and began pacing her almost dark room. My body is buzzing with the shock of the information I've been told. My pulse feels like it's everywhere at once—in my throat, my fingertips, even the soles of my feet.

"This is fucking crazy," she says as she unwraps her headscarf. "What happens now?"

I watch as she fluffs her tight curls absently with her fingertips as she stares up at me, eyes bulging. There's concern there, but also disbelief, like she's trying to make the puzzle pieces fit and they just won't.

"I need to go into the station, there's a new detective that wants to speak with me. The first cop says he'll be able to tell me everything." I sit down again next to her. "Will you come with me?"

She doesn't hesitate, "You're damn right I'm coming with you."

Her certainty steadies me for a moment, like someone putting a hand on your back when you're learning to balance again.

My stomach is churning when I walk through the double doors of the Suffolk County Police station. The place feels colder than I remember, the fluorescent lights too bright, the officers moving with a mechanical efficiency that makes the whole building feel sterile. I glance back at Alyse, and she nods to me as if to say, I got you. I'm so grateful that she agreed to come. Without her beside me, I'm not sure my legs would've carried me past the front desk.

The receptionist at the front desk is a man I've not seen before, and I tell him I need to see Markovich. He walks out almost immediately to greet me. His face looks solemn, and he wordlessly leads me back to a different room. The hallway is long, the floors scuffed, the air faintly smelling of burnt coffee and cleaning supplies.

There is an older white man seated at the table looking at the contents of a manilla file folder. He looks up and gives me a once-over that makes my skin crawl a little. Something about his eyes feels too calculating, too assessing. Neither of them is smiling or seems welcoming. I try to shrug this off, assuming it's because of the nature of the visit.

"Serenity, thank you for coming in so quickly," he says as he stands and reaches his hand across the table to shake my hand. His east coast accent is thick and abrasive.

Too nervous to speak, I nod and shake his freezing cold hand. It feels clammy, and I resist the urge to wipe my palm on my jeans.

"I know Markovich told you that we discovered Mr. Esposito dead in his home today," he begins. "We just wanted to have you make an official statement since he was a suspect in the disappearance and death of your sister, Samaya."

"Yes, of course. Whatever you need," I say, grateful to have found my voice again. Something feels a little too formal about this meeting. I'd given a statement before when Sam had first disappeared, but this was a new detective, and this was the homicide of the main suspect in my sister's murder. My heart keeps ticking up a notch every thirty seconds, like it's trying to warn me of something I don't fully understand yet.

I lay my palms flat on my thighs, trying to appear calm. Detective Adams writes something down on a little notepad, but the folder he was initially combing through is closed. I'm suddenly dying to know what is inside.

"What was your relationship like with the deceased?" he asks, without looking up. I swallow hard and hope he doesn't hear the gulp in my throat.

"We, uh, didn't have much of a relationship. He was married to my sister, and he treated her pretty poorly over the years, so he wasn't exactly my favorite person." I say, treading lightly and trying to hold eye contact with Adams' expressionless blue eyes.

He nods and jots something down in his notepad.

"That's understandable. And you were under the impression that he is — was — the person who kidnapped and murdered your sister?" He asks this so bluntly, and it stings. The matter-of-factness of it makes my eyes burn.

"Yes, I do," I say, my eyes not leaving his. "He's the only one that had any kind of motive."

He looks at me for a beat and then glances at Markovich, who meets his gaze, and they exchange some sort of silent information. Something about it tightens every muscle in my body.

My heartbeat quickens, and I begin to feel uneasy.

"Can I ask what happened to David? How do you know he was murdered?"

Adams looks again at Markovich, who nods slightly, then he slides the envelope towards himself and opens it. He removes three documents and places them before me. My hand flies to my mouth as I take in the first image.

It's a body—presumably David's, lying face down in what looks like a hallway. His face isn't showing since it's facing the opposite direction, but I recognize his wavy dark brown hair. A pool of blood covers the area beneath his neck and chest area, making the tan carpet look a dark brown color. His arms are splattered with blood, and I can see a few dark marks up and down his forearm. Stab wounds maybe? His attacker must've used a knife because they look like defensive wounds.

My stomach flips violently. For a moment, I can't tell if I'm breathing or not.

My eyes drift to the next photo of the wall above the body. It is spotted with blood splatters and bloodied handprints. But more disturbingly, written with what looks like someone's finger is a single, damning word:

KILLER

My hand drifts from my mouth to my throat as I take in the final photo.

It's another shot of David, but someone had turned him onto his back. My mouth becomes completely parched as I take in the disturbing image.

His eyes are wide open, and you can see the look of terror that was in his eyes at the moment of death. His mouth is twisted open into a grotesque grimace or possibly his final cry for help. His throat seems to be split wide open from one ear to the other, and the dark red, almost black blood completely soaks the upper half of his once sky-blue t-shirt. His stomach area is riddled with one-inch bloodied slits where his attacker stabbed him repeatedly. His fingers are gnarled into talon-like shapes, and his nails look bloodied, and some appear to be missing — he fought whoever did this hard.

"Oh my God," I whimper as I close my eyes and cover my face with my hands. I can never unsee these images. They burn themselves into my brain like violent photographs developing behind my eyelids.

Markovich sits down at the table. "I know these images are disconcerting. The forensics team is still analyzing the home, but it appears he'd been dead for just a couple of hours."

"Mr. Esposito was stabbed more than 20 times, and his throat was also slit. Based on the nature of the crime scene and body, we know this was not a random attack—whoever killed him knew him and had it out for him."

He continues to study my eyes. I hold his gaze only because I don't want my eyes to drift back down to the gruesome photos. I can still feel them pressing against the edges of my vision.

"Do you know of anyone who would want David dead?" asks Markovich.

Yea, me.

"I'm not sure. I don't know what kind of stuff he was into. If he treated anyone else the way he treated my sister, I would imagine the answer would be yes. But I don't know who."

Detective Adams scribbles something on his little notepad, and it takes everything in me not to crane my neck to see what he just wrote. My skin prickles with paranoia, hot and sharp.

He clears his throat, and his eyes meet mine once again. "Serenity, when did you return from your trip to California?"

"Earlier today. I landed at around 11 a.m." I say. Then I realize why they're asking me this. "Wait, you don't think I–"

Adams cuts me off, "We are not accusing you of anything. These are standard questions—we are just trying to narrow down possibilities."

I try to calm down, but my breath catches in my throat. My emotions are all over the place right now, and I'm worried that it's making me appear manic. The air in the room feels too tight, too thin.

"I'm sorry, Detective, it's just been a crazy few days. I arrived home just after noon and spent the rest of the evening at home with my roommate, Alyse. She is actually here with me, she's in the lobby."

CHAPTER TWENTY-SEVEN

I pick at the hangnail on my pinky finger as my mind runs through the past hour. Alyse is now giving her statement confirming that I was indeed home with her for the past twelve hours. The fluorescent lights in the waiting room buzz quietly above me, almost drowning out the low murmur of voices from behind the front desk. My leg bounces restlessly, adrenaline still humming through my bloodstream like static.

Initially, I was offended by their insinuation of my involvement, but I felt a little better after I spoke privately with Markovich. The man that I thought kidnapped and murdered my sister is dead—of course, they will have some questions for me. Even knowing that doesn't settle my nerves. My stomach still aches like I swallowed a handful of gravel.

It's been about ten minutes since Alyse went in to give her statement. I reach into my purse to grab my phone and see that I've missed a message from Louis.

Hey, beautiful. Just want you to know that I'm thinking of you

The words pinch something deep in my chest. I text back:

I appreciate you so much. Call me when you can, I reply.

My phone rings, and I glance up to see the receptionist speaking with a worried-looking woman. There's also a man and a teenage boy in the plastic chairs to my left. The boy is picking at the Velcro strap on his sneaker, the sound grating against my already-frayed nerves. Even though it's dark, I decide to head outside to make this call.

I push open the heavy station door and am immediately hit in the face by the cold air. The sky is a deep charcoal, rain misting sideways across the parking lot in thin silver streaks. I wrap my jacket tighter around myself and stay under the building overhang to avoid getting dampened by the rain. I call Louis back.

"Hey, sorry, I'm at the police station," I say.

"All good. Were they able to arrest David? Was he home when they went to serve the warrant?"

I turn and look through the building's window, watching the receptionist shuffle paperwork. "Well, yes and no. He was home, but he's dead. They found him dead last night."

I hear Louis' sharp intake of breath before he responds, "Holy shit, Serenity!"

"Right," I say. "And I just had to give a statement. It was so fuckin' scary. At first, the detective thought maybe I somehow killed him!"

"But how? You've been in California for the past few days."

"I know, but the detective said the blood or forensic or whatever looked like he'd been killed just hours before they arrived. I was home during those hours."

Silence. Heavy, weighted silence. I hear the echo of a car door slamming somewhere across the lot.

"Alyse is giving them her statement right now, though, and luckily I was with her the entire night, so my alibi is legit. It just felt hella scary to be questioned like that."

"I can't even imagine. This is so crazy! How do they know he was murdered?"

"The pictures they showed me were brutal. He was stabbed like thirty times and whoever did it also slit his throat. There was so much blood…" my voice trails off, and my free arm wraps around myself as I remember the photos I'd been shown. I may not like the guy, but I couldn't imagine stabbing anyone once, let alone doing that much damage. The image of his twisted face flickers behind my eyelids, making my stomach twist.

Louis seems to take in what I said, or maybe he's too shocked to speak. I glance back at the window and see Alyse approaching the waiting area.

"I gotta go! I'll text you when I'm done here."

I end the call and scurry back inside, grateful for the warmth but suffocated by the stale scent of the waiting room. I watch as Detective Adams shakes Alyse's hand. She is smiling, but it's a tight, "I'm around white folks," smile, so I have no idea how the conversation went.

"Thank you both for coming in," Adams says once he and Alyse are standing next to me. His face looks softer, and my stomach relaxes slightly. He looks directly at me now, "Serenity, I know these past couple weeks have been hell for you — my condolences about your sister... If you think of anything that may be useful, please give me a call."

He hands me his card, and I meet his eyes again, though my vision now swims with tears. His blue eyes soften further with evident sympathy. The sincerity almost undoes me.

"I will," I whisper. "Thank you."

As soon as he turns to walk away, Alyse and I hurry to leave the station. I've spent so much time inside those walls that it's starting to feel familiar. Too familiar. The automatic door groans as it opens, and the cold air outside feels like a slap, but a necessary one. At least out here I can breathe.

"What happened?" I ask as soon as we are seated in the car.

"Girl," she says as she pushes the button to start her car, "that was intense."

"I know, right?" My heart is still racing, reluctant to calm down.

"So, he first asked me if I knew David, and I was like 'yea, kind of.' Then he asked me about the past twenty-four hours, where I was, and what I did. I just told him that after I picked you up from the airport, we were at home together."

"Did he show you the photos of David?" I ask, giving her a sideways glance to gauge her reaction.

"God no! Oh my God, I can't handle that. You know I can't even watch those True Crime shows. But he did say that it was disturbing." She glances over at me, "Wait, did you see the photos of David?"

I nod solemnly, my stomach becoming nauseated at the memory.

"They are beyond disturbing, girl. The person who did it definitely knew him. It was like, a crime of passion or whatever they call it."

She shakes her head, eyes glued to the road ahead, "This is getting crazier and crazier. I was so sure that he was the person that took Samaya, but now, I don't know what to think."

I lean my head back against the passenger seat's headrest and close my eyes. The rain taps softly against the windshield. My chest feels tight, my brain buzzing like a hive. I can't believe how much my life has changed in a matter of two weeks.

Nothing feels real, and nothing feels safe.

CHAPTER TWENTY-EIGHT

I lay down without even bothering to do anything with my hair, and I can almost feel it frizzing up already. The pillow smells faintly like my shampoo from before California, and the familiar scent makes my chest ache in that quiet, homesick way that hits after too much happens too fast.

But I don't care.

My hair is the least of my worries. I pull my white furry blanket up around my chest and arms as I begin to process my day. My body feels like it's still vibrating from the station, from the pictures, from the way Detective Adams's eyes stayed on me like I was a possibility he hadn't ruled out. I'm happy to be home, even though I'm sad. That mix is confusing. Like stepping back into a version of your life that doesn't exist anymore, but your body hasn't caught up to the truth yet.

Coming home to a sister-less New York felt hollow. I had hope because I thought I'd be coming home to some answers and possibly closure.

But now, I just feel even more lost and confused, and afraid.

What happened to my sister? What happened to David? And is this related? Was something else happening that I was unaware of? Maybe David was involved in something that got Samaya killed, and then he was murdered.

The questions loop again and again, louder each time, like my brain is pacing a hallway with no doors. I keep trying to land on one story that makes sense, but every story collapses into another unanswered corner.

I comb my mind for anything that she might've mentioned that could correlate to this, but I come up with nothing. David seemed to have many secrets, and I am talking more than just the large amount of alcohol he consumed almost daily. His cousins were into some drug dealing shit in New York City, but I thought it was all in the nineties.

I try to picture him. Not the David from the photos. Not the David snarling into my phone. The David Samaya once loved enough to marry. The David who knew how to turn on charm like a faucet. The David who knew how to pretend. And that thought makes my stomach turn, because if he could pretend with her, he could pretend with anyone.

I sigh and flop over to my side, using my arm as a pillow. I stare at the wall until I feel my phone vibrate behind me, alerting me to a call. The vibration startles me harder than it should, like my nervous system is still stuck at full volume.

"Hey, just checking on you," Louis says, sounding a little apprehensive. "I don't wanna bother you, but I just know there's so much happening."

"No, you're good, trust me. I'm literally lying here thinking about shit I probably should not be thinking about. What are you up to?"

"Just at home," he says.

His voice is a soft place to land. Not a solution, not a fix. Just… a steady presence in the middle of this chaos. I roll onto my back and twirl a curl between my fingers. I want to see him, but I also feel like a dick for hooking up with my ex. That guilt has been sitting like a stone in my stomach since Oakland, and now that I'm back, it feels even heavier. Like I brought the mess home with me.

"I could use some company if you feel like making the trip over," I say, trying to sound flirtatious, but falling somewhere between needy and lonely.

I can almost feel his smile through the phone as he responds, "Just tell me what time to be there, and I'm on my way."

When I get off the phone, I jump up to check my reflection. Dismayed, I decide to throw my poodle-esque hair into a high, messy bun. I recheck my reflection. The bun is lopsided but cute enough. My eyes look puffy, but there's nothing I can do about that. This will have to do. I glance around my room and decide that it looks ok. I haven't unpacked my luggage from my California trip, but I'm not worried about that right now. If he notices, he doesn't seem like the kind of man who'd care.

I rap gently on Alyse's door. The door opens quickly and she looks concerned. Even in her own exhaustion, she still checks on me first. I don't know how I got so lucky.

"Hey boo, what's up?" she asks, her eyes searching mine. Poor girl, she looks as ragged as I feel. I reach out and wrap my arms around her instinctively, and she immediately returns the embrace. Her hug is warm and grounding, the kind that says you don't have to speak yet.

"I'm ok. Well, as ok as I can be with all the shit I've seen today." My mind floats to the grueling images I was shown just hours ago, and I inwardly cringe. "Louis is coming over in a little bit."

Her head pops up from my shoulder, and she looks at me again. "Louis! Oh, that makes me so happy," she says excitedly. She rubs my arms up and down with her hands, "I love that for you."

I can't help but smile. She's excited for me in a way that feels pure, like she's holding hope for me when I can't hold it myself. "Yea, I could definitely use the company tonight," I admit. I look beyond her and see her painting supplies. When I crane my neck further, I see a painting of a woman coming out of what looks like a lotus flower. It is beautiful, but not surprisingly—her work is also top-notch. The colors look alive, like they're breathing, like she poured her nervous energy straight into the canvas.

Her eyes follow my path, "You like? I don't know what I'm gonna do with it, I just have to work on something to help with my anxiety," she looks at me and then looks down.

"I love it," I say. "Whatcha sippin' on?" I gesture to her glass on the desk. She strides over and grabs the glass, shoving it into my hands.

"Try it! It's this pineapple concoction I came up with while you were gone."

I take a tentative sip. It's fruity and tangy and sweet. It tastes like a vacation I didn't get to take. I take another long drink before passing it back to my beautiful friend.

She smiles and gently pushes me aside, "I'm gonna make you one. You need a fucking drink after the day you've had."

Midway through my second concoction, Louis arrives, looking more dapper than ever. He's wearing a new look hat, and I can't help but admire how his gray sweats hug him in all the right places. I look over at Alyse and am relieved to find she didn't just catch me looking at him in the way I just did. I suddenly want him physically in a way that feels—well, *primal*. Like I've been starving for softness, for safety, for a body that feels steady next to mine.

Louis says nothing. He just pulls me into his long, strong arms for a hug. I lay my face on his awaiting chest and sigh, the first sigh of relief since I saw him last. I feel his heart beating beneath my ear. It's calm. Solid. It makes me want to cry for a whole different reason.

"Hey," he says into my hair.

"Heyyy, Louis," Alyse says, and I can hear in her voice that she really does like him.

He releases me and smiles a big grin at my best friend, "Alyse! Good to see you." He crosses our living room to give her a hug also.

"I made drinks!" she says proudly, gesturing to the two cups on the kitchen counter. "Want one?"

"Sure, what are they?"

She steps over to the counter and picks up the drink, giving the glass a swirl after she takes a big gulp, looking thoughtful, "Hmmm... I haven't named them, but it's pineapple juice mixed with vodka and a splash of Malibu rum."

He chuckles. "Sounds fruity."

She busies herself making fresh drinks and I turn to look at him. "They're really good," I assure him.

He just stares at me, and his eyes say so many things without him having to utter a word. I feel myself inwardly cringe because I now know I need to tell him about what happened with Dre. The guilt resurfaces sharp and hot. He looks at me like I'm precious, like I'm worth care, and I feel that fraud feeling crawl right up my throat.

Drinks in hand, we enter my room and sit down on my bed. He looks around, probably noting my somewhat messy room and still packed bags. He notices me watching him, and he raises his glass.

"Cheers?"

I raise my own drink to toast. "Cheers, handsome."

We both sip our drinks, and I see Louis nod in approval and then wince slightly. I smirk.

"It's, uh, good. Strong, but good," Louis says after his second mouthful.

I take a few sips of my own drink as I prepare to tell him the news about my mom and regrettable hook-up. He looks at me expectantly as if he knows something is up. I swallow. Hard. My mouth suddenly feels dry, even with the sweet burn of vodka on my tongue.

"So, how was the visit with your mom?" He asks.

"It was tough to see her like that," I begin. "She wasn't responsive at all, and they had a ventilator that breathed for her. I spent two days with her, so I feel good about that."

He nods sympathetically. "I know it must've been really hard. But I am happy that you decided to go and spend time with her. Did they say what her odds are to come out of the coma?"

"Not really. Most likely, she won't come out of it. But because there's a tiny chance that she might, they want to keep her there and on life support for another month or so, just in case. There's very little brain activity they said, which isn't a great sign."

He places his half-drunken drink on my bedside table and scoots closer, enveloping me in his arms. I allow myself to lay my head on his chest, and then a second later, I jerk it up. How can I let him console me and act like everything is the same between us? He may find out about the situation with Dre and never want to talk to me again. I don't know how I would feel if I met someone and stood by them during the most challenging time of their life, just to find out they were drunkenly hooking up with their toxic ex while out of town. The shame feels childish and grown at the same time.

Louis frowns. "What's wrong?"

I take a shaky breath and begin telling him about the night with Dre. He is silent the entire time that I am speaking. When I finish, I stand up and cover my face with my hands as I begin to pace nervously. My heart is pounding like I'm waiting for a verdict.

"Do you still have feelings for this guy?" He asks quietly.

I stop pacing. "What? Oh my God, no! Not even a little bit. I was not myself… I know that isn't an excuse, but with the news about Sam and seeing my mom like that, I just... I don't know. I just lost my head for a minute." I feel like such an ass as I hear my own words tumble out.

To my surprise, he reaches out for my hand. I cock an eyebrow as I cautiously take his hand, and he pulls me down to sit next to him on the bed.

"Ok. Then we are good." He says simply, although I can read the disappointment he's trying to hide on his face.

"Wait, what?" I say, confused and relieved at the same time. "We're good?"

"Serenity, I mean, yea, it sucks to hear it, of course. I like you a lot. Hell, I think I'm falling in love with you. But I get it. You are dealing with more than anyone I have ever met right now. Add some drinks and weed to the mix, you were bound to make some questionable decisions."

My eyes dance between his, dumbfounded at his generosity and compassion. The way he says it feels like a hand on my back, steadying me, not shoving me off a cliff. He squeezes my hand and smiles that half-smile, but there's a hint of sadness in his eyes. "But just don't do it again, ok?"

I throw my arms around him and snuggle my face into his neck, feeling tears prick my eyes. I don't know what I did to deserve this man, but I am so grateful he is in my life. My whole body loosens like I've been bracing for impact for weeks.

"I love you," I murmur into his neck. I stiffen, not knowing how he's about to respond to my admission. He pulls away, and I immediately panic.

"I love you too, Serenity Jones."

My entire being melts as he cups my face in his hands and kisses me deeply. It isn't just lust, it's relief, it's release, it's something safe to fall into. I climb onto his lap, straddling him, and the kiss grows more urgent. His hands find the hem of my shirt, and he gently begins pulling it upwards, and I allow him access, lifting my arms so he can free me from my shirt. His fingers, frantic now, fumble with my bra hooks until it unfastens and the bra falls away, exposing my breasts to him.

He breaks the kiss now and gazes down at my awaiting breast, and my nipples harden even before his lips find them. I gasp when he takes my left nipple into his mouth, and my head falls back as pleasure overtakes me. The pleasure cuts through grief the way light cuts through fog, not erasing it, just giving me air.

"I've missed you," he murmurs into my chest before showing my right breast some attention. I feel him harden beneath me, and I smile between moans. I love what this man does to me and what I do to him. I love the way my body remembers how to want something that isn't pain.

It's the perfect distraction from everything dark happening in my world.

CHAPTER TWENTY-NINE

Being back at work feels like being in the twilight zone. Everything feels strangely familiar, yet absolutely nothing is the same. The walls look the same, the hum of the kitchen is the same, the clatter of dishes and silverware hasn't changed—but it's like I'm walking through a life I used to know instead of the one I'm living now. My body is here, going through motions, but my mind feels suspended somewhere far away, still stuck in California, still stuck at the beach, still stuck in the moment the detectives said "homicide."

It's been ten days since they found David's body in his apartment. So far, they don't have many leads, but they are sure it was some sort of revenge killing based on the bloody message on the wall above where his corpse had lain. Every time I picture that word, *KILLER*, my skin prickles.

Was that about him? Was that about Sam? Was that about whoever took her? Or is someone playing some twisted, violent game we haven't even begun to understand?

I thought coming back to work would provide some sort of normalcy, but it has done nothing but ease some of my financial worries. My mother is still in a coma in the hospital. Samaya is still dead. And my heart is still broken. Each shift feels like pushing through thick fog, like I'm wearing grief as a weighted vest I can't take off.

Alyse, Jason, and I had organized a makeshift memorial ceremony for Sam at the beach near her house. A few of Sam's work colleagues came as well as her college homegirl, Ashley. Louis and Jamal came, of course. It was small and simple. We each lit candles and spoke about what we loved most about her. It was challenging, and even then, it didn't make her death feel real.

Maybe it's the lack of knowing where her body is, or perhaps it's just denial, but it's like my mind can't accept that she's gone. The ocean kept roaring behind us, steady and alive, while my sister was nowhere and everywhere all at once.

"You ok?" Jason asks, bumping his bony hip into mine gently. I tear my eyes away from the dreary scene outside the window. Gray clouds press low over the street, matching the heaviness in my chest.

"Hey, Jay. I'm ok," I say, not sounding very ok, even to my own ears.

He snakes his arm around my waist and gives me a side-long glance, "You have always been such a shitty liar, girl. It's ok to not be ok," he says gently. His voice is soft, the kind of soft only friends of ten-plus years can manage. I lean my head onto his shoulder.

"Thanks, Jay," I say. "I guess I just thought coming to work would bring me some sense of normalcy, but it really just reminds me of how different everything is now. I only came to New York to be near her, and now that she's gone…" my voice trails off. It cracks halfway through, and I pretend I didn't hear it.

"I know. It's going to take some time. A whole lot of time to feel anything other than grief. I'm here for you, booboo. Always."

I hear someone clear their throat behind us, and we quickly turn around in unison.

It's Mario.

"Hey, boss!" I say as cheerfully as I can. He smiles a genuine smile at me, then shoots Jason a stern look.

"You back from lunch, Jason?" he asks, his deep Italian accent booming in the small space.

Jason reaches for the apron slung over his shoulder and begins tying it around his waist.

"Yes, sir," he says in a mocking tone and then rolls his eyes at me.

"Serenity, how's it going? How's it been being back after… everything?" Mario asks, shifting uncomfortably.

Mario and I don't have much of a working relationship, so I know him even asking is taking a lot for him. He's very New York and "business only." The softness in his tone feels almost foreign coming from him.

"It's been nice having something else to focus on," I say. "Thanks for holding my spot for me."

He awkwardly pats my shoulder, "Of course, it's the least we could do."

His touch is brief, almost skittish, like he's afraid grief is contagious. Then he walks away, busying himself with one of the cooks. I scan the restaurant and notice a couple sitting together, and the woman looks concerned. She waves me over, and I make my way to her table.

"Did you need some more water?" I ask as I look at the table. Everything seems to be in order. No empty plates, no sticky spills, no reason for concern except the way she's staring at me like she knows me.

She glances at what I assume is her husband and then looks back up at me, "No, I just—I was just wondering if you're the girl from the news? Your sister was missing several weeks back, right?" Her husband shoots her a disapproving look before turning bright red with embarrassment.

I groan inwardly. This isn't the first time someone's recognized me from the press conferences we'd had a few weeks ago when the police were looking for Sam.

"Yes, I am," I say, not sure of what else there is to say.

"I just wanted to say how sorry I am. I know we don't know each other, but I just feel for you…" her voice trails off, "I lost my sister when I was younger, and it was really hard. I just wanted to say that it will get better. But it will take time."

As uncomfortable as she looks, her tearful eyes are sincere. Her voice trembles like she's fighting back memories as much as tears. I swallow hard to avoid also becoming glossy-eyed.

"I appreciate that," I say in a quiet voice. "What happened to your sister, if you don't mind my asking?"

She wrings her hands together. She looks as if my question has mentally transported her back to whatever that day brought for her.

"She was killed—runk driver. She fought and tried to hang on, but unfortunately, she didn't survive her injuries. She died five days later in the ICU at Shady Oaks University Hospital."

I squat down next to their table and instinctively place my hand over her hand. Her skin is cold, trembling. I look the woman in her eyes, "I am so sorry to hear that. No one deserves that."

She nods, and her tears flow freely now, as do mine. The shared grief hangs between us like a fragile thread. We sit there like this for a few moments, and I am so glad it's the lull in the afternoon between lunch and dinner, so the restaurant is relatively empty. Even the hum of the overhead lights feels softened, like the whole place is giving us space. Her husband even looks teary-eyed now.

"May our sisters rest in peace," she manages.

"And may the bastards who took their lives rot in hell," her husband says, angrily.

"Steve!" she says, then looks at me apologetically, embarrassment in her eyes now. "Sorry, he just gets worked up."

"No," I say, holding his gaze. "I wholeheartedly agree."

His eyes soften a little, like he feels understood for the first time in this entire exchange.

As soon as I step outside of Mario's, I realize I should've brought a warmer coat. We are well into November, and my hoodie is not cutting it anymore. The wind slices right through the cotton and bites at my skin. My breath puffs into the air like smoke.

I wait the million years it takes for my little car to begin warming up. It's seven, and I don't want to go home. I've been staying at Louis' apartment most nights in the past several days for this exact reason. The quiet of my own place is too loud right now. I consider calling him to see what he's doing, but decide to wait until later.

I need to drive by Samaya's house. I do this randomly sometimes, drive by. It was such a large part of my weekly routine. It's like the car goes there on muscle memory, even though my heart clenches every time.

They finished all the forensics and investigative processes weeks ago, so now the house just sits there, temporarily abandoned. Since it is fully paid off and Samaya had no other debts — she was the responsible one in the family, clearly— the house is passed to the next of kin which would be me since mom isn't able to take it on.

But I can't bring myself to stay there. Even though it's been thoroughly cleaned from the crimes that occurred there, I just can't imagine living there. Too many ghosts. Too many shadows that would look like her. Too many rooms where the silence would feel accusatory.

So, here it sits.

I park on the street and peer up at the darkened house. I think I see the light on near the back of the house for a second. My breath stops. I turn the car off, and the interior of my vehicle darkens. I look again.

There is a light on in the back of the house.

My pulse jumps so hard it hurts. I grab my pepper spray out of my purse and decide to text Alyse.

I'm here at Sam's and I think someone has been in the house. Just texting you, so someone knows where I am

Her response comes quickly.

Should I meet you there? DO NOT GO INSIDE!

I switch my phone to vibrate and get out of the car. My palms start sweating around the bottle of pepper spray. What am I doing? Every nerve in my body is screaming at me to get back in my car and drive away, but my feet still move forward, shaky but determined.

When I get closer to the house, I see that the light is coming from the backyard. It looks like the back floodlights are on, which means someone was recently back there. Or is still back there. They are motion sensor lights, and they only stay on for fifteen minutes after the motion is detected.

My skin prickles. I consider calling one of the detectives when the light goes out, leaving me in darkness. The sudden dark feels like a hand over my mouth. I turn quickly and briskly walk back to my car, my heart racing so loudly it drowns out everything else. As soon as I am inside and close my door, I see the backyard motion sensor light come on again.

I call Alyse.

"Hey! What is going on?" she says when she answers on the first ring. It sounds like she's driving.

"Girl," I hiss, "someone is here at Sam's place in the backyard! The backlight is on a motion sensor, and when I pulled up, it was on, which means someone was back there. Then, it went off and came back on a few seconds later!" I say this as one long run-on sentence.

"Maybe it was an animal? Like a neighbor's cat?"

I hadn't even considered this.

"I mean, maybe," I say hesitantly, starting to feel a little foolish.

"Look, I am on my way anyway, so just stay in your car. I'll be there in like four minutes."

CHAPTER THIRTY

Alyse and I sit huddled together in her SUV, peering up at the house. The light hasn't come on again since she got here, but just before she pulled up, I could've sworn I saw a stream of light, almost like the glow of a flashlight upstairs in the house.

My breath keeps fogging up the window in little anxious bursts. The neighborhood is too quiet for what my nerves are doing. Every rustle of wind against the trees makes my pulse jump.

"I swear to God, Alyse, I saw something."

Alyse looks a little scared, but also a lot skeptical. She keeps darting her eyes from the house to me, like she's trying to hold two realities at once. She wants to believe me, but she also wants this to be nothing.

"Babe, maybe we should go home. Or at least call the cops. If you really think you saw something inside, we should not be the ones to investigate. You know black folks are the first to die in a scary movie."

I consider this. My fingers tighten around the seatbelt in my lap. It's like my body knows she's right, but something in me keeps pushing back. I don't want to be scared inside my own sister's life. I don't want to be the kind of woman who drives away from the truth because it's dark and uncomfortable.

"I'm going inside."

"Please tell me you're not serious, Serenity."

Instead of answering, I get out of the car and walk around to the sidewalk. The cold air bites at my cheeks and snaps me awake in a way the heater in the SUV couldn't. I stare up at the house. It looks like a haunted version of itself now, all clean lines and closed blinds and silent rooms that still feel like her.

Alyse joins me, linking her arm through mine. I look over at her, and she looks owlish. Then we both return our gaze to the darkened house. My stomach flips like I'm standing at the edge of a cliff.

Right then, there's a flash of light clearly shown in the upstairs window.

Samaya's room.

The air leaves my lungs. My knees go weak for a second like my body is trying to fold in on itself. I hear Alyse gasp next to me. We look at each other and jump back into her SUV. My hands fumble like they don't belong to me anymore. I fumble for my phone in my bag and dial 9-1-1.

"9-1-1, what's your emergency?"

"There's someone in my house—well, my sister's house. But she's dead, so no one should be inside." I know I probably sound crazy, but I am freaking out. The words tumble out sharp and breathless, like I'm being chased.

"Ma'am, what's the address?"

I give her the information, and she tells me she's sending an officer. My whole body is buzzing with adrenaline that has nowhere to go.

"Can you send detective Markovich?" I ask quickly.

"Only if he's on duty, ma'am. Just sit tight and do not attempt to enter the residence."

I end the call and look at Alyse, who looks as freaked out as I feel. Her lips are pressed tight. Her hands are clenched in her lap like she's holding herself together.

"What'd they say?"

"They are sending an officer," I say. "Who do you think that is?"

She shakes her head, her eyes wide, "Girl, I don't know, but I *definitely* saw the light. It looked like the flashlight on a cell phone."

I nod, whipping my head back to the direction of the house. It's completely dark again now. The silence feels loud. Like the house is holding its breath with us.

"Don't people sometimes break into homes that are abandoned?" Alyse asks. "Maybe someone who's been following the story knows the house is uninhabited and came to see what they could steal."

I don't answer because I see the red and blue lights of the police car pulling up silently behind us. Relief hits me so hard I almost shake. I'm relieved when I see the tall form of Detective Markovich approaching our car. Alyse and I get out to greet him. The cold cuts through my hoodie again, reminding me I'm not dreaming.

"Good evening, ladies," he says, looking up at the house. "Dispatch said you saw someone in the house?"

"I saw a flashlight. Well, first, I saw the motion sensor light in the backyard when I first pulled up, but thought that could've been an animal or something. But when we both saw the flashlight in the upstairs window, I knew someone was inside."

Markovich turns to take in the house. The way he studies it makes my scalp prickle, like he's already running through worst-case scenarios. "How about I go inside and look around?"

I hand him the keys that are already in my shaking palm, and he makes his way up the driveway towards the house. Alyse and I stand there, shaking with cold and fear. The two of us look small out here in the dark while he looks steady and prepared. I see Markovich enter the house with his gun raised and flashlight on. I can see him making his way through the lower level of the house, turning lights on as he enters each area of her spacious home. Every light he flips feels like a heartbeat.

He's still in the front half of the downstairs when I see the light in the backyard.

"Oh shit, do you see that?" Alyse gasps, grabbing my upper arm in a vice-like grip. I nod dumbly. My throat goes dry. My mind starts doing that thing where time stretches but my thoughts race.

I can hear Markovich yell something inside the house, but I can't make it out. Maybe he saw something, or maybe he saw the light turn on also?

We get into the car, unsure who is outside with us on this dark night. We stare out the windows and crane our necks to look behind us, waiting to see some intruder, but see nothing for a long while. My heart is slamming against my ribs so hard it's almost painful.

One minute passes, then five.

Each second feels like someone pulling a string tighter and tighter around my chest.

After about eight minutes, I see Markovich coming through the back gate. The front yard flood lights immediately illuminate him, and he looks a little winded. He walks up to us and motions for us to roll down the windows.

"There was definitely someone in the residence," he confirms. "There's a slat missing from the back fence, and I think that they went through there. I have a couple guys coming to patrol the area. Nothing seems to be missing, and nothing has been broken into."

"So how did someone get inside the house? It's been locked for weeks."

He looks at me with a mix of concern and confusion, "Whoever was inside the house had a key."

That lands like a punch. My mouth opens but no sound comes out. A key means this wasn't random. A key means this wasn't some bored idiot looking for a thrill. A key means whoever was inside belongs to a circle around Samaya's life. Maybe even a circle around her death.

I stand in the center of Samaya's room. It's been completely untouched since her disappearance. The air in here is different from the rest of the house, heavier, like the room is holding on to her. I feel like I'm trespassing on something sacred just by breathing.

Something is different.

I turn in a slow circle, taking in everything I see. I don't remember her closet door being open. I walk over to it and look inside. The clothes look shuffled, not the way they'd been left when we first surveyed the room when she initially disappeared. That detail scrapes at my nerves because I know her. I know how she kept her things.

Samaya was a neat freak. It wasn't just her kitchen that she kept white, clean, and pristine. It was everything in her home. I look at the shirts which had once been folded into perfect squares and see that someone has rummaged through them. The hangers are crooked. The stacks are off. The air in the closet smells faintly like someone else's hands have been in there.

"Someone's been in here," I say, turning to face Alyse and Louis.

Louis rushed over as soon as I texted him what had happened. Once I told him the officer had left and that I was staying to do my own investigation, he insisted that he was coming over. The fact that he showed up so fast makes my chest pinch with gratitude and guilt all at once. I push the guilt down. I need him right now.

"Maybe they moved things around when they were searching the house for clues," Louis says.

I shake my head. "I'd come through and looked right after I was cleared to reenter the house. I mean, yea, they definitely went all through her stuff, but these things weren't touched." I point to the dressers, which were now completely empty, save for the lamp that stood there. They only seemed to take relevant things or had blood on them. Surfaces were swept for fingerprints, and the forensic team took any clothing articles with stains. The closet had been closed and unaffected.

I continue to look at the room. Something was off.

Way off.

"Serenity, that was over a month ago now, and a lot has happened since. Maybe you just forgot," Alyse says behind me.

I whirl around to face her, giving her an incredulous look. The mistrust in my own brain makes me feel crazy, but trusting my gut feels like the only thing keeping me upright.

"I know it's been a crazy few weeks, but this is something I remember." I didn't mean for the words to come out so sharply, and Alyse looks as if I just slapped her. She takes a step back.

"My bad," she mumbles. I can tell my snapping has thrown her off and maybe even hurt her feelings. I let out a sigh, reaching out to touch her arm lightly, "I'm sorry, babe, my nerves are shot…"

"Nah, I get it, girl." She still looks a little thrown off, but I decide to leave it there. I take another look around the room, feeling the strong sense that someone has been in here, but not having any concrete proof of what is giving me that sense. Outside of her clothes in her closet being in slight disarray, things appear normal. Too normal. Like whoever did this wanted to leave quietly.

I turn to look at Alyse and Louis. They both stand there, ready to help, but obviously unsure of what to do since they are unfamiliar with Sam's place. My eye catches something just behind them.

The window.

The window, which I am one million percent positive, was closed and locked since I was last here. It is now open about four or five inches. The cold air sliding in from outside feels like a whisper from whoever was here.

"The window!" I exclaim as I push past them towards it, "The window was closed. I specifically made sure everything was locked up before I left the last time."

"That I remember," Louis says. "I was here when you did all of that last month."

"Call that cop and tell him! Maybe he can get fingerprints or something?" Alyse says.

I shake my head, "I'm going to need more than an open window that I can't even prove was open."

I walk over to Sam's bed and plop down. I set my elbows on my thighs and cradle my face in my hands. My whole body feels hollowed out. Like I keep losing pieces of myself every time something else makes no sense. I try to think of who else would have a key to my sister's house, but my mind comes to a dead end. David had one. She had given one to me. Maybe a neighbor? A contractor? One of the cousins? Someone she trusted enough to stop thinking about?

My phone rings in my pocket, and I absently reach for it. Looking down at it, I see a text from a number that I don't recognize.

I know what happened to your sister.

CHAPTER THIRTY-ONE

"**G**uys, we need to go. *Now.*"

The words come out sharper and more urgent than I intend, but my adrenaline is already spiking. My heart is thudding so hard it feels like it's trying to punch through my chest. I decide to wait to tell them about the mysterious message until we get the hell out of this house. The air inside Samaya's room had felt thick, wrong, almost watching us. The last thing I want to do is stand here and talk about it.

Louis looks confused, and Alyse also seems bewildered. I realize I am probably beginning to sound crazy as hell. I stand and lead the way, hoping that they will do the same. They do, and we head downstairs wordlessly together. Every creak of the steps feels louder than usual, like the house itself is listening. My palms won't stop sweating, and I keep glancing over my shoulder as if someone might be behind us.

"Serenity, what's happening? What's the r—"

"Can we talk about this in the car?" I say, cutting her off. My voice cracks at the edges. I make a mental note to apologize to my friend later for being so bitchy tonight, but right now my brain is racing too fast to form an apology.

Once we are in her car, Louis stands next to my door. The cold hits me again, sharp and grounding, but the dread sitting in my stomach doesn't budge.

"What is going on, Serenity?" he asks. His face is lit by the moon behind me, and I can see the look on his face. He looks tired and confused. I instantly feel bad for dragging him into the craziness that is my life lately. I feel like every time he steps into my world, something terrible is waiting in the corner.

"I just got a text about Sam," I begin. "I don't recognize the number, but I think maybe it's from whoever was in the house earlier. And, I don't know, I just panicked." My eyes fill with tears. My throat tightens. The words feel unreal even as I say them.

His eyes widen, and he looks between Alyse and me. I look over at Alyse, and her jaw is dropped. She looks like someone just told her the ground is made of quicksand.

"What did it all say? Can I see the message?" he asks.

I hand him my phone, and he reads the text. His brow tightens.

"609, I think that's Jersey."

"Jersey?" I say, not understanding. My brain is slow, stuck, terrified.

"New Jersey."

Duh. "Right," I say dumbly, feeling fourteen years old and out of my depth.

Alyse is already sliding the key into the ignition with a shaky hand. "Can we please get out of here though, y'all?" she says. Her voice is thin and tight. "I do not like this."

"I don't wanna go home," I say. The thought of going back to my apartment makes my skin crawl. Too dark. Too quiet. Too many places for my mind to spiral.

"I don't care where we go. I just wanna get the fuck out of here."

I look back at Louis. His face is steady, but his jaw is locked like he's clenching something back. "Can we come over?"

"Yes, please," he says. "We need to figure out who is texting you."

Alyse pulls out of the street with way more speed than usual. The tires crunch over the gravel and fallen leaves, and for a second I think I see movement in the backyard again through the rear window, but I can't tell if it's real or just my nerves. My stomach drops all over again.

The whole time Alyse is driving, my mind is lost in thought. Every bump in the road makes my heart jump. Every passing shadow outside the car windows makes my breath catch. I consider texting the number to find out what they know, but decide against it. My thumb hovers over my screen, though, itching, curious, terrified.

Who is this mystery person that has information on my sister?

And most importantly, can they tell me what happened to my sister?

Because for the first time since Samaya disappeared… it feels like someone out there is finally talking back.

CHAPTER THIRTY-TWO

I didn't sleep a wink last night.

Not one second.

My eyes burned, my thoughts spun, and every creak of Louis' apartment had me thinking someone was standing right outside the door. Now I sit in Louis' bed flipping through his TV with the volume muted. It's 5:30 a.m., so infomercials and news programs are all that's really on. The apartment feels too still, too dark, too aware of me.

I pause on the local news station ABC 7 New York News because I see a photo of David and one of my sisters right next to it. My pulse jumps. I glance over at Louis's sleeping body and turn the volume up slightly to make out what they are saying.

"...of David Esposito, the ex-husband of the missing woman, Samaya Jones-Esposito. We are not yet sure if the two deaths are related. The Suffolk County Police are still waiting on forensics to give them some definite answers on what happened to Mr. Esposito the night he was brutally murdered in his home. If anyone has information about the deaths of Samaya and David Esposito, they are advised to call the Suffolk County Police Department."

My stomach twists at the word murdered. Even though I saw the photos, hearing it out loud hits me differently. Final. Brutal. No going back.

They move on to an update about a possible hurricane near New York City, and I mute the television once again. The sudden silence feels louder.

Could the two murders be related?

At this point, it's hard to fathom that they're not.

I've been so sure that David was Sam's killer that I didn't leave room to consider anyone else. I haven't been around Samaya enough to know the intricate workings of her life to even have a clue who could possibly want her dead. Let alone both of them.

I run my hand through my curls and look back up at the TV. It's now showing a commercial that looks like eHarmony. The cheesy smiles feel grotesquely out of place. I turn and look at Louis again as he sleeps. His broad chest rises and falls with his slow rhythmic breathing. This man has been such a rock in the past couple of months. A grounding force. A place to land.

I reach out and gently run the back of my fingers along his chiseled jawline, tracing his chin. I then do the same to his forehead and cheeks. He stirs but doesn't wake. When I lean down to kiss him softly, I see a slow smile creep across his lips.

"Mornin'," he murmurs without opening his eyes.

"Oops," I say, "didn't mean to wake you."

"You can wake me up anytime." He opens one eye and peers up at me, his smile widening at the sight of me. Then both of his eyes open, and he looks around the semi-dark room, confused. "Wait, what time is it?"

I flip my phone over and see the time, "It's almost 6."

He groans and squeezes his eyes closed again. "Why are we up so early?"

"Well, we couldn't sleep," I say, sarcastically emphasizing we. He smiles, eyes still closed, and pulls me into a horizontal position next to him. I snuggle into him, pressing my body against the length of his warm body.

We lay like this for several minutes, and I think he's fallen asleep until I feel his erection against me. I smile and wiggle my ass against him teasingly.

"You're gonna get somethin' started," he murmurs into my ear, then gently nibbles it between his teeth. The feeling sends a chill throughout my entire body, and I can't help but shiver.

He slides his hand slowly over the length of my body, starting from my hips and working his way upwards. He cups my breast in his hand, and I moan, pressing my body into him again, wanting him, needing him. Needing something to drown everything else out.

"I want you," I whimper, grinding into him. With that confession, he enters me slowly, and I lose myself.

For a few minutes, nothing exists except him.

No fear.

No texts.

Just us.

But it can only last so long.

"Your phone just rang," Louis calls from his room. I rush out of the kitchen and into his room. Diving onto the bed, I grab my phone and check it.

It's a text from the New Jersey number.

669 Bay Ave. Beach Haven, NJ

Meet at 2 pm

COME ALONE

I stare at it for a long second. My throat goes dry. My hands go numb. My heart drops and then slams so hard it hurts. I glance up at Louis, who is staring at me intently.

"Is it them?"

I nod. "Do you know how far Beach Haven is from here?" I ask, turning my phone screen to face him so he can see the address. He shrugs, shooting me a sheepish look.

"Jersey is a couple hours away," he says. Then he pulls his phone from the nightstand and types something into it. "It's about three hours away driving."

"Damn."

"I'm coming with you. I know it says to go alone, but there's no way in hell I'm letting you go there alone."

I consider this for a moment. I really don't want to go alone, but I don't want to drive all that way just to be denied whatever information is being promised because I didn't follow the directions I was given.

"I have to do this alone," I say quietly. My voice shakes, and I feel the moment land between us like a stone.

Louis stares at me, searching my face. Fear flickers in his eyes, and something else… something like hurt. "Serenity, you have no idea who this person or people are. What if it's a setup? What if whoever this is was responsible for your sister and her ex's murders? I can't let you go alone. I'm sorry."

His worry is raw, rough around the edges. I round the bed and stand in front of him, looking up so I can meet his eyes.

"I understand why you want to come, and I even understand why you think it's not safe for me to go do this by myself," I say gently, reaching my hand up to touch his chest. "But I have to do this alone. I will call the police, and I will call you if anything goes down, I promise."

He just stares down at me in disbelief and anguish. He shakes his head at me, but stays silent, jaw clenched.

"This is fuckin' crazy—you going there alone is crazy. Let me follow you in my car."

"No," I say firmly, stepping away from him. "I will be ok." I hope.

I really, really hope.

As I gather up my belongings, I try to ignore the feeling of his eyes boring into my back with questions and frustration. With fear he's trying not to show. With love he doesn't know where to put.

He walks me to the front door, and before I can reach out to unlock the door, he gently grabs my hand and spins me to face him.

"I care about you, and I'm sorry for pressing you about this, but I just feel really fucked up about knowing you are driving into a situation that could be dangerous. You need to call me when you get there, and you need to call me when you are all done. Got it?"

His face is different than I've ever seen it. There's a pained seriousness that makes me feel terrible about leaving him in such anguish.

"Got it," I say.

Then I am gone.

The cold outside air cracks against my skin like a warning. My stomach twists with dread and something sharper: the sense that today is going to change everything.

CHAPTER THIRTY-THREE

I drive past the house twice before parking around the corner and texting Louis and Alyse.

The homes are lavish and look expensive—manicured lawns, perfectly trimmed shrubs, coastal colors, airy architecture. Whoever these people are, they have money. The kind of money that makes me extra aware of my little Toyota parked on their street. My little life entering their world.

I circle back around and park two houses down from the address I was texted this morning.

BE CAREFUL, the text from Louis reads.

My heartbeat quickens as I see it's about ten minutes to 2. My palms are already sweating. My mouth is dry. I consider my options for one quick second and decide to text the number.

How do I know you're not gonna hurt me?

The bubbles showing them responding pop up immediately. My chest tightens.

You are safe.

I stare at the message for so long it begins to blur. Safe. Whoever murdered my sister's husband thought he was safe too. Whoever broke into her house probably thought I wasn't home.

Safe means nothing right now.

I lean over and open my glove box to see if I have anything that I can use as a makeshift weapon.

Nothing.

Not a pen. Not a screwdriver. Not even one of those heavy-ass flashlights people keep for situations exactly like this. Just the thin packet of car manuals and a crumpled parking receipt.

Well, this pepper spray in my purse will be my only defense.

I grip the bottle just to feel something solid in my hand.

I step out of my car and look up and down the street as discreetly as possible. Every passing car makes me jump a little. I walk up the street with two adjacent rows of two-story beach houses. They all look like vacation rentals for people with tax brackets I don't even understand.

As I approach the driveway of 669, I take down the license plate number of the car parked in its driveway in the Notes app on my phone. It's a newer BMW. Sleek. New. A "don't ask me what I do for a living" type of car.

My heartbeat jackhammers inside my chest the closer I get to the front yard of the house. Every step feels heavier than the last. Every inhale feels too loud. I reach out and unlatch the gate that leads me into the yard to get to the front door. The metal latch clicks like a gunshot.

I grip my phone so hard in my hand it's almost painful, but the slight cramp in my death-gripped fingers is the last thing I'm focusing on.

My eyes dart to the front windows, but there are just closed blinds staring back at me. No movement behind them. No silhouette. Just blank, white rectangles giving nothing away.

I step onto the steps that lead me to the front door and take in the porch. It's clean, no signs of children, just two wicker chairs sitting with a few potted plants. Nothing sketchy. Nothing comforting either.

I knock lightly on the door twice with two nervous raps.

I listen for footsteps on the other side of the door, but hear nothing at first. My breath fogs in the chill air. I wait for a beat and consider knocking once more.

Then—

click.

I hear the deadbolt unlock and I brace myself, unlocking the pepper spray bottle gripped tightly inside of my closed fist.

When the door opens, I am greeted by a woman. She's short, but has an athletic build and shoulder-length blonde hair that looks slightly tousled. Her wide-set green eyes look me over slowly as if she's confirming that I am who I'm supposed to be. She's wearing a cropped white tank top that shows a flat, tan tummy in low-slung grey sweatpants.

This woman doesn't look threatening at all. In fact, she appears to be as nervous as I am once I calm down enough to notice—her pupils are a little blown, her breathing a little shallow.

"Serenity?" She asks quietly.

"Yes," I reply, not knowing what else to say. She opens the door wider and waves her hand, gesturing for me to come in with her. I quickly take in my surroundings. The entryway and living room area that I can see are deserted. Too neat. Too staged. Like no one lives here full-time.

"Thanks for coming," she begins. "My name is Stephanie. I went to college with your sister." She points to the tan leather couch, and I sit down, not knowing what else to do.

"Are you the one who's been texting me?" I ask, wanting to get straight to the point. My voice sounds sharper than I expected.

"Not exactly. Can I get you anything?"

I cock my head to the left.

Who is this chic? Why the hospitality? Why the weird evasiveness?

"If you didn't text me, then who did?"

She sighs and sits down across from me in a brown leather chair that looks like the match to the sofa I am seated on. I watch as she runs her hands through her short blonde hair, tousling it even further. Her knee bounces uncontrollably. She keeps glancing toward the hallway.

"I'm not the one who texted. But I can take you to the person who knows what happened to Sam."

A slow electric current runs down my spine. My breath stutters. My stomach twists.

She stands and motions for me to join her and I quickly get to my feet. I am so confused, but I want to know, so I wordlessly follow her through a beautiful kitchen and into what looks like a large office.

The moment we cross the threshold, I feel it.

The shift.

The heaviness.

The sense that whatever comes next is going to change everything.

CHAPTER THIRTY-FOUR

I blink once. Twice.

My brain stutters, lags, tries to buffer like a broken video file.

No.

No.

No way.

I rub my eyes and refocus on the person sitting before me.

And everything inside me drops away.

Sitting on the edge of the couch…

is my sister.

Samaya.

Alive.

Her hair is shorter now, cut bluntly above her shoulders. Bone straight instead of her natural curls. The dark brown I grew up brushing for her is now a warm honey brown — almost blonde. Her face is thinner. Much thinner. Her cheeks hollowed. Her collarbones too sharp.

She looks like a ghost wearing skin.

She lifts her eyes to meet mine, and my entire nervous system shatters.

"Sam," I whisper. It escapes me like a prayer. Like a hallucination I'm begging to be real.

My feet feel cemented to the floor. My breath stays trapped somewhere between my ribs and throat. I feel inside my body and floating above it all at once — watching myself watch my dead sister who is, impossibly, horrifyingly, unbelievably, not dead.

"Hey," she says softly. "I know this is… a lot."

Her voice breaks a little on the last word.

She stands, but she doesn't step toward me. She stands there like I'm a skittish animal she's scared to spook. She just looks at me — exhausted, apologetic, frightened.

My knees buckle at the same time my brain short-circuits. I can't stay upright.

Sam moves instantly, pulling a desk chair over and easing it toward me. I sit before gravity can take me down completely, my eyes glued to her like I'm afraid she'll vanish if I blink too long.

"I'll grab her some water," Stephanie blurts, almost tripping over herself as she backs out of the room.

"I think she's gonna need something stronger than water," Sam mutters.

Stephanie nods quickly and disappears, grateful to escape the emotional explosion in the room.

I stare at my sister, feeling my pulse ricochet in my throat.

"How?" I whisper. My voice cracks. It feels like my lungs collapse around the word.

She exhales — a long, slow release, like she's been holding her breath for months. She sits on the couch directly across from me. And now that I'm finally seeing her, really seeing her, I register the weariness carved into her bones. The tremor in her hands. The shadows under her eyes.

She looks thirty-five going on fifty.

I reach out, my hand trembling uncontrollably, and touch her fingertips. Part of me wants to comfort her.

Most of me just wants to know she's real flesh and not a dream my trauma invented.

I think back to the candlelight flickering at her beachside memorial. How wrong it felt. How unfinished. How my mind never accepted she was gone even when everyone else did. How her missing body never sat right with me.

Stephanie returns quietly from behind me, water bottles tucked under her arms and two glasses filled with amber liquid clinking in her hands. She hands each of us a bottle and a drink.

"I'll leave you girls to it," she murmurs before giving Sam a soft smile and me a gentle squeeze on the shoulder.

Then the door clicks shut behind her.

I set the water down and take a long swallow of whatever she gave us. It burns its way down my throat. I cough.

My heart is pounding so hard now I can barely hear myself.

"So…" I say, swallowing against the lump in my throat. "What the fuck happened?"

CHAPTER THIRTY-FIVE

"The night that we met up with the guys, Jamal stayed over," she begins, her voice low, almost monotone. "We had such an amazing time. I must've passed out, because when I woke up, he was gone."

Her hands shake slightly as she lifts her glass. I brace myself.

"I remember getting up to go pee. I was still pretty drunk. It was like three a.m. As I came out of the bathroom, I saw a man standing in my room, and I immediately realized it wasn't Jamal."

Her eyes flick up to mine, wide and haunted.

"It was David."

My stomach drops.

"He was wearing all black and had this black hat on. He looked… sketchy as hell. It wasn't super light in my room, but I saw he had something in his hands. I freaked out and started yelling at him to leave, which made him panic. He started yelling at me, saying, 'Shut the fuck up! Shut the fuck up!' I tried to see what was in his hands, but I couldn't tell, so I turned the light on."

She pauses. Her throat works as she swallows.

"That's when I saw it. He had a fucking bat, Serenity. A wooden baseball bat."

A cold shiver ripples down my back.

"I tried to talk to him, you know? I thought maybe it was about money, since he's always blaming me for him being broke and not being able to get a job. So I offered him money." She shakes her head slowly, like she still barely believes it herself. "All the while, I was looking for my phone—or anything I could fight with. But I think he'd already taken it."

She rubs her palms on her thighs again. A nervous tic she never used to have.

"He kept coming closer to me. So finally, I just booked it. I ran downstairs toward the kitchen, but he was right there. And he's so fucking fast."

Her voice cracks.

"I was in the kitchen when I felt the crack…"

She trails off. I feel the room tilt. I can almost hear the bat. Feel it.

Sam takes a long drink from her glass, then sets it down with trembling fingers.

"I was on the bed when I woke up," she continues. "I have no idea how I got back upstairs. He must've carried me. I woke up laying on the bed, and he was talking to himself. Loudly. He sounded crazy, Ren—like way past drunk. So I just… faked sleep. I slowed my breathing."

She presses her thumb into the soft skin of her wrist as she talks, rubbing back and forth to ground herself.

"My head was throbbing like nothing I'd ever felt before. I could feel my blood coming out. My hair was wet with it. He must've seen me move—or he caught me with my eyes open."

Her voice dims to a whisper.

"And that's when he started choking me."

The tears fall before she can stop them. She looks so small. Smaller than I've ever seen her.

"He was on top of me, talking more shit. For a second, I thought he was gonna try to rape me because he kept grabbing my boobs, leering, saying shit like 'I used to love these tits.' One hand on my throat. One hand…" She gestures to her chest and looks away, ashamed at the memory even though none of this was her fault.

I take her hand gently, squeezing.

"But when I looked at his eyes… something switched. His face got dark. His eyes looked evil. Then he grabbed my neck with both hands. I tried pulling them off, scratching, kicking, anything, but he was too strong."

She squeezes my hand back, breath shaky.

"Then I remembered the Buddha statue on the table next to my bed. It's not huge, but it's solid stone. And it was right there. I don't know how he didn't notice me reaching for it, but I grabbed it and swung. Hard."

Her voice steadies just slightly.

"He looked stunned. Then he collapsed next to me. He wasn't dead, but it bought me time."

She inhales sharply.

"I was hurt. Where he hit me with the bat was bleeding. My throat was burning and felt crushed. But I made it downstairs again. I heard him coming, and when I looked up at the stairs, he looked crazed. He told me he was gonna kill me. I knew he meant it."

My heart pounds so fast I feel lightheaded.

"I grabbed what I could, but I left almost everything else. There was no time. I ran out of the house and didn't look back. It was almost dawn by the time I got out."

She finally releases the breath she's been holding. Her shoulders sag. Her eyes meet mine, red and raw.

"Sam… wow." It's all I can manage. My voice fails me.

She nods, blinking back tears.

"I know. I've been watching the news like crazy. When I went back a few weeks ago, I was so scared the—"

"Wait," I cut in. "When were you on Long Island? And why?"

She bites her lip.

"Well… I came back to make it look like I was killed. You know… like faking my own death."

I stare at her. Speechless.

"The plot thickens," she adds dryly.

"So, I had Steph drive me back, and I wore a wig, random clothes. I had the clothes I was wearing when I escaped and my purse. I tore it up and put blood on it so it looked like I'd been attacked."

My eyes widen.

"How'd you get the blood?"

She blushes. "Steph's a nurse. She agreed to take some through an IV every day for a few days so I had a stockpile. All those true crime shows paid off."

I can't help it—I smile at her ridiculous genius.

"Well, it worked. And it made it a homicide case. And David was the obvious suspect."

David.

A murderer in theory.

A victim in reality.

"Do you know about David? He's dead."

"That's why I reached out," she says quietly. "When I saw the news, I knew I had to tell you everything."

I stare down into my drink, take a huge gulp, feel the burn at the back of my tongue.

Then another weight hits me.

"Mom is… sick," I say. Immediately my throat clogs. "She had a heart attack and is in a coma. The doctors said she's probably not coming out of it."

Samaya's face shatters. She starts crying again, and instinctively I pull her into my arms. We hold each other and grieve — for her trauma, for our mother, for the months we lost, for the life we thought was gone forever.

After a while, when the silence softens around us, I ask the only question left.

"So, now what?"

She stands and walks to the window, pulling back the curtain like she's checking for someone.

Then she turns to me—taller. Stronger. More like the big sister I know than she's looked since the second I walked into that room.

"Let's go home," she says.

CHAPTER THIRTY-SIX

I am, yet again, sitting inside the Suffolk County Police Station. Tabitha, who works pretty regularly at the triage desk in the front, and I are now on a first-name basis. She greets me with a chipper wave and her usual welcoming smile as soon as I enter the building.

"Markovich is working on another case, but I believe Detective Garcia is here," she says before I can even ask.

She's good, I think.

"Um, hi, Tabitha. Sure, that's fine. I just have an update in my sister's case."

She gives me a knowing nod and a sympathetic smile. "I'll call him now, sweetie." Her New York accent makes even the sweetest words sound sharp and a little confrontational, but still comforting in its own way.

I wander over to the hard plastic chairs and take a seat, settling in for what I know can be a long wait for any officer to be told there's someone waiting — and then the even longer wait for them to actually come out from the back. I gaze at the desk, noticing the festive fall decorations.

My mind drifts to my mother. I make a mental note to call and check on her once we get this police situation handled.

We decided it was best for Sam to stay at the house while I came alone to inform the police that she is most definitely not dead, and is alive and waiting for them at her home. As soon as the media catches wind of her being back, there will be local reporters outside the house in minutes. If we talk to the police first, they can conduct a press release and inform the public properly.

"Ms. Jones?" Garcia calls.

I snap my head around and stand so fast my phone slips from my hand and clatters loudly against the tile floor. My entire face flames with embarrassment as I crouch to pick it up. When I straighten, I shake his hand, still flustered.

"Hi. Sorry," I say breathlessly, suddenly unsure where or how to begin. "Is there somewhere we could talk in, um, private?"

"Of course. Right this way." He gestures toward the same room I've sat in countless times over the past few months.

I awkwardly pass him and enter the room, which is unnervingly cold. I sit in yet another hard plastic chair and yank my sleeves down as far as they'll go to shield my hands from the AC air blasting through the vents.

Is the AC on? Why is it always freezing in here?

Garcia enters behind me and sits in the chair opposite mine.

"So," he says expectantly, pen ready over his notepad, "what's up?"

My heart kicks into a nervous gallop. I swallow hard before launching into this unbelievable tale.

"I got a text the other night — the night I called Markovich to meet us at my sister's house. The message said they had information about my sister's disappearance. They told me to come to New Jersey to talk, and to come alone."

Garcia begins writing feverishly.

"So I went. I had to know what whoever sent the text knew. It was a friend of hers from college, she—"

"What is the friend's name?" he asks, still writing.

"Stephanie. Her name was Stephanie." I pause to let him catch up. "Long story short, she took me into a bedroom… and my sister was there."

The pen hits the table before I even look up at him. His expression is twisted in disbelief, as if I've just told him I saw a giraffe sitting on the bed.

We stare at each other for a long, electrified moment — only ten or fifteen seconds, but it stretches.

He picks up his pen, opens his mouth to speak, then closes it again and sets the pen down carefully.

"Okay," he says slowly. "Let me get this straight. Your sister is alive. In New Jersey?" He shakes his head, maybe without realizing it.

"Yes. Well, she's here now, but yes, she's very much alive." I release a long, slow exhale through pursed lips. I remember how shaken I felt when I saw her in the flesh. I know it will take him a minute to process.

He runs a hand through his short black hair and gives a short, incredulous laugh. "This is, uh… quite the revelation." He tries to pull himself together in real time. "Where is she now?"

"She's home. At her house. We didn't think it was wise for her to come here or be seen out until we spoke with you to figure out how to handle this. She's really worried about the press finding out and bombarding the house before she has a chance to explain anything."

He nods. "Yes, that's smart. Very smart. Honestly, I have never had a situation like this." He stands abruptly. "I'm going to call in Detective Markovich. Can you wait here a moment? I'll be right back."

I agree, and he practically scurries out of the room—half jog, half walk.

I stand, too restless to sit. My nerves feel like exposed wires. I have no idea what happens next, but my gut tells me this is just the beginning of a whole new layer of this mess.

Samaya looks nervous when I walk into the front door. I had called her as soon as I finished speaking with Garcia, and the officers decided they'd come to the house to speak with her directly and document everything.

She's changed clothes and now looks "office-ready" in a button-down blouse and black pants. She glances down at herself, then back up at me when she sees my expression.

"Too much?"

"I mean… it's not a job interview," I say, head tilted.

"I don't know what to wear. What do you wear to your interrogations with the cops?"

"It's not an interrogation," I say. "They just need to know what happened. Everyone thought you were dead."

She takes a deep breath, her shoulders dropping a fraction. "You're right. I'm gonna change. This is too much."

When the detectives arrive, they set up recording equipment and paperwork on the kitchen table. I watch Samaya try to look calm and collected, but a slight tremor in her hand betrays her nerves—a tremor only I would notice.

"Samaya?"

She turns to face the detective with a tight smile, then sits across from him at the table to begin her interview.

CHAPTER THIRTY-SEVEN

I hear the knock on the door and rush over to check the peephole. Louis had promised to bring food since a small legion of reporters is already gathered outside.

The police warned us they'd show up as soon as the media caught wind of Samaya's return, and they weren't lying. Two news vans sit parked at the curb — one from the Suffolk County News, the other from Newsday.

When we walked back inside earlier after what we thought would be a simple grocery run, a petite woman with flaming red hair practically ambushed us, firing questions like bullets: "Do you know who killed your husband?" and "Where have you been all this time?"

I breathe a deep sigh of relief when I see Louis' face through the peephole.

"Jesus Christ," he mutters as I yank the door open and usher him inside. "That one lady just won't stop with the questions."

I roll my eyes and grab the first bag from his hand, already rummaging through it. I'm starving. "What'd she ask you?"

"She asked if I know anything about what happened to Samaya while she was gone. And then she had the nerve to ask if I'm her 'new boyfriend.'"

"Wow," I say between greedy handfuls of fries. Louis raises an eyebrow at me as I continue inhaling food.

"How many of them are out there now?" Samaya asks as she comes down the stairs. She looks exhausted — sad and overwhelmed and frayed at the edges. My heart breaks knowing what she went through before she ran, and the avalanche of new shit she's facing now. None of this is her fault.

"The same two," Louis answers. "Think there'll be more?"

She snorts. "Judging from what the cops said? Probably. And soon."

A phone rings, and both Louis and I look around, but it's Sam's. She answers.

"Hello? Yes, hi Detective… Oh. Uh-huh…"

Louis and I exchange glances. Sam's face slowly crumples at whatever she's hearing. When she ends the call, she sinks into a kitchen barstool and covers her face with both hands.

"Fuck," she groans.

"What? Was that Markovich?" I ask.

"No. It was Detective Adams. From David's homicide case. He wants to come by and get my official statement."

"Official statement? Of what? You weren't even in the state when he was murdered." I put my cup down and rush to her, wrapping my arms around her shaking frame.

"This is standard procedure," Louis says quickly. "They want to rule you out as a suspect."

"A suspect?" Sam pulls away and begins pacing the kitchen, her breath tight. "That's exactly what I'm worried about."

"You'll be fine," Louis says. "You were in Jersey. Your friend can vouch for you. And they'd need actual evidence to even look at you."

Sam stops pacing, but she's chewing her bottom lip so hard it looks painful. I look at Louis again, he gives me a weak smile.

"What time are they coming?" I ask.

"They're on their way right now."

It's been over an hour since Adams and his partner went downstairs with Sam. Louis and I have taken refuge in her room, waiting. I told him he could leave if he needed to, but he refused. I'm not mad about it.

I watch him beside me, answering work emails like we're not in the middle of a true crime documentary.

"If you'd known all the drama you'd be getting involved in when you asked for my number that night," I say lightly, "would you still have asked me for it?"

He looks up with that same crooked smile that melted me the first night I met him, and my heart thuds with the same warmth.

"Absolutely, yes," he says, reaching for my hand. I give it to him, and he pulls me into his chest. I listen to his heartbeat

— steady, warm, grounding — and it soothes me more than any breathwork ever has.

I love this man.

"I love you," I whisper, unexpectedly emotional.

He cups my face, making me meet his golden-brown eyes. "I love you too. And there's nowhere I'd rather be." A beat. "I mean, I wish y'all weren't dealing with all this shit. But I'm glad I get to be here for you."

My whole body softens. I exhale shakily.

"Me too."

I check my phone—another twenty minutes gone. I sigh. Louis sees the time and his eyes widen.

"Damn, it's hella long," he says. I smile at him using my Bay Area slang. Under different circumstances, I'd tease him.

"I know. I'm thirsty as hell," I complain, scanning the room for my abandoned glass of water. I left it downstairs. I consider texting Sam when a knock on the bedroom door nearly sends both of us into cardiac arrest.

Louis and I look at each other with matching startled expressions. He gets up and opens the door.

Adams' partner stands there, face unreadable.

"H—hi," I manage.

"We're all done downstairs," he says. "You can come down if you'd like." His expression stays flat as he turns and heads back.

Louis and I wait until we hear the front door close and lock. Only then do we head downstairs.

Sam is placing something glass on the counter. She barely acknowledges us as we take our seats at the island. She grabs two more glasses and sets them beside the lone one. Then she opens the fridge.

When she turns back around, she has a bottle of Simply orange juice in her hand. Then she bends to the freezer and pulls out a frosty bottle of Tito's.

She pours without speaking, her hand trembling just slightly.

I match her with an equally long drink, bracing myself for whatever she is about to say.

Then my phone rings—loudly—and all three of us jump.

The number flashes on the screen: the hospital in California.

My stomach plummets. Sam's eyes lock onto mine.

"It's the hospital," I say quietly. "It must be about Mom."

CHAPTER THIRTY-EIGHT

I hear the doctor telling me my mother has died.

I hear her telling me to make arrangements.

The words don't land. They bounce around the air like echoes in a cave.

The phone slips from my hands before I even realize I've let it go. I stand up from my chair. Then I immediately sit back down. My knees can't hold me.

The doctor's voice is still coming from the floor—thin, metallic, too calm, too practiced—but I make no move to pick up the phone. I can't. My body refuses to cooperate.

Louis moves first. Of course he does. He bends down, picks up the discarded phone gently, like it's something fragile, and places it to his ear.

"Hello?" he says.

I can hear the doctor repeating the same grim facts to him. The same ones that shattered me seconds ago. Samaya comes around the island and stands beside Louis, her eyes wide, her shoulders tight, her whole body wound up like a spring.

"I'm so sorry," Louis murmurs as he hands her my phone.

I watch Sam's face as she receives the news. Her eyebrows lift, her mouth falls open, and then—like the big sister she has always been—she asks all the questions I couldn't think to ask. Appropriate ones. Practical ones. The ones that require a functioning brain.

Louis stands and wraps his arms around me, rubbing slow circles on my upper back. The circles don't fix anything, but they keep me from floating out of my body entirely.

After a few minutes, Sam ends the call and braces herself on the counter, head bowed like something is physically weighing it down.

"I can't believe this is happening," she says. Her voice cracks, just slightly. "Of all times for this to happen."

I nod, but nothing comes out. Not a sob, not a word, not even a single tear. It's like my body is working overtime to keep me alive, leaving nothing leftover for grief.

I try to inhale fully, but my breath stays shallow, stuck somewhere between my throat and my chest.

"I am so, so sorry," Louis says softly. "Whatever you guys need, I got you."

Sam doesn't move. She keeps her head down for so long I wonder if she's even breathing.

Then she lifts her chin just barely and says, "They think I have something to do with David's murder."

The shock cuts through my fog like a blade.

"What? What are you talking about?"

She lets out a humorless huff, drains her glass, and wipes her mouth with the back of her trembling hand.

"Yup. They're going to talk with Stephanie. Ask her a bunch of questions about how I was acting. Whether I was there the day or night he was murdered."

"But you were there," I insist. "You have nothing to worry about."

She laughs once—short, bitter, exhausted. "Yes, but the one fucking day they care about? Stephanie wasn't home. She was with her girlfriend the night they think he was killed."

A knot forms in my stomach. The timeline. The isolation. The lack of witnesses. It all paints a terrifying picture. A picture the detectives could easily twist.

"Samaya, I don't think you have anything to worry about," Louis says, but even he doesn't sound convinced. "You can prove you were in New Jersey."

Samaya pours herself another drink and wanders into the living room, collapsing onto the couch like she's folding into herself.

"What are we gonna do about Mom?" she asks quietly, looking over her shoulder at us. Her eyes are glossy, her face young and fragile in a way I haven't seen since we were kids. It hits me then, the truth that always existed but feels more final now: it's just us. It has been just us for a long time, but now it's official.

I cross the room, take her hand, and squeeze hard. "I know, babe. I know."

My tears finally break loose. They flow because no amount of mental preparation can cushion the finality of death.

Especially not when grief is piled on top of grief, trauma on top of trauma, loss on top of loss.

Louis eventually has to leave for a potential client meeting. He hesitates three times before actually heading toward the door.

"I hate leaving you like this," he says, rubbing his hands down his face. "It feels wrong."

I touch his chest lightly, steadying him. Steadying myself. "We'll be ok. Maybe it's good for us to have a sisters' night. Talk about Mom. Mourn. Just us."

He doesn't look convinced, but he nods. I peek through the blinds before he opens the door—reporters are still out there—and then give him a slow, lingering kiss before he leaves.

I lock the door behind him.

Sam is curled on the couch in the fetal position, staring blankly at nothing. She tries to smile at me, but her lips tilt in a way that's more pain than comfort.

I reach out. She hesitates, then sits up and takes my hand. We climb the stairs together.

Upstairs, she mumbles something about needing a shower. I flop onto her bed and check my phone.

The last message I sent to Alyse sits at the top of the screen.

Hey girl. My mom died today

The phone vibrates immediately—she's calling. I silence it, my thumb lingering over the ignore button.

Not ready to talk. Taking care of Sam rn. Call you in the AM

Her reply comes instantly.

Ok. I'm so sorry, babe. Love you both. Call me if you need me XO

I toss the phone aside and stare at the ceiling. My whole body feels heavy. Thick. Achy. My mind keeps spinning through the last forty-eight hours like it's trying to put the chaos in order:

My sister is home.

Our mother is gone.

Sam is a person of interest in David's murder.

We need to plan a funeral.

And I'm barely holding on.

Sam emerges from the bathroom in an oversized Sean John shirt that looks like it's from 2004.

"Got another one of those?" I ask.

She nods, rummages in a drawer, and tosses me a red one. I strip out of my sweater and jeans and put it on. It smells faintly like old detergent and the past.

She sits beside me and starts lotioning her arms. I lie back down, staring up at the now-familiar ceiling.

She switches off the lamp. After a moment, I feel her hand searching for mine in the dark. I take it, and instantly we're little girls again — hiding from chaos, clinging to each other in the dark.

She rubs her thumb over the back of my hand in soft, slow circles. I squeeze her hand gently.

"Remember when we were little?" she whispers. "I think you were like three or four. And Mom told us the police were coming, and to not let them get her?"

I nod in the darkness, a sad smile tugging at my mouth.

"And we put peanut butter on the threshold of the door because we thought the cops would get stuck like the peanut butter stuck to the roof of our mouths…" Her voice breaks into a quiet laugh.

"And we hid in that tiny-ass closet, thinking we were geniuses," I add. "And then the cop found us and we were so mad our plan didn't work."

"We were *pissed*," she chuckles.

We lie there talking like this for nearly an hour — trading memories, sweet ones and ugly ones, stories filled with laughter and shadows and complicated love.

At some point, our words fade out.

At some point, sleep pulls us under.

Her hand stays laced in mine the whole night.

CHAPTER THIRTY-NINE

As soon as I open my eyes, I am assaulted by the sun shining through Sam's open blinds. A harsh, overconfitted kind of morning sun. I groan, cover my face with my arm, and roll over, away from the light. Sam lies facing me, curled into a small ball. She looks peaceful — more peaceful than I've seen her since she's been back. A little girl version of her, the version before everything heavy found us.

I gently pull the blanket up around her arms, moving slowly, carefully, as if she might crack if I jostle her the wrong way. Then I roll ninja-style out of bed, praying the frame doesn't creak. I tiptoe to her dresser and grab a pair of sweatpants, slipping into them before padding downstairs.

The quiet feels strange. This house has always been quiet — but right now, it's the kind of quiet that hums with leftover chaos. A quiet that feels too still, too aware.

Downstairs, I rummage through her pristine white cupboards until I find a coffee pod for her Keurig. The familiarity of the motion, press the pod in, hit BREW. settles me for a moment. I sit at the barstool and wrap my hands around the mug, grounding myself.

My mind drifts back to the night before.

And to the dream.

God, that dream.

I dreamed for the first time in months, and it was a nightmare so vivid that even now, awake in the morning light, I can still feel the residue of it crawling along my skin.

In my dream, David approached me. Except his body was just as I'd seen in the photos: the slashed throat, the gaping wound, the blood that had dried in violent rivers. His voice was warped, metallic. And as he spoke, his slit throat slowly spurted blood in sync with his words.

At first, it was impossible to understand him. His mouth moved like a puppet's—stiff, wrong—and nothing matched the sound coming out. All I could see was his bloodied corpse, resurrected and standing before me in that disturbing heroin addict's slump, the kind where the body leans so far to one side you're certain gravity should've claimed it.

He moved toward me without moving his feet.

Just gliding.

Smooth.

Steady.

Wrong.

And then he stood directly in front of me—or stooped, really—his dead eyes locked on mine, and the voice came through clearly, strained and distant, like a recording played through water.

"She did this to me. She did this to me, she did this to me."

Over and over, until his mouth filled with blood, and it began pouring out in a steady stream, running down his chin, splattering onto his shirt.

I remember running.

I remember the hallway.

Endless.

Repeating.

The same hall he was killed in, stretching on forever.

When I finally woke up, I was drenched in sweat, my heart pounding like it was trying to escape my chest.

"She did this to me."

Those words cling to me like cobwebs.

The sound of hot liquid streaming from the Keurig startles me out of the memory. I open the fridge and settle for the oat milk hidden behind the eggs. I stir it in with a little sugar and decide to call Alyse.

"Girl!! Oh my God, how are you? I've been wondering what's happening, but I don't wanna be like all up in ya' shit, you know?" she exclaims the second she answers.

Her voice is a salve. A tether.

A reminder that someone knows me outside of all this darkness.

"Hey, girl… damn, it's so good to hear your voice right now," I say, my eyes stinging with unexpected tears. "Shit's so crazy…"

"Tell me everything. When can I see you? I'm free this afternoon!"

I tell her the latest, everything except the nightmare. I can't bring myself to speak that into existence out loud. When I finish, she goes quiet for a long time.

"Alyse?"

"I'm here. I'm just taking it all in. So wait — do they think Samaya killed David?"

"I'm not sure. She's just super freaked out right now."

We make plans to get together later, and I end the call. I'm heading toward the stairs to check on Sam when—

A knock.

A sharp, unexpected knock.

I freeze.

Phone in hand.

Breath stuck halfway up my throat.

I walk slowly to the door, keeping my footsteps light. I peer through the peephole.

Louis.

Relief floods through me so fast I could collapse.

I open the door just a few inches first—checking the yard automatically. And thank God I do, because the reporters out front notice me immediately.

"Is your sister home?"

"How did your sister escape?"

"What do you know about the murder of David Esposito?"

Their voices are like buzzing insects—high, whiny, relentless.

I yank Louis inside and slam the door shut.

He's holding a white box in one hand and a coffee in the other. He looks like some kind of angel disguised as a man in grey sweatpants.

He hands me the coffee, smiling that melt-my-spine smile.

"Just made a cup," I admit. "But thank you, love. I didn't know you were coming this morning."

Now he looks sheepish. "I couldn't sleep at all. I felt so fucked up for leaving you guys here by yourselves. And I figured if I showed up with coffee and baked goods, I'd get a pass for just poppin' up on y'all unannounced."

He opens the box: blueberry muffins, a weird round brown thing (a scone maybe?), and two glazed donuts.

"Oh honey, you did good. And you are one person I wouldn't mind popping up on me every morning."

The implication hits me half a second too late.

His smile turns softer. Warm.

He wraps those long arms around me and buries his face in my mess of curls.

"I'd love that too," he murmurs.

We eat muffins at the island while I tell him about the dream—and this time, saying it out loud makes it feel even more disturbing.

"That's fucking creepy, Serenity," he says.

"Right?!"

"Who do you think he meant when he said 'she did it'?"

I shrug and take a huge bite of a glazed donut to avoid answering the question I don't want to think about.

"Maybe you should get out of this house for a few hours," he suggests gently. "Happy hour later? Can you get away?"

I want to. God, I do. But —

"I don't know. I would love to get away. I know I need to. I just feel hella bad about leaving Sam here alone with everything going on."

He nods, reading me perfectly.

"Well, I'm never gonna tell you what's right for you. But I think it would help a lot. She could come too."

I laugh. "No, there's no way she's going out in public right now. I'll come. Let me figure out what's going on with Sam, and then I can meet you — maybe around three or four?"

His whole body relaxes at my answer.

His eyes warm.

His shoulders drop.

He pulls me into a hug, and I rest my cheek against his chest, letting myself feel held.

"You are such a light spot in my world right now," I whisper.

"You've been the same for me," he says.

I snort. "Even though since the moment you met me, it's been nothing but drama and crazy shit?"

He laughs, the sound rumbling in his chest. God, I love that sound.

"Yes, even with all the crazy shit poppin' off. Don't get me wrong — the shit is crazy — but you're a good person. I know men who missed out on good women because she came with a little baggage. I think if the person is solid and loyal, the crazy stuff around them doesn't change that."

The word baggage tugs at an old wound. Dre's voice floats up from memory — cold, dismissive.

And now?

Now I understand why his ex had baggage. Hell, why I do.

But I push all that away and focus on Louis — solid, present, sincere.

"I appreciate that you think like that," I say. "I wish more men did."

"So… food later? My treat," he says.

"It's a date."

He cups my face, kisses my forehead, then my nose, then finally my lips. I sigh into him, and he smiles against my mouth.

I watch him walk down the driveway and get into his car before heading upstairs to check on Sam.

CHAPTER FORTY

It feels incredibly strange to be out in a public place. I close the giant door behind me and glance around the restaurant until I spot Louis sitting at one of the high tables near the bar. He waves, and I make my way over to meet him. He looks handsome in his fitted black t-shirt. It makes his arms bulge in the best way. He must've gone to the barber since I saw him this morning because his hair is perfectly cut and lined up.

He looks *good.*

He stands to hug me, and he smells just as good as he looks. His full lips kiss me softly on the cheek, and he whispers, "My God, Serenity, you look beautiful." I actually got dressed for the occasion. I went for the jeans that hug my ass perfectly and a lavender shirt that shows a hint of cleavage and collarbones. I added some boots with heels to feel taller, although I still only come to just above his shoulders. "Thank you," I breathe. "You don't look so bad yourself."

We sit down, and he gestures to his half-empty glass, "Drink?"

"Yes, something strong."

The waitress approaches and looks at Louis with very interested eyes. Then she notices that I am now sitting here, and she looks between him and me as if assessing who or what I am to him. Her face becomes decidedly less interested when she looks at me. She pulls out her little leather pad and asks me with an unmistakable note of disappointment what I would like to drink.

After she walks away, I turn my attention back to Louis. I note that he doesn't glance over at her voluptuous ass as she walks away from us. *Good job, babe,* I think to myself. It's rare for a man to not accidentally sneak a glance behind an attractive woman as she walks away. I inwardly cringe because I am constantly assessing his behavior and searching for any signs of a red flag.

I hate that I'm like this now—hyper-aware, always scanning, always braced for the worst. My body hasn't unclenched in weeks. Even here, in the dim restaurant full of clinking glasses and soft music, I can't shake the feeling that someone is watching me. That someone is watching us.

"So, how are you feeling, babe?" he asks.

"Honestly," I say while I fidget with the black cloth napkin in my hands, "I don't even know. Overwhelmed mostly? I just feel like there's been one huge blow after another, and I can't keep up."

"You can, and you are," he corrects me as little miss not-so-happy-to-see-me approaches with our drinks. I take a quick sip of my Honey Jack and close my eyes. Sweet relief. "Yea, I guess you're right. This whole thing about Sam being a possible person of interest is unnerving. I feel so bad for her because of what she has already gone through, you know?"

Louis nods and then looks away briefly. When he meets my eyes again, they look full of questions.

"What?" I ask.

He shakes his head and looks down. "Nothing. It's nothing."

I reach out and put my hand over his. Something's up.

"What? Tell me, it's ok."

"I've just been thinking about, you know, the case, the murder, and the fact that your sister isn't dead. Do you know anyone else who would want him dead? And someone who would want him that dead. The pictures you described sound pretty fucked up." He is nervously swirling his cup as he stammers over his words.

"No, I mean, I don't know…" My voice trails off. Then he looks me straight in the eyes.

There's a split second, barely half a breath, where the noise in the restaurant seems to drop away. It's like the universe inhales before he speaks. Like it already knows I won't like what he's about to say.

"I guess what I'm wondering is, do you think there's any way that Sam could've had something to do with his murder?"

My whole body stiffens. My eyes dart all around us, surveying who may have overheard his statement. A couple turns their heads. Or maybe I imagine it. Lately, I'm imagining a lot.

"Hell no!" I hiss, leaning forward. "What are you even suggesting?"

He raises his palms in a gesture of surrender. "Hey, hey, I'm sorry. I'm just asking."

I drop my shoulders and lean back in my seat. Crossing my arms over my chest defensively, my mind considers what he's just suggested. I think about how nervous Sam was when she knew the cops were coming to ask their routine questions. I also think about how obsessed she was about not having an alibi for the day of his murder. But that would be normal, right? I know she's had bad experiences with the police in the past. I shake these thoughts out of my mind. Samaya is innocent. I refuse to entertain any ideas that contradict that.

But the seed is planted. A shadowy little thing. And once it's planted, it starts growing on its own.

"Look," Louis says, his eyes genuine. "I didn't mean to upset you and maybe I shouldn't have asked. That was super out of pocket to even bring that up."

I return my hand to his on top of the table, "No, you have every right to ask. That's a valid question. I mean, he did almost murder her. I even get why they are looking at her as a suspect. I just know regardless of how pissed she became with David, she would never hurt anyone, much less brutally murder them."

He squeezes my hand and smiles tightly at me.

"Y'all ready to order?" asks the waitress impatiently, and the sudden arrival of her voice makes me jump.

We order our food, and Louis tells me about one of the new clients he's taken on in the city. I listen as earnestly as I can, but my mind keeps going back to his question about Samaya maybe being involved with David's murder.

My stomach knots. My drink goes warm. I keep feeling eyes on the back of my neck, even though every time I turn, no one is looking.

As I pull up the driveway to Sam's house, it looks as though she'd got every single light on in the place. I frown. This is strange since she's such a stickler about keeping her energy bill down. I pull down the driver's side sun visor and take a quick glance at my reflection. Luckily, I don't feel as buzzed as I should feel. I smooth my curls as much as possible, but between the light rain and the make-out session Louis and I just got in standing outside the restaurant, I'm looking a little disheveled.

I grab my purse and exit the car, closing the car door gently behind me. I hear something behind me, like footsteps, and I gasp, nearly jumping out of my skin. When I whirl around and survey my surroundings in a panic, I see nothing, but then my eyes lower, and I see a black cat standing behind me, looking equally as terrified as he swings his tail hypnotically behind him.

For a split second, I swear I feel breath on the back of my neck. Like someone was right behind me a moment ago. Like I just missed catching whoever—or whatever—was there.

"Holy shit," I mumble, removing the hand from my throat. I continue my journey up the walkway and begin to put my key in the lock, but then I see Sam's face peering at me from behind the sheer curtain that covers the front door's semiopaque window. She swings the door open, and I stand there, stunned, key still in position to unlock the now wide-open door.

"Well, hello," I begin. Sam hustles me inside and then stands in the doorway, her eyes darting every which way. She closes the door and faces me.

"Someone was out there," she says, eyes frantic and red-rimmed. I walk over to the couch and put my purse down, noticing the half-empty bottle of wine and empty wine glass on the coffee table.

"What do you mean?"

"A man was standing outside of my back window!" she says shrilly. I can tell she's at least a little buzzed. "I was coming down the stairs, and right as I was about to turn the corner, boom, there he was. Just standing there, in the middle of the yard standing in the rain."

"Do you know who it was?"

"No, but it was definitely a man. And he was pretty tall. And he just stood there in the rain, he didn't move, it was like he was watching the house, watching me." She shivers, saying the last part.

Her voice shakes. Her hands shake. And something deep in my chest sinks—because this doesn't feel like drunken paranoia. It feels like truth. It feels like danger circling us from the dark edges of this neighborhood.

"Did you call the police yet?"

"No. Well, I was going to, but whoever it was, was gone by the time I'd grabbed my phone off the charger upstairs. I thought maybe I had imagined it, but it was just so real." She reaches for her glass and guzzles a good amount of her drink from it.

"How many glasses have you had, Sam?"

Her eyes grow wide, and her jaw goes slack, "You think maybe I imagined it?"

I consider my following words wisely. I don't know if someone had been outside of her house, but I did know that I'd had a similar experience a couple of weeks ago. A shadow where someone shouldn't be. A feeling of being watched. A presence slipping out of sight just a heartbeat too fast.

"Let's make sure we lock everything up and, for God's sake, close up some of these curtains."

"You sound just like mom," she begins but then stops. We both sit there, not saying anything more, but feeling it all.

"Let's just lock everything up, and we can check in with officer Markovich tomorrow. Maybe we should be staying somewhere else while all of this plays out."

The house feels too bright. Too exposed. Like if we stand still long enough, someone outside will see straight through us.

CHAPTER FORTY-ONE

hen my mind registers the sound of pounding downstairs, I am instantly awake.

The kind of pounding that doesn't sound confused or accidental; the kind that feels intentional, forceful, urgent. My heart kicks into overdrive before my eyes even fully open.

I sit straight up in Sam's bed and look around. She is no longer next to me, so I throw the blankets off and swing my legs out of bed to get up. The knocking grows louder as I descend the stairs, taking them two at a time. Every step feels like a countdown to something terrible. I reach the bottom step just as Samaya opens the front door.

At the door, I see Detective Adams and his partner. Behind them are four other officers. My heart sinks.

A cold rush moves through my body like someone poured ice water down my back.

What is going on now?

"Samaya Esposito-Jones? We have a warrant here to search the property." Detective Adams says in a dead tone. Before Sam can say anything, all the officers push past her and begin talking loudly to one another as they start rifling through the stuff in the entryway and kitchen.

The house fills instantly with the sound of drawers slamming, radios crackling, boots everywhere. It feels invasive, violent — like we're being swallowed whole.

I meet Sam in the entryway, and she looks half asleep and absolutely stunned.

Her face is blank, but her eyes are panicked. Like she's still trying to understand what universe she woke up in.

"May I ask what is going on?" She asks Detective Adams. He looks at her, and his face is expressionless.

"We have reason to believe there may be something here that can aid us in finding out what happened to your husband."

"Ex-husband," Samaya corrects through gritted teeth. She is seething now.

"Well, according to our records, you two are, well, were still legally married," the detective says with a hint of triumphant amusement. "We just need to have a look around. You have nothing to hide, right?"

He's taunting her now, but she doesn't break. I watch her visibly take a couple deep breaths. She glances at me and then back to Adams.

"We'll be outside. Let me know when you've finished 'investigating'," she says this last word with her fingers in air quotes. She grabs my arm and leads me outside, and I turn to look at Adams for some sort of guidance or maybe permission. I have no idea how to read his words.

"Don't go too far," he smirks. I watch as Sam rolls her eyes. She drags me to her car parked in the driveway, and we get inside.

The moment the doors shut, it's like the world collapses into silence — heavy, buzzing silence.

"What the fuck," she yells, slamming her tightly balled fists against the steering wheel, making the entire car jolt. I look over at her, trying to think of something calming or comforting to say.

Her whole body trembles with rage and fear — I've never seen her shaken like this. Not even when she first told me what David did to her.

"This motherfucker tried to kill me. Kill me, Serenity! He was going to rape me. And now, because he's dead, I am the bad guy? Like what in the actual fuck? And why would I write 'killer' on the wall of his apartment? I'm alive."

"Girl, I am on your side, and I totally get what you're saying. You don't deserve this shit," I say adamantly. "They are just grasping for straws. They have to go through their process, no matter how fucked up it is to you."

She leans all the way back in her seat, nostrils flaring. Her arms are locked, and her hands have a white-knuckle grip on the steering wheel. I reach over and tentatively touch her arm. She flinches, and I wince. She looks over at me apologetically.

"Sorry, babe, I'm just so freaked out right now. I don't even know whose life I'm living right now. Nothing feels ok. Nothing is going right."

"I know… I mean, I don't know how you feel. How could I possibly? But I am here for you, and I know that it's going to be ok."

She nods, but doesn't move otherwise. I fix my gaze at the front window of her house, where I can see the shadow of figures moving about the house.

Each shadow passing the blinds makes my stomach tighten — like any moment, one of them will stop, turn, and stare out at us.

I can't handle seeing Sam like this. She was always the person who held it all together and helped everyone around her feel calm and grounded. Seeing her like this makes me want to lose hope. But I know I can't do this because she needs me, and I am all she has right now. She has no one now. Not her daughter, her husband, or even her mother.

It's up to me.

I pull her hand from the steering wheel and rest in her lap. She removes her other hand as if on cue and lays her in her lap. I place my hand on her shoulder and gently push it down. She follows my direction and relaxes her shoulders.

It feels like guiding someone through a panic attack underwater — slow, careful, desperate.

"Breathe, babe. Breathe." I say gently. She audibly exhales. After the second exhale, her head bows, and the tears that she's probably been holding in for the past few days, flow freely.

About twenty minutes later, Detective Adams approaches the car with an officer, and my whole body stiffens. In his hand is a planner or journal.

My stomach drops. I already know — nothing good comes from a detective holding a journal like it's a weapon.

"Mrs. Jones, can you please step out of the car?"

Sam and I look at each other, and her eyes are wide with terror.

"It's going to be ok," I said. But now I'm not sure what to think.

The lie tastes metallic on my tongue.

I watch them walk over to the steps leading up to the front door. Samaya stands facing me, and all I can see is the side of the officer's face and the back of detective Adams's head. I watch as Sam's face goes from worry to fear and then frustration. Her hands are gesturing to the notebook, and then she throws her hands up. I wish I had the keys to crack the window and make out what they are saying.

The silence stretches too long. Too dangerous. Every second builds pressure in my chest.

After a few moments, I can't take it anymore, and I open the passenger door.

"...and almost raped me. Of course, I vented in my journal. But it's just a journal. I am a therapist. I literally get paid to suggest journaling to my patients to help them process their emotions–"

"Fair, but it just so happens that the man mentioned in your journal actually ended up dead. How do you explain that coincidence?"

"I can't explain it. Just like I couldn't the other day. I was in a different state, for God's sake."

"A state that's only about two hours away from here. It is totally feasible that you came here, revenge killed your ex, and then made your way back to hiding in Jersey."

"This is crazy," Sam says, shaking her head in dazed disbelief.

I get out of the car.

"What exactly is going on?" I ask, my hand planted firmly on my hips. Now, I'm pissed.

"Your sister here indicated in her little journal here that she wanted to kill David Esposito." He flips open the journal to the page in question and reads it aloud, "I wish he was dead. If I could, I would kill him myself."

"Operative words being 'if I could'," Samaya spits out angrily. "But I can't. I am not a murderer. I can't believe you can come here and accuse me of murdering my ex-husband."

"Then explain where you were the morning he was killed. Explain what you meant by 'I want him dead' here in your journal. Also, you seem pretty angry right now. Maybe angry enough to kill?" he says and folds his arms across his chest. I watch as the officer next to him tightens his grip on his holster.

Something in my chest twists — this is turning fast. Too fast. They're not investigating anymore. They're hunting.

"Samaya, I think–"

"I want a lawyer," she says suddenly and matter of factly. "We are done here."

Adams' shoulders slump slightly. He was getting off on badgering her this way.

"For now," he says. He gestures to his lackey. "We are done here."

They both walk over to the patrol car, and we stand together on the steps, shoulder to shoulder. We watch as they drive away, and then we walk into the house together.

Once inside, we collapse on the couch. Sam buries her face in her hands and lets out a low sob. My heart breaks for her.

"We will find you a lawyer," I say.

She lifts her head and looks over at me. "Oh, I already know just the one."

CHAPTER FORTY-TWO

We meet with Samaya's lawyer the very next morning. His name is Marcus McAllister, and he practices mainly in New York City, but has a home in the Hamptons, which is where we currently are.

Even the air out here feels different — sharper, colder, like it knows something big is coming.

She didn't tell me that this man was fine as hell. Like, *fine, fine.*

Not the accidental fine. The intentional, crafted-by-the-hands-of-God fine.

First, let me describe the man's home because even his home is handsome. The house is situated near the beach. You can literally see the beach from his front window. Everything inside is black and dark mahogany wood.

The kind of home that makes you whisper without knowing why, like the walls and the furniture and the damn floors all have a bank account.

And speaking of dark, mahogany wood (Lord, forgive me) he is just as dark and handsome and solid-looking.

The kind of man who looks like he reads legal briefs for breakfast and breaks hearts for dessert.

He greeted us wearing a gray suit with a simple white shirt underneath. He wasn't the tallest man, but his chest, my goodness, his chest, filled out every inch of that suit. And although I did my best to keep my eyes towards the heavens, the pants fit just as snugly.

Samaya catches my eye for half a second, and we both bite back a smile like teenagers, the tiniest moment of levity in this hellish week.

Now he sits across from us, one leg crossed over the other, his pointer fingers steepled while his elbows rest on his knees, nodding as Samaya tells him the painstaking details of what happened to her. He says nothing, he just lets her run through her story and nods, while sometimes jots down a few things in his notebook.

His stillness is unnerving—the good kind, the kind that tells you he's listening to every breath and every tremor in your voice.

I take a sip of the water bottle he gave me and try to get my left foot to stop shaking nervously. My anxiety is through the roof.

I swear I can hear my heartbeat in my teeth.

Sam finishes her grueling synopsis of the past few weeks, and we both look at Mr. Handsome, AKA Marcus, with hopeful and expectant eyes. He flips through the two pages of tiny written notes as he chews the end of his pen.

The room feels like it's holding its breath with us.

"Well, first, I am so sorry for what you're going through. It's obviously been a nightmare. I had seen some of this on the news, but hearing the details from you, it's much worse than I'd previously known. The good news is, I can definitely help you. We'll need to meet with the Suffolk County Police, of course, but from what you've shared, there's no way they can link you to David's murder."

My shoulders release, and I let out the breath I didn't realize I was holding.

For the first time in days, the air doesn't feel like glass against my lungs.

"But what about the journal entry? Can they really charge me with murder because I vented in my journal about wishing he was dead?"

"It's definitely a stretch," he says slowly. "But they will try to run with it, which is why it's good you're getting yourself some legal representation."

"What are the next steps?"

Marcus begins to tell Samaya about her options and an action plan. As they go back and forth with questions and prices and answers, I begin to zone out.

The words swirl together—retainer, charges, detectives, options—and all I can hear underneath them is fear.

The more they talk details, the more it reminds me that there is a genuine possibility that my sister could be taken away, again, and this time to prison for the murder of a man who assaulted her. What in the actual fuck is our justice system? White officers can kill a black man dead in the street because they mistook his wallet or phone for a gun, and they not only get out of jail time, but they also often just go right back to work. And yet, here is my sister about to pay thousands upon thousands of dollars to clear her name when she is the real victim here.

The unfairness burns hot in my chest—grief, rage, helplessness all tangled together.

"May I use your restroom?" I cut in, needing to get away and take some space. Marcus stands and gestures.

"Of course, it's just down the hall. It's the last door on the right."

I walk down the hall and into the bathroom. Once inside, I turned on the cold water and cup my hands under the running, ice-cold water. I splash some water on my face and lift my head, one eye squinting open, looking for something to wipe my face with.

My pulse is still hammering. I feel like I'm vibrating inside my skin.

Shit.

With a half-open eye, I spot the door to a cabinet and fumble to open it. I grab the first towel I can find and wipe my face with it. After laying the towel over the counter, I grip the sink with both hands and stare into the mirror at my reflection.

I barely recognize myself— exhaustion has carved out new angles in my face.

My face looks weary, and my curls look wild and unkempt. I gather all my locks up high on top of my head into a big, messy bun. I continue to actually use the bathrooms and then make my way down the hall and back to the daunting conversation occurring in the living room.

"...about payment after we speak to the detectives so I have a better idea of the extent of what you'll need. This is fine for now, thank you," Marcus is saying as I round the corner. "But like I said, we are going to make this go away. You've been through enough."

"Thank you so much, Marcus. Seriously. I'm still freaked out, but I feel a little bit better after this meeting."

"Good. That is good." Marcus says. "Serenity, there you are."

I start blushing, my signature reaction to most situations, apparently.

My cheeks betray me every damn time.

"Hey. Sounds like things went well?" I look between Marcus and Sam. Sam still looks slightly ashen, but is at least smiling now.

Marcus looks at Samaya expectantly, "Yes, I think we have this thing in the bag," he says as if he's a coach discussing an upcoming game.

We say our goodbyes, and Marcus promises to call Sam in the morning when he is on his way to meet with her and Detective Adams.

As soon as we get in the car, Samaya starts talking.

"One, that man is fine as fuck. And two, I think he might actually be able to help me. He thinks they just want to pin his murder on someone, and I agree. All I know is that I wasn't involved, and I have to just trust that the truth will come to light."

"Yes, girl. You've got to just trust the process. I know that sounds like some woo-woo bullshit, but it's all we can do right now, you know?" I say.

Samaya glances in the rearview mirror before signaling to get onto the freeway, "Nah, it's true."

I look out the window and see the few tiny drops on the windshield as it begins to rain.

"How much did you pay him?"

She shoots me a sidelong glance and cringes, "His retainer was $2,500 upfront."

"Damn!" I say, shocked.

"I know, girl, I am in the wrong profession," she says with a crude laugh.

"Wine or Henny?" Samaya asks as she stares into the fridge. I finish chewing the giant bite of pizza I just took. She looks over her shoulder at me and bursts out laughing. "Damn greedy!"

I try not to laugh because I know if I do, stray pieces of pizza will come flying out of my mouth. *"Stmnmwp!"* I manage around my mouthful.

She shakes her head and giggles again as she pulls the bottle of brown liquor out of her cupboard.

"This is possibly the best pizza I've ever had," I say after I finally empty my mouth.

"No wonder you were scarfing it down. And I told you, Gino's is like the best pizza on earth."

I take another, more modest bite and savor the unique, New York-style crust. It's a bit chewy, and the cheese is way different than the stuff we had in California. She slides me a small glass of Hennessy, and I raise one eyebrow as I glance from her to the glass.

"The fuck?" I say. "You ain't got sprite or coke?"

She gives me a half-smile and shrugs, "Come on, little sister. You can do it."

"Bitch, don't you remember I could barely do the Honey Jack by itself, and that shit is hella sweet."

She crosses her arms over her chest and looks me up and down, "I just paid that sexy lawyer $2,500. You are taking a shot with me."

I pick up my glass, "I can't argue with that. Let's do it. But if I get too faded, you're taking care of me."

"Deal."

I hold my head back and took a long swallow, trying to water-fall it into my throat without hitting my tongue. I hit the wrong spot in the back of my throat and start immediately coughing and sputtering as I almost choke.

This is hilarious to Samaya, who shakes her head and laughs, "Rookie."

She proceeds to pour another shot as if I didn't almost just die trying to take the first one. I down the second shit with success and no choking. When the warmth hits my throat and stomach, I feel a little more at ease.

My phone vibrates next to me, and I see Stella's name appear on the screen.

"Hello?"

"Serenity, hello, sweetheart," she says warmly.

"Hi, Stella. How are you?" I clear my throat and try to clear my newly Hennessy fogged mind.

"I'm fine. I called to check in on you… Jason said your sister is home. What a miracle! Is she ok?"

"Yes, very happy she's home. She's as ok as she can be, all things considered. I think she's just happy to be home," I say and glance over at Sam. Her eyes are wide as she mouths, 'who's that?' I mouth back, 'my boss.' She nods, but still looks uneasy.

"That's wonderful, dear. Well, it is so very good to hear your voice. Oh! Mario is wondering if you'd like to work this week—no pressure, of course, but we have a few people out sick with a nasty bug, and we are short-staffed. If not, we can manage. I just figured you may be able to use the extra cash."

Work.

I consider working for the first time in a while. I haven't even thought about work or anything with the craziness of everything going on. With rent approaching two weeks though, I should probably pick up a shift.

"Yea, um, yes. Can I call you back and let you know? I will definitely pick up a shift. I just need to check on a few things first."

"Of course, dear. Call me anytime."

I end the call and turn back to Samaya. "That was my boss's wife asking if I want to return to work this week. I guess a bunch of people are out sick."

She nods, "You should probably go, right?"

"Financially, yes. But I feel bad leaving you for an eight-hour shift."

"Girl, I am fine. If anything happens, I know how to dial 9-1-1." She looks at my face, "Nothing is going to happen. Seriously, make some money this week."

I consider this and then pick my phone back up and text Stella.

"Can I work a shift tomorrow?"

I put my phone back down and reach for my drink, but my phone pings before I can pick it up. It's Stella.

"Yay! 5-9 work?"

"Perfect. Can't wait to see everyone."

"Alright!" I say to Sam, "You'll get some 'me time' tomorrow night. I'm working the 5 to 9 shift."

She raises her glass to toast, "Cheers to you going to work instead of babysitting your big sister."

I lightly punch her arm before picking up my glass to meet her toast.

CHAPTER FORTY-THREE

I have three hours before I go to work, and I'm already dreading it. Not so much the working part. I'm actually looking forward to being busy. It will be nice to focus on work tasks instead of thinking about murders and police and the true crime feel that my life has taken on as of late. Still, the idea of stepping back into "normal" life feels like trying to walk into a room after a fire and pretending you do not smell smoke. I keep waiting for the other shoe to drop, even though my closet is basically full of shoes at this point.

My head was pounding when I woke up–no doubt from the shots of Hennessy Samaya and I took last night before we passed out giggling on the couches downstairs. She is still uncomfortable sleeping upstairs in her bed, and I can't blame her. The things that happened up there are unforgettable. I feel it in my body even when I am not thinking about it. Like my nervous system remembers for me.

I consider texting Stella that I changed my mind about working and then remember the lack of funds in my checking account and think better of it. I look around for my purse and keys before heading upstairs to let Sam know I need to go home and get ready for work. I already feel guilty and I have not even pulled out of the driveway yet.

"I'm glad you're getting the hell out of this house," she says, giving me a hug. "I mean, I'm very grateful that you've been staying with me, but you've got to get out into the world again." She tries to smile like she means it, but there is a tired edge to her eyes that makes my stomach twist.

I snort, "I'm just going to work, babe. Have you gotten updates from your sexy lawyer? When do y'all meet with the cops?" I'm trying to keep it light, keep her light, keep me light. Like joking has become a tiny shield we keep passing back and forth.

"Tomorrow morning at eight." She says it like she is trying not to think about what eight a.m. means.

"How are you feeling about it?" I ask gently, even though I already know the answer in the way she is holding her body.

"Eh, you know, freaked out," she laughs nervously as she smooths her hand over the sheet she just put on the bed. "But I do feel better that Marcus will be there and can do most of the talking." Her laugh barely lands. It falls flat in the room, like she is trying to convince herself more than me.

I grab the opposite corner of the top sheet she tosses over her bed. We each straighten the corners and tuck them under the mattress, just like our mom taught us many years ago. The muscle memory hits hard. The way our hands move without thinking makes my chest ache.

Sam's mind must've gone to the idea because she gives me a sad smile. Her face softens like she is about to say something else, and then decides not to.

"I miss mom," I admit. "I know we didn't have the best relationship, but I guess I just miss having a mom." Saying it out loud makes it heavier. Like the words have weight that my throat cannot quite carry.

Samaya rounds the bed and sits down next to me on the half-made queen-sized bed. She looks older for a second. Not physically, just in the eyes.

"I know what you mean," she says, rubbing slow circles on my back. "It's like, now that she's gone, all the good memories seem to come to the forefront. Totally normal, and totally not a bad thing. Just a little sad." Her voice is steady but I hear what she is not saying through the steadiness.

"Definitely sad. Are you sure you're going to be ok while I'm gone? It's gonna be, like, a lot of hours." I hate the way I sound like a parent leaving their kid home alone. I hate even more that I feel like one.

She laughs and pushes my shoulder before standing up. "I'm the big sister, remember? I will be fine. It'll probably be good to spend a little time alone." She says it confidently, but there is a flicker in her eyes right after. Like the truth is she has no idea what alone will feel like in this house anymore.

I sigh and pick up my purse from her floor. We walk downstairs together in silence. The quiet in this house is not peaceful. It is the kind of quiet that makes you notice every creak and every breath.

She gives me a long hug at the door, and when I pull away, I see that she has tears in her eyes. That tiny crack in her armor makes me want to cry all over again.

"What's up, babe?" I ask, instantly concerned. I am already bracing myself for whatever new fear just landed. She quickly wipes her eyes and straightens her shoulders.

"Nothing is wrong. I just - I just love you. Thank you for everything, sissy." Her voice catches on the word love, like she is afraid if she says too much, she might unravel.

I reach out and squeeze her shoulder, holding her gaze, "Of course. I know you'd do the same for me." I do not add what we are both thinking, which is that she already has.

When I get in my car, I text Louis to tell him that I'm going to work and that he should stop by the restaurant later. His response is immediate and affirmative. I smile. I miss spending time with him, and I feel like I haven't spent much one-on-one time with him since Sam's been back. I make a mental note to set up a date night with him as soon as possible. I need something that feels like mine again. Something that is not death or detectives or survival mode.

I back out of Sam's driveway and see a Suffolk County Police car coming up the street. The car slows as they approach the house and once they see me driving, they wave and continue around. My stomach drops anyway.

Perfect, I think. Officers must be patrolling her neighborhood. Are they patrolling to watch her whereabouts or to protect her? These cops are a fucking trip. I keep replaying the way Adams looked at her yesterday. Like he already decided what he wanted the story to be.

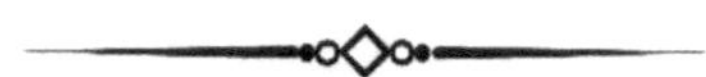

When I approach Mario's, the first person I see is Johnny. His eyes bulge with surprise when he sees me, and then his tan cheeks turn rosy. He composes himself quickly and takes on his usual "I'm trying to appear cool because I like you" bravado. I forgot how much his nervousness makes him talk with his whole body.

"Serenity," he says, opening the door for me. "Long time no see. Hey, I'm really sorry about what happened to your sister." His voice is softer than usual, like he is afraid to scare me.

I'd forgotten how thick his New York accent was. "Hi, Johnny. Thank you for that." I appreciate his kindness but I also feel that familiar tightness in my ribs. Like people saying sorry is a reminder that this is real.

He stands there, shifting from one foot to the other, hands shoved deep into his pockets. It's strange to see him nervous around me, and it's almost making me nervous. Luckily for both of us, Stella approaches. Her arms are outstretched, and she pulls me into a big hug before ushering me into the back room of the restaurant. Her hug is the kind that makes you want to collapse into it.

"Sweetie, how are you?" She asks her hands on my shoulders. Her dark brown eyes search mine in a motherly way, and it makes my stomach tighten. Needing to shift the energy, I step back and turn to hang the purse on one of the hooks on the wall. I do not trust my voice with the truth right now.

"I'm doing ok. Thank you again for being so flexible about my… life stuff. Knowing that I still have a stream of income has been super helpful." I say it like I am explaining something normal. Like life stuff does not mean funerals and police interviews and nightmares.

"Of course, honey." Her eyes look concerned. "Have you eaten? Do you want to eat before you start your shift?" The question is so gentle it almost breaks me open.

I glance down at my body and blush. I have lost some weight over the past month. I feel it in my jeans. I feel it in my face. Grief is a thief.

"I'm ok, Stella. I just want to start working. It helps take my mind off everything happening." I need movement. I need noise. I need something that does not feel like waiting.

I'm relieved when she leaves me to help one of the new girls with a customer's gift certificate. I pull my cell phone from my pocket to remind Louis to stop by later. I type his name in and pause first, just staring at it for a beat because even this small normal gesture feels like a lifeline.

When I wander out of the break room, the first person I see is Jason. I squeal and rush over to him, throwing my arms around his skinny waist. He giggles and squeezes me back just as enthusiastically. He smells like cologne and comfort.

"I thought you were out today?" I say breathlessly when we separate. I'm already smiling harder than I have all week.

"Girl, when Stella told me you were working, I brought my ass right up in here! The fuck? I had to come to see my work wifey." His voice is pure sunshine.

"I'm so fucking happy you're here. Everyone keeps asking how I'm doing and saying how sorry they are, and I just want to work, you know? Not unpack the trauma while asking people what they wanna eat." I say it quick, like if I slow down I might start crying.

He nods sympathetically. "Girl, right? Well, I am your bodyguard, baby." He shimmies his hips and wiggles his eyebrows at me as he says bodyguard, and I laugh. I immediately clamp my hand over my mouth when I see an older couple turn to look at our noise. Even their disapproving glance cannot touch me right now.

Having Jason here changes my mood entirely. We make our way through the shift, laughing, teasing each other, and talking shit about the guests who are the most uptight and uncomfortable with his flamboyant gayness. When one of the older white women asks me if my hair is naturally curly or if I "paid for a perm," we completely lose our shit. For a while, I almost forget there is a storm waiting back at Sam's house. Almost.

It's about an hour before my shift ends when Louis walks into Mario's looking as fine as ever in a black peacoat over a blue and white checkered button-down shirt. His eyes light up when they land on my face. I smile like a fool as I cross the space between us. It hits me how badly I needed to see a face that means safety.

"You look happy," he breathes into my ear as he gives me a quick hug and peck on the cheek. His voice is soft, like he is trying not to startle something fragile inside me.

"Happy to see you, my love." I guide him to an empty table near the back of the restaurant. He sits down, and I hand him a menu. The way he moves like he belongs here with me makes my chest ache in a good way.

"What would you suggest, ma'am?" he asks in a mock voice as he eyes the pages of our impossibly long menu. The thing is three pages long and printed in size 9 font. People always say they never know what to order because the options are quite literally endless. He is trying to make me laugh, and it works.

"Well, you mi–"

"The alfredo fettuccine is one of my favorites," I hear Jason say from directly behind me in a low baritone voice. I jump, startled, not realizing he was there.

"Jason," I hiss, "you scared me!" My heart is already on edge, and he about gave me a heart attack.

He ignores me and is practically drooling over Louis, who is removing his jacket and his broad chest in the well-fitting shirt now exposed. I watch Louis clock it and try not to laugh.

"Hi Louis, remember me?" he asks. Louis glances at me, looking a little less than comfortable.

"Of course. You're Serenity's friend Jason, right?" Jason beams at this recognition, and I roll my eyes so hard I fear they may get stuck staring at the inside of my skull.

"Yes, Jason. This is my boyfriend, Louis." I say, crossing my arms over my chest pretending to be territorial. I lowkey love saying boyfriend out loud.

Jason throws his hands up in surrender, "I was just saying hello, honey." He turns his attention back to Louis, "So good to see you again."

He swings his hips so hard as he saunters away I wonder if he might actually throw his back out. I turn back to Louis and slide in the seat across from him.

"I'm so happy you're here," I say, stroking the top of his free hand. His hand is warm and solid. It steadies me.

"How's it been? Weird being back?"

"No, actually, it's been really good. I haven't felt this much like myself in a long time." I surprise myself by how true it feels. Like for these few hours, my life belongs to me again.

He smiles at me and then looks back at his menu. "You have no idea how happy that makes me. Now, what the hell should I order?"

I laugh as I stand up, smoothing my apron. "Well, Mr. Carter, I've got to get back to work, so you'll have to just flag me down when you're ready to order." I don't want to leave his table, but I do.

Louis stays until my shift ends, and we stand outside under the awning. The rain is freezing and so am I. The weather app on my phone had said we may actually get some snow flurries. Louis tells me he's got to go home for a bit, but that he'll stop by Sam's house later. The sky looks heavy, like it is holding something back.

"Maybe I can come to spend the night at your place?" I ask, running my fingers up and down his chest. I look up at him through my lashes, "I could use some… you know." I want to feel like a person again, not a walking grief case file.

"Some dick?"

We both start laughing, and I smack his chest. He pulls me in close and stares deeply into my eyes. We kiss, and it's long and slow and sensual. He kisses me like he is trying to remind me I am still alive.

"I love you," I say breathlessly, my body already beginning to respond to his touch. I say it like a confession and a prayer.

"I love you too," he says, staring down at me. Then he leans in close to my ear, "And I can't wait to deliver what you need later. I miss tasting you on my tongue." His voice is low enough to make my knees wobble.

I melt against him as my knees go weak. I forget the cold. I forget almost everything.

This man is heaven on earth.

He walks me to my car and waits until I have started my engine to walk over to his own vehicle. The way he does not leave until he knows I am safe makes my throat tighten.

A freak and a gentleman, could he be any more perfect? I wish perfection could protect us from what is waiting at home.

The rain pelts my windshield as I pull out of Mario's and make my way to check on Samaya. I crack my window to feel the cool air and sprinkles on my face. The road looks slick and dark, and for the first time all day, that old crawling feeling starts to return in my chest.

I have not felt this much like myself in weeks, and it feels so good. But even as I drive, I cannot shake the sense that the peace I just borrowed is about to be collected with interest.

CHAPTER FORTY-FOUR

I frown as I pull up to Sam's house and see that all the lights are on. I glance down at my car's clock and see that it's nearly 8:30 p.m. She must've gotten spooked again. It's not like her to have every single light in the house on with the blinds wide open at this time of night. The brightness feels wrong, like a stage set for something nobody wants to watch. My skin prickles before I even kill the engine.

I cut the engine and remove my key from the ignition. When I exit the vehicle, I notice a little black Honda parked in front of the house.

Is someone here?

My stomach dips like I missed a step. My mind starts flipping through names, faces, possibilities, and none of them feel good.

I gently close my door and shift my bag on my shoulder, slowly approaching the house. When I draw closer to the front door, I realize I can see a tiny sliver of light. I stop on the walkway for half a second, listening. The air feels too still. Even the rain sounds quieter, like it's holding its breath with me.

The door is pulled to the jam, but not completely closed.

My pulse turns ugly. Not fast. Heavy. Like it's trying to pound its way out through my ribs.

Using my pointer finger, I push the door open and look inside the entryway of Samaya's house. No one seems to be downstairs, so I walk inside, closing the door behind me. I walk over to the kitchen and place my bag and keys onto the center island. My hands feel clumsy, like they don't belong to me. The whole house smells faintly like wine and fear.

Then I hear it.

Someone is talking. Aggressively.

The sound makes my blood go cold in one clean sweep, like someone opened a freezer door inside my chest.

At first, it sounds like maybe Sam is having a serious conversation on the phone. But there's a low, male voice talking also.

Is she on speakerphone? I walk slowly to the base of the stairs and listen. My body moves on autopilot, my brain lagging ten feet behind like it's too scared to catch up.

"...why I set you up with Dr. Maslow..." I hear my sister's voice say faintly.

"... didn't want to work with me. You didn't want me anymore!" Says a male voice that I don't recognize.

The words hit me like a slap. That voice isn't just upset. It's unhinged. It's a voice that has already decided what it deserves.

I hear Sam speak, but I cannot understand what she's saying.

Dr. Maslow? Who is up there, and what are they talking about?

My mind scrambles for context and comes up empty. The emptiness is terrifying.

I hear the sound of something glass breaking, and Samaya screams shrilly.

"Shut up!" The man's voice demands.

The scream threads straight through my spine and yanks everything tight.

I freeze. My entire body goes rigid, and my stomach turns to lead.

I glance around for my phone and see it sitting forlornly on the kitchen's center island. I glance up the stairs and then back at my phone before walking over to pick it up. I get halfway to the base of the stairs and stop again. The house suddenly feels too big, too quiet, too full of corners that could hide a nightmare.

I have no idea who is upstairs with my sister, and I am damn sure something is very wrong up there. I look back over the shoulder towards the kitchen and decide to find a weapon of some kind. I will not be the dumb blonde in the movie who goes upstairs asking, "Hello… Is anyone there?" and then wondering why my ass is dead on the floor five minutes later. The thought flashes hot and mean and I hate that it's where my brain goes, but my brain is right.

Even though I have never wielded a knife for more than the occasional steak, I opt for a large knife. I look back over my shoulder towards the stairs to ensure that no one has come downstairs. Turning my attention back to my weapon options,

I slide open one of Sam's drawers. I see a rolling pin and then shake my head.

This knife is going to have to work.

My palm is slick as I grip it. I keep thinking, please let me not need this, and at the same time, please let it be enough if I do.

Knife in hand, I walk back to the stairs and listen. The door must be closed now because all I hear are the muffled sounds of angry voices. Well, the male voice is angry. Sam's voice is small and hard to make out. The difference between them makes my throat burn. I hate how small she sounds. I hate more that someone made her sound that way again.

Hands shaking, I find the banister and walk gingerly up the stairs. Each step brings a new bead of sweat, and another tightening of my gut. My legs feel both too heavy and too light, like I could either collapse or sprint through the drywall.

I hear a loud thud, and it is immediately followed by a scream.

Sam.

My vision tunnels. That scream is not a scared scream. It's a hurt scream. It's the sound of a body meeting something hard.

My sweaty hands fumble to unlock my phone, and I text Louis.

"Come now. Call the police." I hit send and shove the phone into my back pocket. I walk up the remaining steps and cross the hallway until I am directly outside of Sam's bedroom door. My heartbeat is so loud I'm scared it can be heard through the wood.

"Shit, shit, shit, shit, *shit,*" the man's voice says. He sounds… panicked. I press my ear to the door, waiting to hear something from Samaya. Anything. I need her voice to anchor me. Silence is worse than screaming.

My ear is met with silence. I stand there for a beat.

The kind of beat that stretches too long. The kind where your brain starts making up pictures you don't want to see.

Ring-Ring! My cell phone's rhythmic phone bell sounded in my pocket.

Shit.

The sound rings out like a flare gun in a dark forest.

I cower away from the door, my jaw slack. I reach back and grab my phone, switching the volume button on the side of my phone to the mute position. But I am way too late.

How could I be such a fucking idiot?

My stomach drops through the floor. I can feel the moment I lost the advantage I never even had.

I weigh my options. I consider running downstairs, but I am not leaving my sister behind. I take a deep, jagged breath and reach for the door handle. My hand is shaking so hard the metal rattles.

Just as I am about to turn the knob, the door flies open. Stunned, my phone falls from my hand.

The air in the hallway feels sucked out, like the house flinched.

A large man stands before me. He is a few inches taller than me, but stalky and barrel-chested. His eyes are dark - not just the color, but also the feeling. His left eyeball has tiny red dots like he's been hit, or maybe he strained his eye and some of the blood vessels burst. The kind of eyes you don't reason with. The kind of eyes that already broke something inside themselves and are looking for somewhere to put the pieces.

His hair is a dirty blonde color. But it looks a strange yellowish color, like the color of unhealthy urine. It's moist with sweat or rain, and it sticks unflatteringly to his forehead like maybe he'd been wearing a hat and peeled it off of his wet head just moments ago. His skin is flushed, feverish. He looks like a man who has been sprinting through his own rage.

He's wearing a black shirt with dark jeans and on his feet are raggedy black tennis shoes. His breath is sour, and he is panting. Hard. It smells like alcohol and metal and something rotten underneath.

When he sees me, his eyes go wide and scan my body, lingering briefly at my cleavage, and when his eyes meet mine, he grins. His grin looks loaded and full of dark intentions. I retreat one involuntarily step back. My body moves before my brain has words.

"Where ya going, pretty lady?" he asks, and with a quickness I didn't realize someone who looked like him could possess, he grabs my arm and hurls me into the room. I stumble backward and fall on my butt, unable to catch myself before falling. When I land, I drop the knife I'd been precariously holding behind my back in a lame attempt at being stealthy. The room spins. The carpet feels like sandpaper against my palms as I try to reorient.

That was a cute idea.

The thought is bitter and fast, like my brain is already trying to survive with sarcasm.

His eyes flick to the knife when mine do, and he grins again.

"Oh, you're a sneaky little bitch, aren't you?"

The way he says it isn't playful. It's possessive. Like he enjoys the idea of me trying.

I say nothing, but I glance back to the knife and assess the odds of me getting to it before him. He definitely has strength on me, but I'm pretty quick. My breath is shallow and sharp. I can hear it. I can't slow it down.

I reach out to grab the knife, but his right boot comes slamming down onto my forearm, and I cry out a fire engines' wail of pain. The pain is white and instant, a lightning strike that makes everything else go blurry.

"There's no way in hell I'm letting you get to that knife, sweet-pea."

He says sweet-pea like a threat.

He removes his heavy foot from my arm, and I whimper as hot tears fill my eyes and blur my vision. I slowly slide my arm in towards my body, wincing at the awful pain as it shoots from my elbow to my fingertips. Without looking at it, I can tell that it's broken. I dare to peek over at my arm and see that it's in an angry red, and in one area near my elbow, his boot broke the skin, and blood has risen to the surface of my arm. It throbs in pain, and my vision swims. I feel nauseous. The world tilts and rights itself wrong.

I watch as he steps over me and bends down, so I crane my neck to see if it's Sam that he is tending to. As if on cue, I hear her moaning from his corner of the room. It's a sound that doesn't even feel human. It's stripped down to survival.

"Sam?" I say weakly. "Sam, are you ok?"

My voice is thin, like it has to fight its way out.

I hear her gurgling and trying to respond. I roll over to my good side and pull up slowly to my operable hand and knees, searching frantically around me for something, anything to attack this guy with. My fingers scrape over fabric and hangers. Everything normal in here feels obscene right now.

But all I see around me are shoes and hangers and clothes. I spot one of Sam's stiletto heels and grab it with the hand of the arm that works. The heel feels like a tiny weapon in a world of too-big threats.

I slowly pull up to a couch and face them. The big man is bent down over Sam, stroking her hair and whispering something into her ear. I inch closer and pause. The tenderness in his movement makes me feel sick. It's not tenderness. It's ownership.

"The fuck away from me." I hear Sam say in a hoarse whisper, and I can tell she's fighting for consciousness. The loud thud that I heard must've been her hitting her head. Her voice sounds like it crawled through broken glass to get there.

"But I did all this for you," he says, his voice quiet, but clearly disappointed. "I killed him for us. I know how you really feel, Samaya, I always knew."

Killed him for us?

The sentence lands like a grenade. My brain can't even process it all at once.

I raise the shoe up over my head, the heel part protruding out towards this greasy stranger. My whole body shakes with the weight of the moment.

But he whirls around.

His eyes go dark, darker than I've seen since laying eyes on him a few minutes ago. He grabs my arm, the one holding the shoe, and twists it behind my back. The movement is smooth. Practiced. Like he's done this before.

I hear and feel something pop. My shoulder? The pain is instant and searing. I howl. It's not a scream I recognize. It's animal.

The next thing I know, I am lying on the ground, and his other hand is now pressing firmly into my chest, pinning me to the carpeted floor. I hear Sam stirring and telling him to stop. His weight crushes the air out of me. Every breath feels like trying to inhale through a wet towel.

"You were gonna just hit me with the shoe, you feisty little bitch?" he says, his voice now seething with anger and amusement. His spit lands warm on my cheek. I want to vomit.

"Spencer, please stop. Leave her alone!" I hear Sam say from behind him. Her voice sounds more alert now. Spencer.

A name. A person. Not a faceless monster. That makes it worse.

"Shut up!" He screams this, looking over his shoulder, but not letting go of my chest. "You lied to me. You fucking lied to me!"

I can feel his anger intensifying, and spit flies from his mouth as he says the words.

He's losing control.

Control was never about us. It was about what he thought he deserved.

My heart pounds so hard it feels like a jackhammer in my chest. I feel my breath getting shallower as he increases the pressure pushing down on my chest. My vision speckles. The edges of the room start to dim. I fight to keep my eyes open because I know what happens when you close them.

My eyes shift side to side as my anxiety and fear become more and more palpable.

Then I hear it.

Sirens, far off in the distance. Samaya must hear them too, because she points them out frantically to this deranged intruder. The sound is faint but it's everything.

"The police! The police are coming. You need to go."

Her voice is pleading and commanding at the same time. Like she's trying to take her life back with syllables.

"Do you really think I give a flying fuck about the police?" His eyes are wild as he says this, and the free hand still holding the knife waves around above me. I swallow hard. The knife glints under her lamp like a threat in neon.

"Please just let my sister go," Sam whispers through her tears. "Just let her go Spence, and we will tell the police to go. I'll tell them that everything is ok here."

She is bargaining the way you bargain with a hurricane.

He snorts bitterly. "You're such a fucking liar, Samaya. *A liar!* You've been lying to me and leading me on since day one." He looks down at me with a new spark of interest in his eyes. "So, this is your sister, huh?"

The way he says *sister* feels like he's claiming a prize.

He takes the knife's edge and traces my jawline with it slowly. I gulp for air and glance over his shoulder, searching for Sam. The blade is cold and light, but every millimeter of it feels like it's burning my skin.

The sirens get closer, and I can tell they are close to the house. I can hear doors in the driveway, voices shouting from downstairs, the thump of boots. Hope flares stupidly in my chest, and that hope makes the fear worse.

The next forty seconds happen fast. *Too fast.*

I see something switch in this man's eyes. Maybe it was the seemingly impending doom as the sirens reached the house. Maybe it's a psychotic break or memory surfacing at the worst possible time.

I see the moment he decides there is no version of this where he walks away with what he wanted.

He removes his hand from my chest, and I gasp for air, trying to wriggle away with my upper body. He flashes that same grin he greeted me with, except this time, his eyes remain dark and sad and blank. There is nothing human left in them. He grasps the knife in both hands and raises them high. The movement is almost ceremonial.

"Stop!! *No!!*" I hear Sam scream in a shrill voice that I've never heard from her before.

It's the sound of someone watching their worst nightmare take shape in real time.

He brings the knife down hard and without hesitation directly into my chest.

I hear the loud, dull crack and feel the knife as it hits bone and then continues deeper into my body.

The impact is not what I expected. It's like getting punched by a wall.

There's no pain at first. Just shock.

Like my body can't believe what it's feeling, so it delays the message.

I hear Samaya screaming. I see this man's blank face pause as he watches my face.

Then he pulls the knife out of my body, and I see my blood on it. He stumbles off of me.

The air rushes out of the hole in me like a secret escaping.

My breath comes in slow sharp, labored spurts.

I stare up at the ceiling, taking these slow, shallow breaths. My eyes fill with tears. Not from pain. But from fear and shock.

Because my body understands before my mind does that something has shifted forever.

Now I see Sam crawling over to me and pressing something against my chest. She is screaming and crying while the stabbing man sits there and watches. He is entirely still. The stillness is somehow scarier than the violence. Like he used up all his feeling already.

I hear yelling coming from the stairs. I hear Sam yelling back, "In here, we're in here."

Her voice is a lifeline and a siren and a prayer.

I'm hovering near the ceiling now. Well, I'm not, but yet I am. I see my body lying on the floor, twitching slightly, eyes wide open in a stricken panic. I see two officers grabbing the man who stabbed me and jerking him up from the floor. He is just as silent as I am, and he yields to the officers' demands. His face is blank, like this is all done and he's already left the room inside himself.

I hear them call for an ambulance, and I watch as an officer peels my sister away from my body and begins to tend to me. I want to tell her to stay. I want to tell her I'm still here. I can't make my mouth work.

There is no sound now. I see everyone bustling around, but I don't feel the same urgency anymore, and it is like watching a strange silent movie. My shirt is completely drenched in blood and is spreading onto the floor beneath me. I watch as my body takes a breath and then more time than should passes before the next one. Each breath feels like it has to climb a mountain to get to me.

And everything goes black.

CHAPTER FORTY-FIVE

The first thing I see when my eyes begin to open are the almost blinding fluorescent lights. The ceiling swims above me, white and endless, like I've been dropped into some sterile afterlife. There's a faint chemical smell in the air I can't place at first. I squint and then squeeze my eyes tightly shut. It's so bright.

"She's awake!" I hear a voice say, but it sounds far off into the distance, almost like it's underwater or in a long, far away hallway. The words bounce around my skull like they don't belong to me yet. I hear a beeping sound next. It's slow and low and seems to be somewhere near my head. Each beep feels like a tether snapping tight, reminding my body to keep doing the one thing it knows how to do right now.

I frown, still not ready to attempt opening my eyes again.

What is happening?

My mouth feels like sand. My tongue is heavy. My limbs are foreign. I rack my brain for some sort of context. Without opening my eyes, I try to roll over. The pain that shoots through my right arm is shocking, and my eyes fly open as I cry out. It's a lightning bolt that drags me all the way back into myself.

I squint but keep my left eye open, trying to make out my surroundings. It is so fucking bright. And my arm, holy shit. I'm in a hospital bed, raised slightly, surrounded by machines that look like they're breathing for me. A clear tube runs into my hand. My chest feels like it has a brick sitting on it. I swallow and even that hurts, like my throat is wired tight.

"Serenity?"

Sam.

That voice hits me in the lungs. I open both of my eyes and try to follow the location of her voice. My eyes slowly focus on her. She's smiling, but has a worried look in her eyes. She looks like she hasn't slept in a week, and like she's been holding her breath for even longer. I try to roll over again.

"Hey, hey," she begins gently, rising to stand next to me. "Don't move too much. Your arm is pretty fucked up." Her hand hovers over me like she's afraid to touch me too hard and break me again. I clear my throat. "Where am I?" My voice sounds froggy, and I cough. My throat is so dry it feels scraped raw.

She strokes my hair, and I notice that her eyes are filled with tears. She looks so relieved, but so exhausted. The kind of exhausted that comes from terror finally letting go of your throat.

"You're in the hospital, Ren. Do you remember anything?"

Her voice is careful, like she's walking barefoot across shattered glass.

My mind shows me short bursts of memories, like a strange slideshow, as if triggered by her question. The bright lights of her bedroom. The wet sound of the rain. His eyes. The knife. The weight on my chest. The crack. The way the air punched out of me. I squeeze my eyes closed again and begin to cry. Not pretty tears. These come like a dam breaking.

"Oh, honey… Please don't cry. Everything is ok now. You're safe." She continues to stroke my sweat-dampened forehead gently. I can feel her trying to pour calm into me through her hand. I take my left arm that actually works and feel around my chest, remembering the events with the crazed man at her house. My eyes search hers as I feel the bandages under what must be a hospital gown. The gauze is thick, wrapped tight, and it makes it real in a way my brain is still rejecting.

"I don't know what you remember, but you were stabbed. And your arm is broken."

The words drop like stones. My mind reels again with the memories of that night. I remember getting my arm stomped on by the guy's giant boot. I wince at the memory, the phantom pain rising like a ghost.

"Who was he?" I ask, looking back up at Sam. My voice is smaller than it should be.

She sits back down as if she needs to be seated to explain his relevance to our lives. Her shoulders sag like the whole story is a weight she's been dragging around by herself.

"Do you remember the patient I had that I had to let go of? You know, the one I told you I saw at the coffee shop that day?"

My eyes bulge in recognition. I nod slowly. That day flashes behind my eyes too, but now it has teeth.

"That was him. Apparently, the times I saw him after I referred him were not coincidental. He'd been following me for months after I stopped working with him. Somehow, he thought I was, like, into him. And he began coming to places he knew I'd be. He was my patient during the time that Samantha died also." She drops her eyes to her lap at the mention of her deceased daughter's name. The room seems to dim around it. I see her jaw tighten, that grief and rage living side by side inside her.

"Oh my God," I whisper as I stare at her in disbelief. My skin crawls thinking about all the times she'd been watched and never knew. "Wait! I bet you he was the guy you said you saw standing out in the backyard that one night!" I try to sit up again and wince. Every movement reminds me my body is not mine right now. Samaya reaches over and presses a button on the side of the hospital bed. It slowly rises while making a mechanical whining sound as it lifts my head and shoulders into a more seated position.

"Oh, *girl*. It gets crazier than that. He confessed to David's murder."

My jaw drops to my chest as I stare at her. It's like the floor slides out from under my whole understanding of reality. "Are you fucking serious?"

She nods vigorously. "Girl, yes. Apparently, this dude was obsessed with me, and I didn't even know it. I mean, I knew something was off with him and that it was weird and made me uncomfortable, but I didn't think it was specific to me, you know?"

Her voice shakes on the last part like she's sick thinking about how close she was to being swallowed whole by him.

I nod, completely engaged and blown away. We'd spoken about this guy briefly while we drove to the event at the Bayport Inn, and I had thought nothing of it. Now the memory feels haunted, like it was warning us and we didn't understand the language.

"Anyway, yea," Sam continues. "I guess he heard about my alleged kidnapping and that David was a suspect, and he went after him when he saw on the news that I was presumed dead. In his mind, he was avenging my death or some shit. He confessed everything yesterday evening to Detective Adams. He told them that he felt like I was in love with him too, and that was why he did all of this."

I can see the disgust on her face when she says love. Like the word itself makes her want to scrub her skin. Like his delusion tried to drape itself over her life and call it destiny.

I shake my head in disbelief. I'm trying to breathe through the weight in my chest and the horror in my throat. "Then why was he hurting you that night?"

The question tastes like fear.

She takes a slow jagged breath, smoothing her pants and not meeting my eyes. She looks up, and her eyes look older than I've ever seen. They look like they've been staring at the dark for too long.

"I told him I wasn't in love with him and never had been. I think that's why he snapped like that. Like, in his mind, somehow, he thought we'd be together. Then when he realized he'd basically killed David for nothing, he reacted. You coming in was unexpected, but probably saved my life." Her tears fall now, and mine do too. The thought of what would've happened if I hadn't come in lands heavy and sick inside my stomach.

"You're awake," I hear a deep voice say from the doorway. I tear my eyes away from Sam and see Louis standing there with a bouquet of pink roses. For a second I can't tell if he's real or the morphine is trying to comfort me with hallucinations. But then he moves, and the relief hits me so hard I feel it in my bones. He instantly crosses the room and is on the other side of the hospital bed.

I begin to cry harder. He gently places the roses at the foot of the bed and leans down to carefully embrace me. His familiar smell makes me cry even harder as I cling to him with my good arm. I feel him shake a little too, like the fear is finally leaving his body now that he can hold me. He straightens and pulls over one of the hard plastic hospital chairs and sits as close to me as the big mechanical bed will allow. The look in his eyes is pure and unfiltered love and awe, but there's also something feral there, like he's still ready to fight anyone who tries to take me again. He strokes my chin and cheek.

"How are you feeling?"

I search my mind for the correct adjectives, but nothing seems to fit the magnitude of what I feel. My brain wants to say everything at once. My body wants to sleep for a year.

"Alive. And grateful. And like I need more pain meds."

He chuckles, but looks as if he might cry. His eyes are glossy and wide and I love him for not hiding it. "I fucking love you, Serenity."

"I'll go grab the nurse," Sam says, standing to go. She squeezes Louis' hand and goes out into the hall. Louis and I stare at each other, not needing to speak to convey our emotions. His eyes never leave mine, even as the nurse comes in with her vital-checking machine. He moves aside as she fusses over me, placing something on the tip of my pointer finger and putting my arm into the blood pressure cuff.

"Well, look who's awake," she chirps brightly. She continues to punch things into the computer attached to the wheeled apparatus. She pulls a needless syringe out of her pocket and shows it to me. "This is Morphine, and I am going to give you some through your IV. It's going to help with the pain." I nod eagerly. While it is great to see two of my favorite people, my body is in pain. This sharp pain in my chest area is brutal, like there's a hot iron pressed against my ribs from the inside. We all watch as she slowly pushes the syringe's plunger in, expelling the medication into my IV.

I feel the effects almost immediately, and my eyelids droop. The nurse leaves the room, and I see Louis and Sam whispering near the door. I smile slowly, definitely feeling the effects of the medication now. Their silhouettes look like safety.

When I open my eyes again, I am almost face-to-face with Alyse's big brown eyes.

"Babe!" She cries out as she kisses my cheek. "Oh my God! You have no idea how happy I am to see your motha-fucking ass."

Her voice is a balm. She's crying too, trying to hide it behind jokes the way she always does.

I smile groggily, trying to keep my heavy eyelids open. "I do, trust me."

She sits down in the hard plastic chair that Louis was occupying earlier. I look around the room, suddenly confused. The clock on the wall is fuzzy. The day feels like it got chopped into pieces.

How long was I asleep?

"They'll be back," she says, reading my mind. "They just went to get food."

"Oh, ok."

"Samaya told me everything, so you don't need to waste any energy on giving me the play-by-play. How are you feeling?"

Her hand stays on mine like she's afraid I'll disappear if she lets go.

"High," I chuckle. But while the intoxication part of the pain killers has worn off, the pain isn't all the way back yet. I can feel it waiting in the wings though. "I'm just in shock, girl. Like, I know it all happened, obviously, but it feels surreal. I don't know. It's hard to explain."

It feels like a nightmare I woke up from, but the bruises and bandages are still there to prove it wasn't.

She is holding my hand and stroking my arm. "You ain't got to explain shit, girl. All that matters is that you're alive and that all this crazy mess is over finally. You can finally get on with your life!"

The word over makes my chest ache. I want to believe it. I need to. I begin to nod as I take in her words.

The door opens, and Sam and Louis walk in together with huge smiles. Louis' smile widens even more as he focuses his eyes on my face. I look between the three of them, and my own face cracks into a smile. The fear doesn't vanish all at once, but it loosens, just enough for breath and gratitude and something that almost feels like hope.

It's over.

And everything that I thought I'd lost, everything I'd been searching for—even before Sam went missing—is standing right in front of me now. The love, the family, the companionship. It is here in this tiny little room. My heart bursts with ease and joy that even the morphine couldn't recreate. I didn't just survive a nightmare. I got my people back on the other side of it. The truth finally has a body now, not just shadows and headlines.

I am ok. I am alive. *I am home.*

Later, when the nurses have come and gone a few more times, when the morphine has dulled the edges of the pain into something I can actually sit with, Detective Markovich steps into the room. He looks different without the rain and chaos behind him, almost softer, like even he can't believe how this ended.

"Ms. Jones," he says, voice low. "How you feelin'?"

"Like I got hit by a truck and then stabbed by the truck's cousin," I mumble. Alyse snorts. Louis lets out a breathy laugh that sounds half relief, half disbelief.

Markovich gives a small, tired smile and then looks at Sam. "We have Spencer Caldwell in custody. He gave a full confession for David Esposito's murder and corroborated it with details only the killer would know." His eyes shift back to me. "And there will be charges for what he did to you both last night. Attempted murder included."

Samaya's whole body slumps like someone finally unclipped a weight from her spine. Her hand flies to her mouth and her eyes spill over. Not a pretty cry. A real one. A body finally letting itself believe safety is possible again.

"So… I'm cleared?" she manages. Her voice sounds like a little girl's voice trapped in a grown woman's throat.

"Yes," Markovich says firmly. "You're cleared. The media will be informed. Marcus already called this morning, so he'll help handle any last legal cleanup, but this is done on your end." He pauses, and for once he doesn't sound like a cop. He sounds like a human being. "I'm sorry we put you through hell."

Sam nods, swallowing hard, like she's not sure what to do with an apology that shows up this late. But I see her shoulders loosen anyway, just a fraction. Sometimes that's all your body needs to start coming back home.

Markovich gives me a final look. "You saved your sister's life. You know that, right?"

I blink. That sentence tries to land and can't. Not yet.

"I… I just didn't want her to be alone," I say quietly.

He nods like that's the whole point. "Get some rest." And then he leaves us there, in the quiet after a storm.

That night, when the room is dim and the hallway noises are softer, Samaya crawls carefully into the chair beside my bed and rests her forehead against my blanket.

"I'm so sorry," she whispers.

"For what?" My voice is thin.

"For all of it. For him. For David. For you bleeding on my carpet because some man decided my life was his weird sick fantasy or movie." Her words crack at the end.

I reach for her hand with my good one and squeeze. "Stop. You didn't do anything wrong. You survived—that's not a crime."

She nods, but more tears come anyway.

"Mom would've been so proud of you," I add quietly. The words surprise me as they leave my mouth, but they're true. Our mom was complicated and messy and broken in a hundred ways, but she loved us in the way she knew how. And she would've been proud of Sam for fighting like hell to live.

Samaya closes her eyes and leans into my hand. "We gotta take her home, Ren."

"I know."

"We'll do it right. For us. For her."

"I know," I repeat, and this time I let myself mean it.

For the first time since all of this started, I can picture something beyond the next emergency. A funeral that isn't rushed. A beach day that isn't a memorial. A night of sleep that doesn't end in sirens. A future that doesn't require survival mode to enter.

Louis shifts in his chair on the other side of the bed and reaches across the rail to touch my knee.

"We're gonna get through the rest of this," he says. "The real rest. The paperwork rest. The grief rest. The learning-how-to-breathe-again rest."

I smile because only Louis would say something like that and make it sound normal.

"I'm holding you to that."

"Good," he says. "Please do."

Alyse stands up and stretches like she's been keeping watch over us for a hundred years. "Okay, so when you get out, I'm taking care of you for the first week—I'm serious. You can't argue. I'm coming with groceries and sage."

Samaya laughs wetly. I laugh too and it hurts my chest but I don't even care.

We sit in that shared laughter for a while. Not because everything is suddenly perfect. Not because grief evaporates just because justice finally shows up. But because right now we're alive. We're together. We have each other in the wake of the worst thing we've ever survived.

And in the quiet, between the beeps and the soft hospital lighting, I feel something I haven't felt in months settle inside my body.

Closure doesn't arrive like a ribbon tied on a box. It comes like breath returning. Like your sister's hand in yours. Like truth finally catching up to the monsters. Like waking up and realizing the story didn't end the way you were afraid it would.

I close my eyes again. Not to escape. Just to rest.

Because for the first time in a long time, I actually can.

EPILOGUE

One Year Later.

I feel a hand on my bare shoulder and peel my gaze from the large crowd inside. I turn around to see Sam's smiling face. I smile back.

"I can't believe you're married," she says, snaking her arm around my back.

Married.

"It doesn't feel real, yet that's for sure," I say ruefully as I return my gaze to the reception inside the Bayport Inn.

She bumps her hip into mine playfully. "It never does on your wedding day." She gives me a small peck on the cheek. "Come on, let's get you back in there."

"I'll be right there," I say and watch her saunter inside the venue. She looks beautiful in her backless, powder blue bridesmaid dress. I let her and Alyse choose their own dresses as long as they were the same shade of blue. My eyes shift to see Jason in his powder blue tuxedo, and I can't help but grin. He's my brides-man and was more than pleased when I told him he would get to wear a blue tuxedo. He'd gone into Manhattan to find a blue pair of dress shoes, and he is in there now looking like a sassy Smurf.

I see Alyse chatting up one of Louis' friends from college, and just by her body language, I can tell she's in flirt mode. Get it, girl.

The soft glow spilling from the Inn makes the whole place look enchanted—like nothing bad ever happened to us. Like the life I fought for finally arrived on my doorstep and asked me to dance.

I absently run my fingers along the two-inch scar on my chest. It's been almost two years since the night I was stabbed. The nightmares finally stopped about a year after lots of therapy and nighttime CBD gummies. Moving in with Louis helped a lot too.

For a long time after the attack, I couldn't look at that scar without feeling the phantom weight of a knife pressing into bone. But tonight, as my thumb glides over it, the sensation is different. Softer. A reminder of survival rather than pain. A reminder that I lived—and that I get to choose what kind of life I step into now.

Samaya sold that big, beautiful house near the ocean as soon as she possibly could, and until it sold, she crashed on our shabby brown couch until she got us a two-bedroom apartment. We spent an enjoyable and healing year together in that cozy apartment, and after mom dying and all the other craziness that happened, it was the best decision we could've made.

She stopped offering therapy sessions after that night. She now teaches other people how to become therapists at the Shady Oaks University here on Long Island. Her successful career, coupled with her unique personal experience, made her a great candidate for the job, and while I don't think she'll ever want to take on individual clients to counsel, I know she enjoys teaching about it. I'm happy for her.

Watching her reclaim her life, slowly, intentionally, was its own kind of miracle. There were mornings she couldn't speak, nights she couldn't sleep, days when grief and guilt welded themselves to her bones. But she kept choosing to stay. To rebuild. To rise.

And I watched her grow back into herself the way flowers push through concrete—soft, but unstoppable.

As for me, well, here we are.

Things worked out with Louis, and despite my issues trusting men and myself, he turned out to be every bit of the amazing guy he presented himself to be. We've had a few minor issues, but it's healthy and safe and growing.

Sometimes, late at night, when his arm drapes over my waist and the rhythm of his breathing lulls me to sleep, I still feel that flicker of disbelief. Like I stepped out of a nightmare and into a story where love wasn't dangerous. Where home wasn't something you tiptoe through in the dark.

Turns out, healing looks a lot like ordinary joy. Like burnt pancakes. Like laundry. Like soft kisses before work. Like peace that doesn't ask you to earn it.

I hear the door open behind me, and I whirl around, plastering a big "I'm Married" smile on my face.

Louis appears with a similar cheesy grin as if my thoughts summoned him. His eyes are extra glossy, probably from the many "you're married!" shots his boys encouraged him to take.

I take him in, and I'm sure my face mirrors his goofy grin. He still makes my heart skip a beat sometimes, even after the two years we've been together.

"My love," he says, reaching for me. He nuzzles his face into my neck. "How's my beautiful wife?"

Wife.

Swoon.

I cup his face in my hands and kiss him deeply. He tastes like mint and whisky, which makes me smile beneath his lips.

"You taste like whisky, Mr. Carter," I say coyly, looking up at him through my lashes. He chuckles and runs his hand along the back of his neck, looking sheepish and mischievous all at the same time.

"I gotta drink enough for the both of us," he says and places his hand on my belly. "But I can bring you two a water or lemonade if you'd like."

You two.

I sigh and place my hand on top of his big hand. "Do you think I'll be a good mom? Honestly?"

His eyes sober up, and he straightens. "Of course. That's probably the silliest question you've ever asked." He leans down and kisses me gently on the forehead. "There's no one else I'd rather become a father with."

The last of my fear dissolves then. Not because life is perfect—because it isn't. Not because danger is impossible—because it isn't. But because we've learned how to survive.

How to rise. How to choose each other again and again, even when the world tries to take that choice away.

I melt against him as I've done countless times over the past twenty-four months. This man was exactly what I was searching for in a man, but exactly what I wasn't sure I was worthy of. He hugs me back. Hard and strong, but gentle and tentative at the same time.

"Um… excuse me, love birds?" I hear a voice call from a few yards away. "You've got some guests in here that would love to celebrate with you."

I see Sam and Alyse standing together, both with their hands on their hips. Their faces ooze joy and love. I feel my eyes tear up for the hundredth time today as I look at my two leading ladies.

"Oh Lord, she's crying again," says Alyse as she walks over to me. I giggle through my tears and straighten up, looking down and smoothing my dress.

Sam approaches and links her arm through mine, and she gives me a sideways look and winks.

"Let's get you inside to get the adoration you deserve."

"I love you," is all I can manage through my happy tears. Sam says nothing because her eyes say everything her words could never accurately describe.

I take one last look at the night sky—the same sky that held my scream the night I almost died, the same sky that carried my prayers when Sam was missing, the same sky under which we buried our mother, and healed, and grew, and chose to stay alive.

Tonight, it feels different.

Gentler.

Like it's been waiting for this moment too.

I breathe deeply, straighten my dress, and walk inside with the people who saved me, the family I fought to keep, and the man who promised to walk the rest of his life beside me.

For the first time, my future feels wide open.

Safe. And like *mine*.

A NOTE FROM THE AUTHOR

Dear Reader,

Thank you for reading Serenity's Search. This story took me on an unexpected journey while I was writing it. I thought I was crafting a simple thriller, but it pulled me into something deeper. A story about siblings. A story about survival. A story about how we find our way back to ourselves even when life feels like one long string of losses and wrong turns.

Every character in this book asked me to look at fear, family, and longing in ways I did not expect. Serenity surprised me. Samaya surprised me. Even Louis surprised me. And if they surprised you too, I am grateful. That is the magic of writing. It teaches me as I go, and somehow it offers pieces of healing I did not even know I needed.

If you made it here to the end, please know how much I appreciate you. There are so many books in the world, and the fact that you chose to spend your time inside this one means everything to me. If you loved this story, telling a friend or leaving a review truly helps my work reach other readers who love thrillers with heart, heat, and chaos.

If you want more of all that, you will absolutely want to dive into the interconnected standalone to Serenity's Search, Things We Shouldn't Do. It is darker, steamier, and just as twisty. Keep reading for the first chapter.

Thank you for being here :) Thank you for letting me tell stories. Thank you for holding space for these messy, complicated, fearless women. They mean so much to me, and I hope they stay with you too.

With love,

Lindsey

ABOUT THE AUTHOR

Lindsey Cacy is a thriller author who believes the darkest stories reveal the brightest truths. Her novels, *Serenity's Search* and *Things We Shouldn't Do*, blend suspense, heat, heartbreak, and the complicated, tender resilience of women who have survived more than the world will ever know. She writes the kind of thrillers that make your pulse spike, your jaw drop, and your heart ache, often on the same page.

Born and raised in California and now rooted on Long Island, Lindsey brings her lived experiences, sharp intuition, and deep love of human behavior into every story. Her characters are messy, brave, wounded, loyal, chaotic, and real, and they carry the emotional grit that her readers come to crave. Whether it is a sister vanishing without a trace, a town hiding too many secrets, or a love interest who is dangerous in all the right and wrong ways, Lindsey's books always ask one question. What happens when the truth finally claws its way to the surface?

When she is not writing thrillers, Lindsey teaches yoga, supports women in reclaiming their power, and fills notebooks with ideas for her next twist. She lives for slow mornings, messy buns, found family, fictional chaos, and the magic of creating worlds where women save themselves.

Thank you for reading her work. It means more than you know!

If you want behind the scenes updates, sneak peeks, bonus chapters, and first access to upcoming releases, join Lindsey's newsletter at **lindseycacy.com**.

Every marriage has secrets
Some you don't survive
THINGS WE
SHOULDN'T DO
LINDSEY CACY

CHAPTER ONE

I know he's lying, just as surely as I know he fucked her two weeks ago.

If there's anything I've learned in my thirty-nine years on this earth, it's that men will lie to cover their asses every single time. It's instinct, like breathing. And as I look at him standing there, hands on his hips, staring at me as if I'm the problem, I feel disgust. Not surprise. Disgust. The deceit rolls off his tongue like it's second nature, and his audacity is almost comical.

Eight and a half years.

For nearly ten years I've given this man my love and loyalty. I gave him the best years of my life. I gave him my fucking thirties. And if you ask any woman over forty, she'll tell you the same thing: your thirties are when life finally starts to get good. You outgrow the dumb naivety of your twenties and step fully into yourself. I gave him that.

"Are you even listening to me?"

I return my gaze to my husband and realize he's still talking.

Oops.

"No," I admit. "I'm just trying to process everything."

He throws his hands in the air and sighs loudly, pure exasperation.

Men really are immature.

Here is this grown-ass man, five years older than me, standing in our bedroom like a child throwing a tantrum because he got caught.

Gross.

"I'm leaving," I say, matter-of-fact, turning to the desk to grab my purse. When I look back at him, I catch a flicker of fear in his eyes.

"Leaving? Like *leaving me* leaving? Aren't we going to talk about this?"

"Apparently we have nothing to talk about, since you claim you didn't do anything." I sling the purse strap over my shoulder. "I need space. Time to myself."

His caramel-colored face flushes red. "I don't know how many other ways I can tell you, Constance is just a lady at my job—we went to have drinks and nothing else happened!"

I start tossing a few things into my oversized purse: leggings, a sweatshirt. Then I move into the bathroom attached to our bedroom, scoop up my toothbrush and deodorant, and drop them into my little essentials bag from Forever Twenty-One.

When I walk back out, he's sitting on the edge of the bed, head in his hands, muttering to himself.

Pathetic.

"I saw the messages, John. Friends from work don't talk about 'how good you felt last Saturday,'" I say, calm but cold. My heart pounds in my temples as I watch him, waiting for the panic to surface on his face.

"This is crazy," he blurts, flustered. "She was talking about a conversation we'd had. She told me about some guys she was seeing, so I was just being a supportive friend. The conversation made her feel better, and I'm sure that's what she meant by that."

"I'm sure," I say, flat.

Something I learned long ago: when a man doesn't have an answer, he doesn't admit it. He buys time, ransacks his brain for an excuse, and hopes you'll back down first.

Not me.

I shake my head and walk out. The long hallway of our lavish Long Island home stretches ahead of me, and with each step I take, the air feels lighter. By the time I pull my phone out of my yoga pants, I'm already texting Jenna to say I'm coming over.

"Oh, yeah, he's definitely cheating," Jenna says as she takes my bag from me. "I can't believe he tried to say she was referring to a conversation."

I set my purse down on the small glass table next to Jenna's sand-colored couch, then flop onto the couch.

"I know girl," is all I can manage. I lean my head back and close my eyes. I feel her sit next to me.

"Well you know you can stay here as long as you need. I'll be at work most of the time anyway."

Jenna is a big-time criminal defense attorney who works upward of sixty hours a week. At least. Looking at her—with her petite stature, long blonde hair, and big blue doe eyes—you wouldn't know it. But she's a shark in the courtroom. If I ever became a criminal, she'd be the first person I'd call, not just because she's a good friend.

"Thanks, babe," I say with a weak smile. "I need some time to figure shit out. After all these years and everything we've been through together, I can't believe he could do this to me—and then have the audacity to lie in my face."

She's shaking her head, her big blue eyes dark and narrowed. "It's disrespectful! And gross—guys are just gross."

"Well lucky for you, you only have to deal with them in a professional sense," I say.

She lets out a short bark of laughter. "Women can be just as scandalous in relationships, Lo. Trust me."

"People just suck in general I guess," I mutter, suddenly feeling defeated and worn down.

Jenna slaps her hands on her knees and stands. She grabs my hand and pulls me up so I'm standing beside her.

"Let's stop going down this road and have some wine," she chirps. I listlessly follow her into the kitchen. I feel a little lighter as I sit on the barstool she gestures to at her kitchen's center island.

I take a large gulp of the cool, crisp liquid when she hands me my glass. Setting it down, I close my eyes. When I open them, I see Jenna staring at me with a concerned look.

"What?" I ask, reaching for my long-stemmed glass again.

"Nothing," she says quickly, playing with a long blonde lock of hair. Her eyes meet mine again and she sighs. "I hate that you're dealing with this, you don't deserve it."

"Nobody deserves this, Jenna. It's the blatant lying in my face for me, the fact that he could look me in the eyes and tell me earnestly that what I saw wasn't real—it's disturbing."

"It's gaslighting," she says.

I look down at my hands, my vision blurring. I quickly swallow hard, determined to keep it together. John doesn't deserve a tear. I take another sip of wine, draining the glass.

"So," I say after a steadying breath. "Now what?"

"I'm going to get the guest room ready for you, then let's grab some food, maybe? If you're hungry."

I nod. "Thanks again for letting me crash here."

She waves her hand dismissively as she takes a sip from her glass. "I live alone and am looking forward to some company! Think of this as an extended sleepover."

I can't help but laugh. Jenna refills my glass and pecks me on the cheek before heading past me to the guest room.

I sigh and look around for my purse. Spotting it on the couch, I stand and walk over. I rummage until I feel my sleek plastic phone case. There are several notifications, and from what I can see on my lock screen, they're all from John. Rolling my eyes, I return to the kitchen island and, more importantly, my glass of wine.

I scroll through his nine text messages. They range from "Where are you?" to "Come on, babe, can't we just talk?" I decide to ignore them for now.

Good, I think. Let him squirm.

"Ok! The room is ready for the taking," Jenna says from behind me, and I almost jump off the barstool at her sudden presence.

She smiles sheepishly before giving me a quizzical look. "You ok? I'm not used to seeing you so jumpy."

"I'm ok. John sent some messages."

"*Ew,*" she says, wrinkling her nose. "Saying what?"

"Oh, you know, the usual. I'm sorry, come home, where are you," I say with a dramatic eye roll.

Jenna shakes her head. "Well, fuck him. Let him wonder what you're up to for a change."

I nod, liking the sound of that. I'd spent countless hours waiting for him and wondering where he was. It felt rewarding to know he was at home, probably doing the same thing right now.

"That's a great idea," I say, flashing Jenna a wicked smile. "Now, where should we eat?"

She unlocks her phone and starts searching. "There's this little taco place that just opened downtown. It's supposed to be amazing and they have margaritas."

"Perfect," I say, standing and stretching. "I'm going to get changed, then I'll be ready to go."